ROMANTIC TIMES PRAISES BOBBI SMITH, NEW YORK TIMES BESTSELLING AUTHOR!

LONE WARRIOR
"Fast-paced, swift moving and filled with strong, well-crafted characters."

EDEN
"The very talented Bobbi Smith has written another winner. *Eden* is filled with adventure, danger, sentimentality and romance."

THE HALF-BREED (SECRET FIRES)
"Witty, tender, strong characters and plenty of action, as well as superb storytelling, make this a keeper."

BRIDES OF DURANGO: JENNY
"Bobbi Smith has another winner. This third installment is warm and tender as only Ms. Smith can do. . . . Ms. Smith's fans will not be disappointed."

BRIDES OF DURANGO: TESSA
"Another wonderful read by consummate storyteller Bobbi Smith. . . . Filled with adventure and romance, more than one couple winds up happily-ever-after in this gem."

BRIDES OF DURANGO: ELISE
"There's plenty of action, danger and heated romance as the pages fly by in Ms. Smith's exciting first book in this new series. This is exactly what fans expect from Bobbi Smith."

THE PRISONER AND THE PROTECTOR

"Are you sure you're all right?" Cord asked, concerned.

"Yes, thanks to you. I don't know what I would have done if you hadn't shown up when you did."

"Don't even think about it," he said, not wanting to think about it himself. "Miles is gone, and he won't be back. And I won't leave you again. I'll be right here if you need me."

At that moment, all Autumn wanted to do was go back into the protective circle of his arms and draw on his strength, for she had felt safe there before. She knew what she was feeling was ridiculous—he was the sheriff and she was his prisoner—but it didn't change what was in her heart.

Cord felt suddenly awkward standing there with her, although he wasn't sure why. He told himself this was Grace Thomas. Certainly, she didn't deserve what had just happened to her, but she was a part of an outlaw gang, and he had to keep her locked up.

"Do you need anything?" he asked, ready to return to his desk.

"Only my freedom—"

BOBBI SMITH

FOREVER AUTUMN

LEISURE BOOKS NEW YORK CITY

A LEISURE BOOK®

January 2003

Published by

Dorchester Publishing Co., Inc.
276 Fifth Avenue
New York, NY 10001

ISBN 0-8439-5087-0

Printed in the United States of America.

Visit us on the web at www.dorchesterpub.com.

Prologue

Sagebrush, Texas, 1877

It was late when Pete Miller heard someone riding into his campsite. He wasn't expecting anyone, so he got his rifle just in case there was trouble. He waited, watching cautiously until the rider drew near.

"Grace—" There was surprise in Pete's voice. "What are you doing here? It's the middle of the night."

"I know. I was looking for you," Grace said boldly as she reined in.

"Why were you looking for me? Has there been trouble?" He was instantly worried as he set the rifle aside.

Grace was wearing pants, as Pete knew she

usually did when she rode, and he had a hard time not watching as she dismounted before him.

"There's trouble, all right," she declared, walking toward him.

At eighteen, Grace considered herself a woman, and she had a woman's desires. She wanted Pete, and she was determined to get him.

Grace had been in love with Pete for what seemed like her whole life. He was a quiet, shy man, though, and she had trouble getting him to talk to her whenever she saw him in town at the socials or the occasional dance. Until now, he had always treated her as he would a little sister, but she had made up her mind to put an end to that. When she'd heard several of the hands on her ranch talking about how they'd run into Pete camping out here tonight at the border of their two ranches, she'd decided to sneak away from home and go to him.

"What kind of trouble?" Pete asked, anxiously waiting for Grace to tell him what had happened. He knew it had to be serious if Grace had been sent to find him after dark. He was ready to pack up immediately and ride for home.

Grace stopped before him and looked up at him. She thought Pete was the most handsome man in the world with his dark hair and dark eyes. She gave him a small smile.

"I love you, Pete," she said in a lower, softer voice. "I've loved you for as long as I can remember, and I'm tired of waiting for you to notice me."

Pete was caught completely off guard by her declaration. He frowned as he stared down at her in the flickering campfire light. He'd always thought of Grace as a nice, sweet young girl, but as she stood before him now, she looked like a woman—a woman who knew what she wanted. He didn't say anything, for he couldn't think of what to say. He only continued to stare at her, unsure what to do.

In the fantasy Grace had relived over and over in her mind on the ride to the campsite, she'd envisioned Pete sweeping her into his arms after her declaration of love. In her dream, he had kissed her and declared his undying love for her, too. But none of that had happened. Her profession of love was greeted by silence.

Disappointment pounded through Grace as she stood there. Tears threatened, but she fought them back. She told herself she had come this far; she couldn't give up. Grace knew Pete was a bit shy, and she told herself that she only needed to show him how much she loved him. Then he would respond.

Grace was a woman of action. She was not a woman who gave up easily, and she decided it was time to do something about her feelings for Pete. She moved closer and lifted her arms to link them around his neck. He stiffened a bit at her touch, but that didn't stop her. Grace rose up on her tiptoes and kissed him.

When Pete didn't respond at first, Grace almost panicked. She had never been so forward before, and she had risked everything coming here tonight.

Pete was holding himself as rigidly as he could while he tried to be logical and think through what was happening.

Grace was a lady. She shouldn't have been there alone with him at night. She had her reputation to think of. He knew he should put her away from him and insist on taking her home right away.

And then Grace moved even closer, deliberately rubbing herself intimately against him as she continued to kiss him.

Pete hadn't had much experience with women. There had been a saloon girl one night in town when he'd had too much to drink, but other than that he didn't consider himself to be much of a ladies' man. But having Grace kiss him and rub against him that way was changing everything.

"Kiss me, Pete. Please—" Grace whispered against his lips.

Her words and the feel of her soft, ample curves against him erased all logic from his mind. They were alone out under the stars, and Grace was irresistible.

Pete reacted instinctively. He crushed her to him as his mouth slanted over hers in a demanding exchange that left them both breathless.

He was lost.

Grace's spirits soared at Pete's response. She met him in kiss after devouring kiss, loving him, wanting him. She was an innocent. She had no idea what would come of this, and she didn't care. She only wanted to be with Pete.

Caught up in his desire, Pete began to caress her. Grace did not resist. She had never let anyone touch her so intimately before, but this was Pete. It seemed so right.

He drew her down with him on the bedroll that he'd spread before the fire. They lay together, her hips tight against his. The pressure was so exciting that Grace found herself moving restlessly against him. He unbuttoned her blouse to caress her bared breasts, and she gasped at the excitement that trembled through her. When his lips traced the same path over her silken flesh, she gave herself over to him fully and without reserve.

With eager hands, they stripped away the barriers of their clothing. They wanted only to be close to one another, to know the fullness of loving one another.

Grace was an innocent, but she learned quickly. She wanted to please Pete, to make him want her. She loved having him in her arms. When Pete claimed her virginity there by the campfire, she cried out his name in ecstasy. The heat of their passion branded them both forever.

"I love you," Grace whispered, knowing in that moment he was the love of her life.

Pete responded only by kissing her again. Lost in a haze of desire, they reached the heights of love's pleasure and collapsed in each other's arms. They lay together, sated.

Grace was certain she would love Pete forever. When they finally moved apart, she rose up on one arm to gaze at him. He looked so handsome to her. Unable to resist, she leaned down and kissed him once more.

"How soon do you want to get married?" Grace asked with complete innocence.

Pete had been lying there quietly, trying to come to grips with what had just passed between them. He had never known passion so intense, but—

"Married?" he repeated.

Grace went still at the tone of his voice. Slowly she realized that though they had made physical love, Pete had never told her he loved her.

"You do love me, don't you?" she asked, suddenly feeling like an awkward young girl again and not the seductress who'd come here to entice him.

"I, uh—"

Pete hesitated, and that was her answer.

Tormented by the truth, Grace tore herself from his arms and quickly dressed.

"Grace, wait—"

"There's nothing to wait for!" she declared, trying not to cry.

She was too humiliated even to look at Pete. She had given him her greatest gift—she had given him her love. She had thought Pete was the most wonderful man in the world. She realized now that she'd been wrong. He had been willing to take what she had so brazenly offered, but he didn't really care about her.

"Grace—" Pete hastily began to pull on his pants as he got to his feet.

Grace ignored him. It was too late for explanations. She all but threw herself on her horse and rode away without even looking at him again.

Pete stood there, watching as she disappeared into the night. What had happened between them all seemed like a dream, yet the passion he'd experienced in her arms had been real—and it had been wonderful.

Pete knew that he had taken Grace's virginity, and the knowledge that she had come to him so willingly left him confused and unsure of himself. She said she loved him. He'd had no idea that she felt that way, but now he knew. Did he love her? Introspective, quiet man that he was, he wasn't sure of his feelings for her or of what he was supposed to do.

Pete did not follow Grace. He bedded down for the night. Troubled by all that had passed between them, he did not sleep.

"Where the hell have you been?" Paul Thomas demanded in drunken outrage as he caught Grace climbing in her bedroom window back home at the Lazy T. He had discovered she was missing a little before midnight and had been sitting there in her room, waiting for her to return so he could confront her. He'd been drinking heavily the whole time, and his fury had only grown with each passing hour and drink.

"Pa!" Grace had been miserable on her ride back to the ranch. She hadn't thought things could get worse, but they just had.

"You're damned right it's me!" Paul snarled. "Or were you expecting somebody else?" He got up and lit the lamp, then turned to look at her. "Look at you! You look like a slut!"

Grace suddenly realized how she must look—her hair was loose and her clothing was wrinkled.

"Answer me! Where have you been?" He closed on her, furious.

"I couldn't sleep, so I went for a ride," she answered, and it wasn't a lie.

"And just *who* were you riding?" Paul accused in crude, hateful tones. "You're just like your mother! You're worthless!"

At the thought of his wife—the beautiful Lori, who had walked out on him and never looked back—he backhanded Grace.

Grace cried out in pain at the abuse. Her father had been mean to her before, but he'd never hit her.

"Every time I look at you, I see your mother! Every time!"

"I'm sorry, Pa—"

"You're sorry, all right! And I'm gonna make you even sorrier! Who were you with? Who was it?" He grabbed her arm in a painful, bruising grip. "Or was it more than one boy? You been down at the bunkhouse with all the hands?"

"No! I told you I just went for a ride, that's all!"

He slapped her again, then shoved her down on her bed. "You don't leave this room until I tell you you can! I'm going to find out just what you've been up to!"

With that, he slammed her window shut and locked it. He stormed drunkenly from the room and locked the door behind him.

Grace was beyond shock. Her father had always been distant and cold, but he'd never been physically cruel to her before. She tasted blood in her mouth and knew her lip was swelling already. Thinking of the look upon his face, she feared for her very life.

Panic seized her. What if he found out she'd been with Pete? What if he tried to force Pete to marry her? The humiliation and embarrassment were too much for her to bear.

Grace knew she had to do something. She had to get away. She couldn't stay at the ranch, not anymore, for once her father did find out what she'd done, things would be even worse between them.

Grace waited several days, until she was certain she could get away from the Lazy T unseen. Then she took what little money and jewelry she had and escaped through the window of her bedroom again. She left the ranch that had been her home for all her life. It didn't matter anymore, though, for there was nothing to hold her there. Pete didn't love her—and neither did her father.

Chapter One

"No! I ain't going upstairs with you!" Missy cried as she fought to free herself from Hal Sheridan's painful grip on her arm.

"The hell, you ain't," Hal swore, tightening his hold on her. He wanted her, and he was going to have her. If she gave him too much trouble, he'd take her right there on the saloon floor in front of everybody. That'd teach her to tell him no. The idea excited him even more.

"Let me go!"

Missy needed someone to come to her aid, but those around her paid little mind to the scuffle. It was payday, and everybody was intent on having a good time. They were drinking, gambling and dancing in the crowded Sundown Saloon. Wild times were the norm there, and one

screaming saloon girl wasn't anything for anyone
to get upset about.

"C'mon, Missy," Hal said, leering at her as he
jerked her toward him. "You'll love every minute
of it. You know you will."

Missy was desperate to escape his cruelty. Hal
was a mean drunk. She'd seen what he had done
to Kate the last time he'd come in looking for a
good time, and she wasn't about to suffer his
abuse. As he pulled her closer, she panicked.
Frantic, and knowing her only chance for escape
would be lost if he dragged her upstairs to the
rooms where the girls plied their trade, she
slapped him with all the force she could muster.

"Why, you little bitch!" Hal erupted in fury.
He backhanded her violently. "Is that how you
like it? Real rough?"

Missy sagged weakly against him, stunned by
the force of his blow.

Hal smiled cruelly, glad that she was now
more submissive. He was hot for her and
couldn't wait to get her on her back.

And then a deep voice rang out.

"Let her go!"

The command was loud enough that the other
boisterous, drunken cowboys and saloon girls in
the Sundown Saloon suddenly went quiet. Even
the piano player stopped pounding out his rau-
cous tune. Everyone watched as the man who'd
spoken stepped away from the bar. No one knew
his name, but talk had it he was the new gunman
Mike Watson had recently hired on as a regu-

lator out at the Bar W. Someone had been rustling Mike's cattle, and the ranch owner had let it be known he was determined to see it stop.

The gunman strode toward the couple now, a look of fierce determination on his face. He had been quietly minding his own business until Hal had hit Missy.

The crowd sensed his fury and parted before him. People moved nervously back as he confronted Hal, a man well known for his bad temper and fast gun.

Hal studied the stranger who dared interrupt him. He wanted to get Missy upstairs, and he was ready to fight anyone who got in his way. The stranger was young, but he wore his gun like he knew how to use it. Hal wasn't worried, though, for he believed his own reputation would back the man down.

"You know who you're talking to?" Hal snarled.

"A man who enjoys beating women," he answered.

"That's Hal Sheridan. You don't want to make him mad," one of the other working girls warned in a low voice.

The stranger ignored her advice. He kept his gaze fixed on Hal.

"Missy's enjoying herself. She likes it when I play rough with her. Ain't that right, Missy?" Hal glared down at the saloon girl, daring her to protest.

But Missy knew this was her only chance to

save herself from a hellish night. "No!"

There was a gasp from those gathered around at her cry of denial, and the tension in the room built even more.

Sam, the bartender, had been keeping a close watch on what was going on, and he was getting worried. He didn't want any trouble in his saloon, and he knew Hal could be trouble.

"Hey, Hal, how about I buy you a drink? What the hell, I'll buy you both a drink," he called out.

He'd seen these kinds of situations get out of hand before, and the last thing he wanted was a fight with Hal Sheridan tonight. Hal and his friends were a mean bunch when they were sober, and even rougher when they were drunk. Sam liked their money, but he didn't like them. He was just glad Hal's friends hadn't shown up with him, or the shooting would already have started.

"I'll take you up on that offer—right after I get done with Missy." Hal started toward the steps, taking the saloon girl with him.

"*I said—let her go.*"

Hal's temper was hot. He wasn't about to back down. He made his move quickly, determined to gun down the stranger and then go on upstairs. In one quick, violent action, he shoved Missy to the ground away from him, then drew his gun and fired.

To the shock of everyone present, the stranger anticipated his move and drew faster.

Hal's expression turned to one of complete disbelief as the other man's bullet tore through him. He collapsed on the saloon floor and lay still.

Missy screamed as the shots rang out. She scrambled to get away from the blood and gore.

Shouts erupted as everyone realized what had just happened—Hal Sheridan had been gunned down in a fair fight.

"Somebody run and get the doc," Sam ordered as he hurried from behind the bar to check on the wounded man. He knelt down beside Hal and knew immediately that there was no need for a doctor. "Forget the doc," he told them. "Get Sheriff Gallagher."

The stranger, satisfied that the man wouldn't be hurting anyone else, slowly holstered his gun. He went to Missy's side and took her arm to help her up.

"Are you all right?" he asked.

"Yes." Her eyes were shining with gratitude as she stared up at her rescuer. Tall and darkly handsome, he had a compelling aura of power about him, and she thought him the most wonderful man in the world. "Thank you."

There was a gentle strength in his grip as he steadied her on her feet, and Missy felt suddenly bereft when he let go of her arm. She had enjoyed his touch. She glanced down at the fallen Hal and shuddered visibly.

"What happened?" Sheriff Gallagher shouted as he burst through the swinging saloon doors, gun in hand. Then he saw Sam kneeling beside Hal's body.

"Hal Sheridan's dead," Sam offered. He stood up and went to the lawman to explain. "It was a fair fight. This one here outdrew him fair and square." He pointed out the man standing with Missy.

Sheriff Gallagher faced the stranger. "What's your name?"

"Cord Randolph," Cord answered.

"Well, Randolph, come with me. I've got a few questions I need you to answer down at my office."

Cord nodded.

"Have you seen Hal's friends anywhere around?" the sheriff asked Sam, knowing there might be more trouble.

"I ain't seen them tonight, but that don't mean they're not in town somewhere."

The two men shared a look of understanding.

"Come on, Randolph," the lawman said.

Cord started to follow him. Missy touched his arm, and he stopped, glancing her way.

"I'll buy you a drink when you get back." She smiled up at him.

He nodded.

"Somebody go get the undertaker," the sheriff ordered; then he led the way out of the saloon.

A short time later, Mike Gallagher faced the young gunfighter across his desk in the sheriff's office.

"And that's everything that happened?" Mike

asked, reaffirming the story Cord Randolph had just told him about the way the gunfight had come about.

"Yes. I told him to leave the woman alone, and he drew on me."

"All right. No charges will be filed against you. Like Sam said, it was a fair fight, and you had plenty of witnesses."

"I can go?" Cord asked. He was more than ready to get out of the lawman's office.

"Yes."

Cord stood.

"A word to the wise," the sheriff began. "Hal Sheridan had friends, and they aren't going to be happy about what happened. Watch your back."

Cord nodded, but didn't say anything. He started to leave.

"And another thing."

Cord looked back.

"You look like a smart young man. You ought to think about a better way to make a living. You're damned good with a gun—you proved that by taking Hal down—but remember, there's always going to be some hothead out there trying to make a name for himself by outgunning you."

"I appreciate your advice, Sheriff."

The lawman could tell he wasn't taking him seriously. "Go on—go, but think about what I said."

"Yes, sir."

Cord left the office. His mood was somber as he started down the street. He hadn't wanted any trouble when he'd gone into the saloon, but there had been no way he could just stand by as the others had done and watch the violent drunk deliberately hurt Missy. No woman deserved to be treated that way.

Cord hadn't gone more than a block when the attack came. A shot rang out, winging him in the upper left arm. He reacted swiftly, drawing his sidearm and returning fire as he dove for cover behind a watering trough.

Jess Lawrence and Max Carter, Hal's two friends, had been alerted by others that he'd been killed. Though they'd been told it was a fair fight, they were drunk and bent on immediate revenge. They'd hidden outside the sheriff's office to wait for the chance to shoot Hal's killer. They began firing as soon as they thought they had a clear shot at the man who'd gunned down their friend.

Sheriff Gallagher heard the gunshots and grabbed up his rifle. He could see from his office window that Randolph was hunkered down, returning the ambushers' fire. Racing out the back door so he wouldn't be seen, he circled around and managed to come up behind Hal's friends.

"Drop your guns!" he ordered.

Jess and Max weren't about to obey anyone. They turned on the lawman, guns blazing.

It was the last thing they would ever do.

Sheriff Gallagher got them both. He hated bloodshed. He had always wanted to be a peacemaker, but Jess and Max had given him no choice.

"Randolph!" he called out when the shooting was over.

"Yeah." Cord got up and ran across the street to the sheriff's side.

Sheriff Gallagher saw the blood on Cord's sleeve and knew he'd been hit. "How bad is it?"

"A shot just winged me." He flexed his wounded arm to test it. The flesh wound hurt, but he could tell it wasn't serious. "I'll be fine—thanks to you."

"You were a lucky man today, Cord Randolph, but luck don't always hold."

"I've never relied on luck—just my gun."

"Well, remember what I told you. There are better ways to make a living than hiring out as a gunman."

"Like being a lawman?" Cord retorted.

"That's right—using your gun to bring peace and keep people safe."

"I appreciate the advice, Sheriff, but I don't know that I'm the lawman type."

"You'd make a good deputy, and I could use one here in town," the sheriff told him.

"I'll think about it."

"Good. You do that. Now, go wake up the doc. You need some bandaging."

"Thanks." Cord holstered his gun, then shook hands with the sheriff before walking off.

Sheriff Gallagher watched the young man move away. He wondered how long it would be before someone else called Cord out and tried to outdraw him. He hoped Cord would be ready.

Chapter Two

One Year Later

The dark clouds and chilly drizzle matched the mood of those who'd gathered at the cemetery. The mourners stood over the new grave, their heads bowed in prayer as the minister intoned his final blessing over the deceased.

"Into your hands we commend Michael Gallagher's spirit. He was a brave man, a man of honor, a man who gave his life in the defense and protection of others. Welcome Michael into your kingdom, oh, Lord, and bring peace and comfort to his wife, Beth. Amen."

Beth's choked sob was the only sound that broke the silence that followed.

The mourners began to slowly file forward to

pay their respects to the weeping widow.

Only Cord Randolph stood apart.

Unmindful of the rain, Cord remained staring down at the grave of the man who had been his friend. Pain ate at him, and rage filled him over Mike's murder at the hands of the violent Martin gang.

He finally made his way to where the widow stood.

"Beth—"

"Oh, Cord." His name was torn from her. "Why did it have to be this way? Mike was a good man—a fine man. He didn't deserve to die like this—shot down by cowards." She looked up at Cord, her agony visible in her tortured gaze. "They shot him in the back, Cord. In the back."

Cord was grim. "I'll find them, Beth. I give you my word."

"I want those killers dead. All of them." There was fierce hatred in her voice as she grabbed his forearm and held on to him with a claw-like, desperate grip. "I know you're good with a gun—Mike told me you were the best he'd ever seen. Make them pay for what they've done."

"I will."

At Cord's words, what little inner strength Beth had collapsed under the weight of her anguish. She let her hand fall away from his arm, and an older man came quickly to her side. He gave Cord a knowing look as he put a supportive arm around Beth and escorted her to the carriage.

Cord stood alone, watching as they drove away. He and Mike had become friends after the night Mike had saved him. He'd found himself thinking about the lawman's offer and had heeded his advice after another month. He had taken the job as his deputy and had learned a lot from Mike. They had worked well together.

Cord's father had taught him early how to use a gun, and he'd been good at it. His parents had died of a fever when he was only fourteen, and he'd suddenly been alone in the world with no one to help him. He'd been fending for himself ever since. He had never had a close friend like Mike before. Cord had known he owed Mike, but he never figured he'd be paying him back like this—by hunting down his killers.

Cord took one last look at the grave, and a terrible resolve filled him.

A small group of mourners remained behind, and he saw that the mayor was among them. He walked over to speak with him, knowing what he had to do.

"You need a new sheriff," Cord said with serious determination.

"Yes," Mayor Baker answered.

"I want the job," he told him.

"It's yours." The mayor had been hoping he could convince Deputy Randolph to take over. He knew Mike had trained Cord and had thought thought highly of him. He trusted Mike's judgment. He dug in his pocket and pulled out the sheriff's badge. "This was Mike's." He held it out.

Cord took the badge and pinned on his friend's star.

Mike had tried to stop the outlaws. He'd managed to track down and arrest Joe Simons, one of the members of the elusive and deadly gang. Leaving Cord in charge of things in Sagebrush with the other two deputies, Miles Harris and Thatch Edwards, he'd been escorting the prisoner to Dry Spring to stand trial before the circuit judge. Two days had passed before Cord got the wire from the judge letting him know Mike had not shown up. Cord set out to search for him and had found him murdered and Simons gone. The rain had washed away all traces of the gang's trail, leaving Cord frustrated in his attempt to track the killers. He would always live with the regret that Mike had insisted he stay behind with Thatch and Miles.

Cord didn't know how long it would take, but he knew one thing for sure—he was going to find a way to bring down the Martin gang.

Sheriff Cord Randolph smiled grimly as he mounted up to lead his deputies out of town. The telegram he'd received a short time before was the best news he'd had in a long time. The lawman in Dry Spring had wired him that he thought the notorious Grace Thomas, a member of the Martin gang, was in disguise and heading into Sagebrush right now on the stage.

In the two months since Mike's death, Cord had followed every possible lead, trying to track down Rod Martin and his gang of killers. He'd had no success in locating them—until now. This help from the sheriff of Dry Spring was just what he needed.

Cord didn't know why the Thomas woman was traveling in disguise, but he was certain it was part of a bigger plan by the gang. He and his men would intercept the stage outside of town and arrest her there, so there wouldn't be any chance of bloodshed in town. Once he had her in custody, he hoped to get vital information out of her about the gang's whereabouts so he could bring the rest of them in. It had been too long already. He wanted Rod Martin and the others locked up behind bars, waiting to stand trial.

"Let's ride," Cord ordered, and he led the way out of town.

Autumn Thomas stared out the stagecoach window at the passing Texas countryside. She found it hard to believe that there could be so many miles of open, dusty, seemingly endless land without any sign of civilization. Everyone had warned her that she was going to the "Wild West," and now she knew what they meant. How had her sophisticated life in Philadelphia come to this? She gave a slight, disbelieving shake of her head, for she truly had no idea. Everything had happened so fast.

"Are you all right?" James Dodson, her fiancé, asked, noticing her slightly troubled expression.

"I'm fine," Autumn replied. She managed a smile at James, but it wasn't easy.

It seemed it had been just a short time ago that everything had been simple in her life. Though she still missed her mother, who'd passed away some three years before, Autumn had believed she was in control of her destiny. Her inheritance had left her more than well-to-do, and she spent much of her time doing charity work and working with other women in trying to get the right to vote. The latter was proving an uphill battle, but she found the challenge invigorating. Six months ago her engagement to James had been announced, and though they hadn't set the date yet, she knew their wedding would be the highlight of the Philadelphia social scene.

Her life had been perfect, just the way she'd wanted it to be.

Then the telegram had come from a lawyer named Ralph Baxter in Sagebrush, Texas. And her whole life had changed.

Autumn could still remember the exact wording of the lawyer's telegram:

"This is to inform you that your father Paul Thomas has passed away."

The shock and the pain that had followed had left her both furious and in tears.

Her father had been alive all this time, and she'd never known it!

Outrage had filled her at learning that her

mother had lied to her her whole life about her father's death. She had grown up believing he'd been killed in a tragic accident in Philadelphia. The fact that he had been alive was bad enough, but to realize that he had never tried to contact her made her even more furious over the whole situation.

A letter from Mr. Baxter had followed, explaining in more detail that Autumn was his sole heir and due to inherit his entire estate. And so, here she was making this unexpected trip to Sagebrush, Texas, to claim the ranch her father had left her in his will.

Autumn had had a feeling that this trip would be an adventure, but she hadn't thought it would be *this* much of an adventure or this difficult. The dust—the heat—the roughness of the travel, not to mention the crude accommodations they'd been forced to endure, were making the trek a true test of her determination to learn the truth about her family.

"Are you sure you're all right?" James asked again.

"I'm just a little tired, that's all."

Autumn wasn't about to give James the satisfaction of knowing how truly exhausted—mentally, physically and emotionally—she was. He had been decidedly negative about making the trip from the start. He'd encouraged her to just hire the attorney who'd contacted her and have him sell off the property. He had wanted her to forget about the entire incident—in essence, to take the money and run.

But Autumn was a fighter. She never backed down from a challenge. She'd felt compelled to come to Texas to learn about her past. It was only when she'd announced her intention to travel to Sagebrush that Muriel Williams, a long-time friend of her mother, had come forward to tell her what little she knew about her parents' relationship.

Autumn had been numbed by Muriel's revelations. The older woman had told her that she had been born in Texas, not Philadelphia. Lori, her mother, had hated living out West so much that she had gotten a divorce and returned with Autumn to live with her own family in the East.

"I'm beginning to understand why your mother hated living here so much," Muriel remarked from where she sat beside Autumn. She was a woman accustomed to city living, and this was an entirely new experience for her. She wasn't quite sure yet whether it was an experience she was going to enjoy or not, but there was no way she could have let Autumn make the trip without her.

Autumn glanced outside again. "It is deserted looking, and I don't think it could have changed much since she left—there's really nothing to change."

"I don't think your mother ever missed her life here. Never once did I hear her say she regretted returning home."

"I still don't understand how she could have lied to me about my father, though."

"I don't either, but I knew better than to question her about him or the time she'd spent here. She confided very little to me about what really happened between them. She would only say that the past was over and she never wanted to think of it—or your father—again. I guess it was easier for her to deny his existence to you, and to everyone else, than to explain why they'd divorced. By claiming he was dead, she didn't have to answer all the questions about why they were no longer together."

"And she would have had a lot of questions to answer," James put in arrogantly.

Learning the news about Lori Thomas's divorce hadn't changed James's feelings for Autumn—or her money—but he definitely looked upon her mother in a new light now. He thought it was good that she'd died before the truth had come out about her divorce. A divorce was quite a scandal in their social circle.

Autumn knew James was right, but it still angered her that he'd remarked on it. She expected him to be supportive, not condemning. She ignored his caustic comment and said to Muriel, "Thank you for coming along on this trip with me. I know it hasn't been easy for you."

"The trip hasn't been easy for any of us, darling, but when your mother was ill, I promised her I would watch over you." Muriel patted her hand reassuringly and gave her a gentle smile.

The blond and beautiful Autumn looked so much like her mother that Muriel's heart ached. "And I will."

"I appreciate your kindness more than you'll ever know."

"This has been so difficult for you—finding out about your family this way—but your mother begged me never to reveal what I knew, and I told her I wouldn't." Muriel was still feeling a bit guilty over breaking the promise.

Autumn quickly reassured her. "It's all right. Mother had no way of knowing my father would put me in his will. I'm glad you were honest with me. What still puzzles me about their whole relationship is why my mother ever married him in the first place."

"Paul was a very handsome man." Muriel's expression turned a bit dreamy as she recalled Paul and Lori's whirlwind courtship so many years before. "Your mother was quite smitten with him. All the women wanted him, but your father only had eyes for her. He swept her off her feet and they married quickly. Your mother's family had money, but Paul was proud and wanted to make his own fortune. They had been married for only a short time when he decided he wanted to go to Texas. Your mother was so in love with him at the time, she never gave a thought to what she'd be giving up. She only cared about pleasing Paul."

"It's so sad that their marriage didn't work out."

"They were both strong-willed, determined people—and your mother was very used to getting her own way."

"I wonder why my father never came to see me."

"I often wondered the same thing, but your mother wouldn't speak of it. You know now that he did love you, though. He made you his sole beneficiary."

Autumn knew money was important. She had seen in her work with the poor how difficult life could be without it, but she also knew that in life, love was the most important thing of all. Loving and being loved meant more to her than all the riches of the earth.

Autumn thought of her father—the tall, dark-haired, handsome man in the small wedding portrait she had of her parents. He was a stranger to her, and when she'd received the telegram, a deep yearning filled her to learn everything she could about him. That was why she was here, on this stagecoach, heading for Sagebrush, Texas.

"How much longer until we get to this godforsaken town?" James asked in irritation.

"It's only midday," Autumn told him, her thoughts of her father interrupted. "The driver said when we started out this morning that we wouldn't get there until late afternoon."

James looked thoroughly disgusted. He leaned back, seeking what ease he could get on the wooden seat, but there was no comfort to be found in the jostling stagecoach.

James was a socially and politically connected man of wealth and privilege. He was accustomed to all the comforts of civilization. He was accustomed to having his instructions followed. With each passing mile, he was becoming more and more annoyed with Autumn because she hadn't taken his advice about her inheritance and handled everything from Philadelphia. He certainly hoped she proved more malleable once they were married.

The stage continued on over the endless miles, and the heat grew even more oppressive as the day aged.

"Whoa!"

The driver's unexpected shout and the sudden reining in of the horses jarred Autumn, Muriel and James.

"What's wrong?" Muriel asked, wide-eyed with fear.

"I don't know," Autumn answered, unable to see the road ahead from the passenger window.

"The driver's slowing down—but we haven't reached any town yet." James was puzzled. The area looked so deserted, he could see no reason for the driver to stop.

"We aren't being robbed, are we?" Muriel asked, suddenly terrified. "I've read all about stage robberies in dime novels. Outlaws are everywhere out here! Or it might be Indians attacking. We might be taken captive or shot."

Autumn clutched her reticule more tightly to her. She was suddenly glad that she'd secreted her mother's small derringer in her purse before they'd left on the trip. When she'd first discovered the gun among her mother's possessions, she'd been shocked, but after hearing Muriel's stories about the difficulty of life here in Texas, she'd understood why her mother owned one. James was quite capable of protecting her and keeping her safe on the streets of Philadelphia, but this wasn't Philadelphia.

As the stage came to a complete stop, James leaned out the window to get a better look and saw three men on horseback blocking the way. He couldn't hear what they were saying to the driver, but he feared Muriel might have been right about the danger.

One of the men rode back and reined in close beside the stage, stirring up a thick cloud of choking, red dust. The man reached out and threw open the door beside Autumn.

"Everyone out of the stagecoach!" he ordered harshly.

Chapter Three

Cord recognized Grace Thomas immediately as she emerged from the stage. She was all dressed up like a real lady, but there was no mistaking her. Had she been any other female, Cord would have thought her quite beautiful, but he knew the truth about the Thomas woman—and it was a truth that a pretty face and nice clothes couldn't disguise. Grace Thomas was a member of the deadly Martin gang, and if she was heading into Sagebrush in disguise, it could only mean that trouble was on the way.

"Come on! Get down!"

Autumn moved quickly to obey the man's gruff order. She looked up through the haze of dust created by the stirring horses. The fierce-looking man was sitting on his mount before her,

33

and he had his six-gun drawn and aimed directly at her.

He was an outlaw! It was just as Muriel had warned!

Fear filled Autumn. Desperate for a way to defend herself, she reached into her purse, wanting what little protection the derringer would give.

Cord was watching the Thomas woman closely. He didn't trust her at all. He knew how dangerous the Martin gang was, and he wasn't going to give her any opportunity to try anything. He reacted instantly when he saw her slip her hand into her purse. Maneuvering his mount to the side of the stage, he leaned down, snared her around the waist and hauled her up bodily against him. He held her tight, her arms pinned to her sides so she couldn't reach the weapon he was certain was hidden in her purse.

"Help!" Autumn let out a shriek as she found herself crushed to the hard-muscled width of her assailant's chest.

"James! You've got to help her! Do something!" Muriel cried.

James started to get out of the coach to go to Autumn's rescue. One of the other men who'd forced the stage to stop rode up beside the first gunman and pointed his weapon at James.

"Don't try anything!" the second man ordered.

"Let her go!" James insisted in his most authoritative voice, watching as Autumn continued to struggle against the stranger's hold. James had known that coming to Texas was a stupid mistake. He just hoped Autumn would listen to him from now on.

"Just hold it right there."

James froze as he stood in the stagecoach doorway. These men looked deadly, and he certainly didn't want to be shot.

Autumn had no intention of giving up. She kept fighting the man she believed to be a bandit. Using all her strength, she tried to break away. Her hair came tumbling loose from the neat bun she'd styled it in that morning, and she could feel her gown tearing as his iron grip held her locked against him. But there was no way to escape. When he made a grab for her reticule, she was even more certain the man's motive was robbery. Her terror grew as she wondered what the outlaws would do to them after they'd stolen their money.

And then the other man who was holding his gun on James called out, "You got her all right, Sheriff Randolph? You need any help?"

"She's every bit the wildcat I thought she'd be, but I've got her," Cord growled. It wasn't easy, but he managed to keep control of his captive.

Autumn couldn't believe what the man had said. She went suddenly still.

"Sheriff?" she repeated, shocked. "You're a sheriff?"

"That's right," Cord answered. He kept one arm tightly around her as he tore her reticule from her grip and tossed it to his deputy. "Take a look in there, Thatch."

Thatch quickly dug through it and found the derringer. He held the small gun up for Cord to see.

Cord smiled a cold, satisfied smile. She had been armed, just as he'd expected.

"You're under arrest, Miss Thomas," he said.

"What?" Autumn twisted around to stare up at him in disbelief. At any other time, she might have thought him handsome, but at this moment he seemed the devil incarnate. His chiseled features were harsh, his expression dark and condemning as he glared down at her.

"You heard me."

"You're arresting me?" she repeated.

"That's right, *Miss Thomas*," Cord said coldly.

"How do you know my name?"

"I know a lot more than that about you."

Autumn was chilled to the depths of her soul. "I don't understand—"

"You will. You're under arrest for the murder of Sheriff Mike Gallagher."

"I don't know what you're talking about!" she protested.

"Tell it to the judge."

"See here, Sheriff, this is some kind of terrible mistake," James broke in.

Cord glared at the man, and the threatening look silenced James. "Both of you—get down out of the stage—now!"

James hastened to obey, then turned to help Muriel.

Cord knew the men who ran with the Martin

gang, and this man wasn't one of them. Still, he couldn't be too careful. "Search him and the other woman," he ordered Thatch.

Thatch did as he was told while Cord's other deputy, Miles, dismounted and went to help Cord. Cord handed his prisoner down to him.

Autumn cringed as the big, beefy, mean-looking deputy lifted her from the horse's back. His hands were harsh and groping upon her. She struggled to hold the bodice of her dress up. The seam that had been torn left her chemise partially revealed, and the deputy was leering down at her.

"Sheriff—I haven't done anything wrong!" Autumn protested angrily. High color stained her cheeks as indignation overwhelmed her. She wanted to cower, to hide from these awful men, but she forced herself to stand tall. She had never been treated so terribly in her life. She was being manhandled! The bodice of her dress had ripped. And through all her peril, James had done nothing. He had been helpless to come to her defense.

Had he not despised the gang she rode with, Cord might have admired the spirit Grace Thomas was displaying in standing up to him, but instead he felt only fury at her continued claims of innocence. He ignored her protests as he stood before her. He saw how her dress was gaping open and caught a glimpse of pale flesh.

"Let her go, Miles," he dictated. "Fix your dress."

The deputy obeyed, and Autumn was relieved

to have his hands off her. She suppressed a shudder as she quickly covered herself as best she could.

"Thank you, Sheriff," she said. For a moment, she hoped she would be getting back on the stage, but her hope was dashed.

"Put your arms out," Cord ordered.

"What?"

He took her wrists and bound them before her.

Autumn couldn't believe she was being restrained. "Why are you doing this?"

"It's just an extra precaution for the ride to town." Cord didn't trust her. He knew how dangerous she could be.

"They're unarmed," Thatch announced after searching James and going through Muriel's reticule.

"All right, let's ride."

Autumn assumed she would be riding on the stagecoach for the balance of the trip into town. She was shocked when the sheriff swept her up in his arms and put her on his horse.

"What are you doing?" she demanded.

"Taking you to jail," Cord said with satisfaction as he mounted behind her. He pulled her tightly against him, allowing her no freedom to move at all.

"This is ridiculous!" Autumn continued to argue. "Gentlemen—you have to help me!"

She looked at the stage driver and the man riding shotgun, but found their guns were trained on her, too. Shock radiated to the depths of her being as the realization came to her that this was no mistake—no nightmare from which she would awaken. This man holding her really was a lawman, and he was deadly serious in his intention to arrest her.

"Shut up right now or I'll gag you," Cord said.

Autumn fell silent. She didn't doubt for a moment that he would do as he'd threatened.

Cord was glad she offered no further resistance, and he urged his horse toward town.

Miles and Thatch mounted up and wheeled their horses around to gallop after them.

"What are you going to do about this?" James looked up at the stage driver in outrage. "How can you just sit there and do nothing? You can't let them ride off with her this way!"

"That was Grace Thomas the sheriff just arrested," the driver explained unsympathetically. "She's wanted by every lawman in West Texas. She runs with the Martin gang. There will be some big celebrating in town tonight once the word gets out that Sheriff Randolph's brought her in."

"Who? *Grace* Thomas?" James repeated the name in confusion. "That's ridiculous. I don't know any Grace Thomas. The woman the sheriff just rode off with is my fiancée, Autumn!"

"Maybe he really is one of them," the man riding shotgun said to the driver. His gaze narrowed as he pointed his gun at James again. They had just picked these passengers up in Dry

Spring and knew only that they were headed to Sagebrush.

James saw the threat in the man's eyes and fell silent.

"That's better."

"James—" Muriel clutched at his arm, terrified by all that had happened. "What are you going to do?" She wanted him to take charge, to go rescue Autumn. She was angry that he had just let the sheriff ride away with her like that and had not done anything to stop him.

"Right now, the only thing you're both going to do is get back on the stage," the driver ordered. "We got a lot of time to make up if we're going to get to Sagebrush before sundown."

Cord and his deputies were watchful as they cut across country on the trek back to town. Martin and his men had to be around somewhere close, and Cord didn't want to be caught off guard as Mike had been. The woman was holding herself rigidly before him. He was glad, for he wanted to make the trip quickly and without incident. He didn't have time to fight with her. He wanted to get her safely locked up as fast as he could.

They reached town without incident, and Cord reined in before his office. He dismounted and tied up his horse, then helped his prisoner down.

"What are you going to do with me?" Autumn demanded as she stared around, getting her first look at Sagebrush.

"Lock you up. Let's go."

She did as she was told, realizing there was no point in resisting.

Cord led her toward the office and opened the door. He waited for her to enter before following her inside. He pointed her toward the jail cells.

"Go on right back there."

Autumn stared at the barred cell through the open door in the rear of the sheriff's office. The cell door stood open, but she balked at going in. She turned to her captor and glared up at him in defiant indignation.

"You're making a mistake, Sheriff! My name is Autumn Thomas—"

"So you're using an alias now."

She stared at him in confusion. "An alias? Why would I need an alias? I haven't done anything wrong. You can't lock me up for no reason."

"I've got plenty of reasons, Miss Thomas. You may not have been the one who pulled the trigger, but you ride with Rod Martin."

"I've never heard of anyone named Rod Martin! I'm from Philadelphia! My father was Paul Thomas, and he owned a ranch near here."

"I know all about your father and I know all about you," he said, ignoring her arguments. "Are you going in the cell of your own accord or do I have to pick you up and carry you in there? I can do it, you know." He glared down at her, more than ready to do whatever was necessary to get her locked up.

Autumn wanted to rage at him, but she held her tongue. With as much dignity as she could muster, she lifted her chin and walked past him into the small, cramped jail cell, her head held high. As she stood there, her back to the lawman, she heard the loud clank of the door being closed and locked behind her.

"Turn around," Cord told her. "I'll untie you now."

She faced him and held out her wrists. He reached between the bars and untied the rope, freeing her.

"Thank you," she bit out as she rubbed her chafed wrists.

Never in her entire life had Autumn been treated so ignominiously, and she was beginning to wonder if James hadn't been right. Maybe she should have just sold the ranch and stayed back East. Right now, the thought held great appeal, but it was too late to change anything. Fighting down the panic that threatened, she tried to be logical as she watched the lawman through the bars of her cell.

"Sheriff, I can prove who I am," she began.

"Oh, I'm sure you can," he returned tightly. "I'm sure Rod Martin thought of everything when he helped you with your disguise. It's a good one. You actually look like a lady."

She gasped at his insult.

"I just want to know why you're here in Sagebrush," Cord went on. "Did Martin send you into town to check things out ahead of time for him? Is he after the payroll that comes through town, or has he got something else in mind?"

She didn't know what he was talking about. "If you'll just listen to me, I can explain everything. There's a lawyer in town—his name is Ralph Baxter. He wrote to me and requested that I come here. I'm sure he'll vouch for me."

Cord regarded her suspiciously. She had obviously done some checking around if she knew Baxter's name. "So, you know Ralph Baxter?"

"No—I've never met him, but—"

Her words only confirmed what he'd believed. She was trying to lie her way out of jail, but it wasn't going to happen.

"I'll see about talking to Baxter tomorrow," he said to humor her. "You go ahead and make yourself comfortable, Miss Thomas. You're going to be in there for a while."

"But, Sheriff!" Her panic grew and she found herself clinging to the bars, peering through them at the stern lawman.

Cord ignored her pleas. He turned his back on her and walked away. Certain that she was safely locked up, he closed the door to the office to prevent her from hearing his conversation with his deputies.

Autumn stared after him, filled with shock and disbelief. She looked around the tiny cell and fought down a shiver of apprehension. She wondered how her life could have changed so dramatically so quickly. How had she come to be locked in a jail, accused of being a party to murder? Autumn knew she was trapped. There was no way out until the sheriff decided to listen to reason and check out her story.

The mystery of her dilemma left her baffled. The sheriff had known her name was Thomas, but how could that be? She'd never been in Texas before. How could he have known who she was? Had someone alerted him that she was on her way? The lawyer, perhaps? But even if he had notified the sheriff that she was coming to claim her inheritance, there was no way anyone could have known what stagecoach she would be arriving on. And why had she been arrested?

Autumn knew she had to find out what was going on in Sagebrush and learn everything she could about the notorious "Martin gang." She'd never heard of it before today, but she had a feeling she'd be hearing a lot more about it from now on.

Autumn made her way to the cot and sat down gingerly on the edge. It was hard and uncomfortable, and she couldn't help wondering who'd slept on it last. She realized she had no choice in her accommodations, though. Right now, she was helpless to do anything to improve her lot. She would have to bide her time until the stagecoach arrived. She just hoped the stage didn't run into any trouble on the way into town. She wanted to get out of that jail as quickly as possible—and she couldn't wait to see the look on the sheriff's face when the truth of her identity became known.

Autumn smiled smugly at the thought.

Sheriff Randolph was the man's name, and it was a name she wouldn't soon forget. He was arrogant and intimidating. If he was an example of the kind of law and order that ruled here in the West, then Texas was in serious trouble.

Frustrated at not being able to help herself, Autumn awaited James's and Muriel's arrival.

"So far, so good," Cord said as he sat at his desk.

Miles and Thatch took the two chairs before him.

"We were lucky," Thatch said.

"Very. If it hadn't been for Sheriff Bannecker's wire, we would have missed the opportunity."

"But now that we got her, what are we going to do with her?" Miles asked.

"Question her," Cord told them. "She wouldn't be here unless Martin had something planned."

"It must be important if he sent her into town ahead of him," Thatch agreed.

"The army payroll is due to come through, but not until the end of the month," Cord remarked thoughtfully. "I doubt she would have come this early if that was his plan."

"The bank?"

"Could be. Both of you take a walk around town and see if you notice anything out of the ordinary. I wouldn't put it past Martin to try to break her out once he learns we have her."

The deputies started to leave the office.

"And, Thatch?"

The deputy looked back at him.

"Stop by Baxter's office and tell him I need to see him."

"You think her story is true?" They had heard her arguments with the sheriff while he'd been locking her up.

"No, but I've got to do my job. I don't doubt she's lying, but I'll contact Baxter just to make sure. Then stop by the telegraph office and send a wire to Sheriff Bannecker. Let him know we got her."

"We will." Thatch nodded and followed Miles outside.

Cord cast a glance back toward the cell area. Grace Thomas's continuous denials angered him. He knew who she was. He'd seen her wanted poster. By contacting Baxter, he was calling her bluff.

Everyone in town knew her story—how her father had disowned her and how she'd worked at one of the saloons over in Eagle's Nest before taking up with Rod Martin. Cord had to admit he was surprised by her disguise. It was a good one. If he hadn't known the truth about her, he would never have suspected she was an outlaw's woman.

Cord looked down at her derringer lying on his desk.

He smiled to himself.

Miss Thomas could lie her pretty little head off, but there was no denying it—she'd been armed and dangerous.

Chapter Four

"James, you haven't said much," Muriel began tentatively as the stage rolled into Sagebrush. An ominous silence had stretched between them for the duration of the trip, but now that they were in town, she could wait no longer to find out what he planned to do to help Autumn.

"There isn't much to say right now," he bit out tersely, barely casting a glance her way. "I told Autumn this trip was completely unnecessary, but she insisted on coming. I hope she's satisfied. And what on God's earth was she doing with that gun in her reticule?"

"It was her mother's gun. Don't be angry with her," Muriel said defensively.

"Her mother's gun?" James looked at Muriel

in amazement. His opinion of Autumn's mother had just fallen even lower.

"From what I understand, Autumn found it in her mother's things after she died. I guess she had it when she lived here in Texas. I don't really know. Autumn probably brought it along just in case there was trouble."

"If she'd stayed in Philadelphia as I suggested, none of this would have happened. She could have arranged for the lawyer to handle everything. He could have sold the ranch for her, and Autumn could be back in Philadelphia right now—not locked up in a jail cell!"

Muriel gave him a censoring look. "How could you expect her to stay home after finding out that the father she thought was dead had been alive all this time?"

"Well, you know what?" James said caustically. "The man is dead now. Obviously, he didn't care much about Autumn while he was alive. Why should she care about him now?"

"Maybe it's not that she cares about him, but that she wants to understand her past. You have to admit, her mother kept a great deal from her."

"Yes, her mother lied to her and probably for a very good reason. Just look where Autumn has ended up!"

"So what are we going to do to help her?" Muriel demanded of him.

"Oh, I'll get her out of this, all right, but once it's over and we're back in Philadelphia, I hope she starts heeding my advice a little more closely."

"I'm sure she will," Muriel said soothingly, but all the while she was thinking of how hateful James was being. Autumn deserved his sympathy and love, not his condemnation.

It was still daylight when the stagecoach drew to a stop before the stage office. James immediately descended and helped Muriel down.

"The sheriff's office is down the street. I saw it as we drove past," he told her. "Wait here and take care of our luggage."

"I will not! I want to see Autumn and make sure she's all right. I'm sure she needs all the help she can get right now."

"All right, let's go," he said, disgusted with the entire situation. He just wanted to deal with the sheriff man to man and get Autumn freed as quickly as he could arrange it.

"We'll be back for our things later," he told the driver.

They hurried off to see Autumn.

Cord looked up from his desk as his office door opened and the man and older woman who'd been on the stagecoach came in.

"Where's Miss Thomas?" James demanded. "I'm James Dodson, her fiancé, and I want to see her immediately."

"You're her fiancé?" Cord eyed James coldly as he stood up behind his desk. The other man's claim surprised him. Grace Thomas was Rod

Martin's woman. Cord frowned, wondering about this man's connection to the gang. His hand settled on his sidearm. "She's locked up nice and safe in the back, and she's going to stay that way."

"We have to see her," Muriel told him, stepping forward.

"There will be no visitors."

"But this is all such a terrible mistake," Muriel went on. "I don't know who you think she is, but you're wrong! The woman you have locked up is Autumn Thomas, and she's from Philadelphia. We were making the trip—"

"You can save all your talk," Cord interrupted. "I'm not releasing her."

"Then send for the lawyer Ralph Baxter. I'm sure *he's* a man of intelligence," James dictated, making his opinion of the gunslinging lawman quite clear. "He can straighten this whole situation out for you very quickly. We even have a letter from Baxter."

Cord's expression darkened at the man's implied insult. "I left word for him."

"You left word?" James repeated sarcastically. "If you can't be bothered to find him, I'll go get him myself. Where's his office? I'll bring him back here right now."

Cord had had enough. He didn't know who this man was, but he was losing patience. Thatch had already reported that the lawyer wouldn't be back in his office until the following day. "Baxter won't be returning to his office until tomorrow."

"Tomorrow? You mean you're planning to keep Miss Thomas in jail overnight?" James demanded.

"I'm planning on keeping her in custody longer than that," Cord told him in a tone that was deadly serious.

"But that's ridiculous! She's a lady! You can't lock her up this way—"

"I already have." Cord's gaze never wavered from the demanding stranger standing before him.

"James—we'd better go." Muriel suddenly felt frightened by the tension growing in the room. Autumn's situation was far more serious than she'd thought. Something was horribly wrong here.

"You'd be a smart man to listen to your lady friend," Cord said quietly.

James backed away from the desk. Without another word, he strode from the office, leaving Muriel to follow.

Muriel looked up at the lawman, her gaze challenging his as she bravely asked, "Autumn will be safe here with you, won't she?"

He didn't know why the woman insisted on calling his prisoner by a different name, but he answered, "Miss Thomas isn't going anywhere."

"That's not what I asked you, Sheriff. I want to be sure she's safe, and I'm holding you personally responsible for her. I'm sure we can clear all this up just as soon as Mr. Baxter returns."

"She'll be safe."

Muriel nodded. Still worried about Autumn, but momentarily satisfied by the sheriff's assurance, she left the office.

Cord didn't sit back down right away. There was something about James Dodson that he didn't like or trust. When one of the deputies returned to the office, he would send him to keep an eye on Dodson. Cord went to the window and watched Dodson until he and the woman had gone from sight.

Cord considered what the woman had told him, and he wondered for the first time if there could be some kind of mistake. As quickly as the doubt crossed his mind, he dismissed it. He'd seen the picture of the female outlaw, and there was no mistaking the identity of the woman he had locked up. It was the same woman as the one on the wanted poster. It was Grace Thomas.

Autumn heard the sound of voices out in the sheriff's office. She couldn't make out what they were saying, but she recognized two of those speaking as Muriel and James. Excitement and relief filled her. They had come for her. Soon the lawman would come to set her free. Surely James would convince him that a mistake had been made in arresting her.

Autumn went to stand at the cell door. She couldn't wait to be out of jail. But time passed, and still the sheriff didn't come for her. She kept straining to hear what was being said, but silence had fallen over the office.

Her hopes faded after a while, and she sank back down on the cot. It was almost sunset, and the thought of spending an entire night behind bars unnerved her. The last few weeks had been trying enough without ending up locked in a jail cell like a common thief.

Cord was feeling restless. He went to look out the office window and saw Gail Yohe, a pretty young waitress in town, coming toward the jail carrying a tray laden with food.

"Gail, let me help you with that," he said, opening the door.

"Hello, Cord," Gail said, smiling brightly as she allowed him to take the tray from her. "Thatch stopped by and said you had a prisoner and needed a dinner for her tonight."

Her gaze was hungry upon Cord. She thought he was the best-looking man in town, and she was determined to find a way to get him to the altar.

"I appreciate your bringing it down." He was surprised by her actions; usually she just gave the tray to Thatch. He set the food on his desk top.

Gail was willing to try just about anything to get Cord. She had insisted to Thatch that she could bring the tray to the sheriff's office. She was glad for the chance to have a few moments alone with Cord. Usually, the only times she got to talk with him were when he came into the restaurant to eat or at church socials or a town dance. On those occasions, there were always a lot of other people around, ruining everything. Right now, they were basically alone except for the prisoner locked up in back, and she wanted to take full advantage of this rare privacy.

"I brought along something for you, too," she said in a throaty voice.

"You did?" Cord looked at her questioningly, wondering what she was talking about.

"Yes, the pie is for you." She slid the plate from the tray onto his desk.

"Thanks. That was kind of you." He knew the desserts from the restaurant were delicious.

"It's my pleasure. Thatch mentioned that you arrested somebody really important today." She gazed up at him adoringly. She had honestly paid little attention to what the deputy had been telling her. She'd been too excited at the prospect of being alone with Cord. "Who was it?"

"Grace Thomas," he answered.

"That horrible woman who rides with the Martin gang?" she asked, aghast.

"That's the one."

Gail deliberately overreacted, shuddering visibly. "I can't imagine living that way."

From the talk she had heard about the Thomas woman, Gail believed her to be a slut. What other kind of woman would choose to lead the life she was leading?

"She won't be causing any more trouble while I've got her locked up here."

"Thank heaven."

"I'll take the food back to her now before it

gets cold," Cord said, picking up the tray. "Thanks again. I really appreciate your help."

Anyone else would have accepted the dismissal, but Gail was not so easily discouraged.

Cord had not thought she would follow him as he went back to give the food to his prisoner.

Gail was curious about the notorious female outlaw, though, and wanted to get a look at her. She trailed behind Cord.

When the door that connected to the office swung open, Autumn looked up, hope springing to life within her. She'd heard voices again and believed her release was imminent.

Autumn expected to see the sheriff and the lawyer coming, keys in hand, to free her. She expected to see James and Muriel waiting for her in the outer office. Instead, she saw only the sheriff—and he was carrying a tray of food.

Her spirits sank.

"You're not coming to release me?" She was thoroughly disgusted.

"No. I'm bringing you dinner," Cord answered.

"But I don't need any food! I need to get out of here!" she argued. "Have you spoken with the lawyer yet? Will you be letting me out tonight?"

"No. Baxter's out of town," he informed her, sliding the tray beneath the cell door to her.

"He's not here?" Autumn was aghast at the prospect of spending endless days locked behind bars like a common criminal while she awaited Baxter's return. "When will he be back?"

"Tomorrow."

"Tomorrow? So, I'm going to be forced to stay here all night?"

"Yes, Miss Thomas, and judging from what I know about your activities and the fact that you tried to draw a gun on me when I was taking you into custody, you're lucky you weren't shot."

"She is a nasty one, isn't she?" Gail said smugly from behind him. This Grace Thomas looked every bit as wild and despicable as Gail had imagined. Her hair was down around her shoulders in utter disarray. The dress she wore was soiled and partially torn.

Cord was surprised that Gail had come after him. He walked away from the jail cell, wanting the other woman to go back into the outer office where she belonged.

"Enjoy your dinner," Gail called out to the prisoner in a sickeningly sweet tone as Cord ushered her away and closed the door behind them.

Autumn had never been so angry with anyone in her life as she was with the arrogant lawman. She wanted to throw the whole tray of food at him and almost picked it up to do just that, but somehow she managed to control the impulse.

Autumn had faced difficult times in her life before and had persevered. She told herself she could overcome this adversity, too. Though Sheriff Randolph had thwarted her at every turn so far, she was certain she could find a way to convince the hardheaded lawman of her innocence. She admitted to herself that it had been foolish to try to use the derringer, but when he'd come charging up to the side of the stagecoach, she'd thought he was an outlaw and had only been trying to defend herself. She would say no more, for her explanation would be wasted on him until the lawyer showed up with proof of her identity.

Disgusted, but suddenly realizing she was hungry, Autumn sat down and began to eat.

"She really tried to shoot you?" Gail asked Cord, looking up at him wide-eyed with worry. She couldn't bear the thought that something might have happened to him.

Cord nodded. "She had a derringer in her purse, but I got it away from her."

"I'm so glad you weren't hurt. I hope she never gets out of jail!" she said spitefully.

"I want the whole Martin gang locked up." His tone was dark and determined.

"You'll get them. I know you will." Gail was about to say more when Miles returned. She was irritated by the deputy's unexpected appearance in the office, but couldn't reveal her true feelings. She smiled sweetly. "Well, I'd better be going. I hope I'll see you soon, Cord."

There was no denying the invitation in her voice, but Cord paid no attention. He wouldn't allow himself to think about anything but bringing Mike's killers to justice.

Gail was smiling as she left the sheriff's office, but once she was out of sight, her smile faded.

She was irritated. Cord had changed in the months since Sheriff Gallagher's death. She used to be able to flirt with him and get a response from him, but lately he'd been completely indifferent to her charms—and it was making her mad. She wasn't about to give up in her quest to marry him, but she did occasionally need some kind of encouragement. She had to find a way to win him over.

Cord was glad when Gail had gone and he and Miles were alone.

"Thatch is down by the hotel," Miles explained. "Everything seems all right. The man and woman checked in and went up to their rooms."

"Good. Did you notice anything else unusual going on around town?"

"No. It's quiet, just the way you like it."

"You're right. That is the way I like it." Cord nodded, satisfied that things were peaceful for the time being.

"Do you need any help here?"

"No. Everything's fine for right now."

"Well, I'm going to go eat; then I'll see how Thatch is doing. We'll check in with you later."

When Cord was alone again, he sat back down at his desk and lost himself in thought. He stared down at the pie Gail had left him, but had no appetite for it. Thoughts of Mike besieged him. Cord longed for some way to turn back the clock and change what had happened, but there could be no changing the past. He could only take care of today, and he'd done that.

He'd arrested Grace Thomas.

It was the least he could do for Mike.

Chapter Five

"So this is their best hotel," James muttered as he escorted Muriel down the second floor hall in the Sagebrush Hotel.

"It's their *only* hotel," Muriel pointed out as they stopped at her room.

James unlocked the door and held it open for her. They walked in, and he looked around in disgust. His room was right next door, and he imagined it was probably the same.

"At least the linens look clean." She was trying to be optimistic as she eyed the bedding.

"I should hope so."

Granted, the room was cleaner than anything they'd stayed in for the last week, but the stark accommodations made James long for the comforts of higher-class civilization. He knew there was no point in even thinking about home now, though, not with Muriel by his side. The woman had given him no peace since they'd left the sheriff's office nearly an hour ago. In all that time, she had not stopped badgering him to take further action to try to set Autumn free.

James had to admit he was tempted to do nothing more and let Autumn spend the night in jail. He thought it might teach her to heed his counsel more closely in the future. He certainly had no intention of dealing with a situation like this ever again. The fact that she'd been arrested and he'd been held at gunpoint still shocked him. Once they were married, she would obey him, just as the wedding vows dictated. If Autumn had done what he'd told her to do from the very beginning, everything would be fine right now.

"It doesn't matter how good or bad our accommodations are as long as Autumn is in that . . . that jail! We won't be getting much sleep for worrying about her." Muriel went back to the doorway. She looked down the hallway to see if the porter was coming with their trunk. "I still don't understand how this could have happened to her."

"Perhaps this is why they call it the Wild West," he told her. "Lawmen can arrest anyone they want, any time they want, and hold a prisoner for no reason."

"But Sheriff Randolph really believed she was some outlaw named Grace. He sounded so certain."

"Any idiot can be confident," James sneered. He had little respect for the lawman and was going to enjoy the moment when he realized he'd arrested an innocent woman. "We'll get the letter from the lawyer and show it to him, then he'll have to let Autumn go."

The man from the stagecoach office finally appeared with a load of luggage. They'd requested that he bring Autumn's trunk up first.

"Let me see if I can find that letter in here," James said after the man had gone to get more of their things.

James's expression turned serious as he opened Autumn's trunk and began to dig impatiently through her belongings. He hoped the actual document with the lawyer's signature would convince Sheriff Randolph that he'd made a mistake in arresting Autumn.

James was relieved to find that Autumn had safely stowed the missive in an easily accessible side compartment.

"You found it?" Muriel asked excitedly, peering over his shoulder.

"Yes. As soon as the rest of our luggage has been brought up, we can go and speak to Sheriff Randolph again."

"Thank heaven, we've got the letter," she said as relief filled her. The idea of any lady spending a night in the Sagebrush jail was horrific and unacceptable, and she now knew they would be able to save Autumn from that horrible fate.

It was almost dark by the time James and Muriel made it back to the sheriff's office. Sheriff Randolph was there, and so was one of his deputies.

"We need to speak with you again," James announced as he and Muriel entered.

"What is it?" Cord had been expecting them. Miles and Thatch had been watching the hotel and had seen them leave and head this way. Miles had hurried over to alert him.

Miles stayed in the background as the man confronted Cord, but he didn't relax. He hated the Martin gang as much as Cord did and wanted the Thomas woman to pay for her involvement with them. He would be ready if this man tried anything.

"I have Ralph Baxter's letter to Miss Thomas right here," James announced arrogantly as he presented the envelope to the sheriff. He was confident the letter would serve as indisputable proof of Autumn's identity. "This verifies everything I told you. You can release her now." The last was a command.

Cord took the letter out of the envelope and unfolded it. He quickly read it.

Miss Autumn Thomas,
    This is to inform you that Paul Thomas has passed away and you have been named sole heir to his estate.

Cord glanced back up at James. "This letter doesn't prove a thing," he told him, letting it drop to his desktop.

"What? Of course it does!"

"You could have forged it."

James had never dealt with this kind of situation before. Few people ever dared to defy his authority. It was only with great effort that he managed to control his temper. "I want to see Miss Thomas—now!"

"Like I told you before—no visitors," Cord replied harshly.

Muriel touched James's arm to get his attention. "We'd better go—"

"All right, but I'll be back tomorrow—with the lawyer!" James snarled. He snatched the letter and stormed from the office taking Muriel with him.

Miles looked at Cord once they'd gone. "You want me to spend the night here with you?"

"No. You don't have to stay all night, but I do need you to take over for me for a few minutes, before it gets too late. I want to go see Beth and tell her that we've arrested Grace Thomas." Mike's widow deserved to know what had happened.

"It'll be good for her to hear the news straight from you," Miles agreed.

"I won't be gone too long," Cord said, leaving the deputy in charge.

Miles sat down at the desk, thinking about Grace Thomas locked up in back. She was a damned good-looking woman. She had managed to look like a lady today, but he knew the truth about her. He felt no pity for her. She was only

Rod Martin's whore and deserved whatever she got.

Miles thought about giving Grace Thomas something right then—

A forbidden spark of heat flared within him.

The more he thought about it, the more he liked the idea. The heat grew in his loins. Miles knew Cord wouldn't be back for a while. He was alone with her, and who was there to care what he did to her while he had her to himself? He was sure Cord despised her as much as he did. It didn't take much for Miles to justify to himself what he wanted to do. If she spread her legs for Martin, she could spread them for him, too. She was an outlaw and a prisoner. She had no rights. To his way of thinking, she'd forfeited her rights by riding with the gang that killed Sheriff Gallagher.

Miles pulled down the shades and locked the office door. He got the keys and went back to the cell area. The prisoner was seated on the cot. She watched him warily as he came to stand before her.

"Where's Sheriff Randolph?" Autumn asked, a little unnerved by this deputy's presence.

"He's gone. He left me here to take care of you." Miles liked his own choice of words. He was going to take care of her all right.

His gaze turned leering as it settled on the torn bodice of her gown. She'd tucked the material in as best she could to repair the damage, but he still remembered the glimpse of cleavage he'd seen earlier that day.

Autumn grew tense as the deputy continued to just stand there staring at her. The look in his eyes made her uncomfortable, and she remembered how his hands had felt upon her when he'd held her. For the first time since she'd been locked up, she was glad she was safe inside the cell.

And then the deputy took out the keys.

"Are you going to release me?"

"Hell, no." His voice was husky with the lust that filled him.

Autumn went a bit pale as he fitted the key in the lock and turned it. "What are you doing?"

Miles didn't bother to answer as he pushed the door open, leaving the key in the lock, and let himself into the jail cell.

Autumn stood up, ready to flee, but there was nowhere for her to run. She was trapped.

"Now, a smart woman in your situation would be real willing to cooperate with the law," Miles began.

"I will cooperate with the law. I'll cooperate with Sheriff Randolph. When is he coming back?" she demanded. She hoped by using the sheriff's name she could strike some fear in this animal who passed himself off as a deputy.

"I don't know. He didn't say."

Autumn backed away as the man came toward her. Desperately she looked around for some escape—some way to save herself.

"I'll scream if you come any closer!" she warned.

He chuckled. "Go ahead and scream. Nobody's gonna hear you."

Autumn took another step back and came up against the cell wall. The deputy had left the cell door open, and she knew her only hope was to somehow find a way to get past him so she could run outside. She offered up a silent prayer for help as she made her move, trying to dart around him.

Miles had seen the frantic look in her eyes and knew what she was going to try. He grabbed her arm as she tried to elude him and dragged her over to the cot, where he shoved her down on her back.

"No!" Autumn wasn't sure what she could do. She tried to scramble away, but he loomed menacingly over her. The look on his face sent chills of terror through her. She saw only his horrible, grinning face as he leaned down toward her.

Miles leered at her. He had the prisoner just where he wanted her. He reached down to free himself from his pants.

Cord had wanted to be the one to tell Beth Gallagher about the arrest, but she had not been at home. Returning to the sheriff's office, he was surprised to see that the shades had been drawn. He started to go in, but found the front door locked. Suddenly worried that Rod Martin was inside trying to break Grace Thomas out of jail,

Bobbi Smith

he ran around to the back of the building. He
had a key for the back door, and he let himself
in. Gun drawn, he moved silently inside.

"Go ahead and scream. Nobody's gonna hear
you."

Cord heard Miles talking, and then he heard
Grace Thomas cry out.

"No!"

Cord charged into the cell to find his deputy
about to attack the helpless prisoner. In one swift
move, Cord hit Miles across the back of the head
with his gun. Miles collapsed, unconscious, falling halfway on top of Autumn as she lay on the
cot.

Autumn screamed. She struggled and fought
against his suffocating weight. She tried to get
away, expecting him at any moment to start tearing her clothing from her.

Then suddenly the evil deputy was gone—
lifted bodily off of her. And she was free.

"What—?" she gasped, shocked by all that had
happened so quickly.

She looked up to find Sheriff Randolph standing over her attacker, his gun in hand.

The sheriff had saved her. Without thinking,
she launched herself into his arms.

Cord saw her very real terror. He holstered
his gun and held her in a sheltering embrace.

"Are you all right?" he asked. "Did he hurt
you?"

"No—you got here in time. Oh, thank you."
Autumn clung to the sheriff, feeling his iron

strength and thanking God that he'd shown up in time. She could only imagine what the other man had planned to do to her.

Cord felt her trembling. Until that moment, he'd thought her a strong, willful woman, but in his arms, she felt delicate and helpless—a far cry from the woman who'd resisted him so fiercely earlier. He knew a great desire to protect her. He grew angry with himself for the danger he'd put her in, for trusting Miles and leaving her alone with him. It was his job to keep her safe while she was in custody, and he had almost failed miserably. He was just thankful Beth hadn't been home when he'd gone to speak with her. If she had been, he wouldn't have returned in time.

Cord had trusted Miles. The deputy had worked for Mike, too, and Cord had kept him on, along with Thatch, when he'd taken over as sheriff. Miles was going to have one hell of a headache when he came around, and Cord was glad. Miles deserved worse than that for what he'd tried to do.

Miles gave a low groan and started to roll over. "What happened?"

Cord put the woman gently from him and reached down to tear the deputy's badge from Miles's shirt. "Get up and get out of here! You're fired."

Miles put a hand to his aching, bleeding head and slowly started to get to his feet. "I'm fired? For what?"

"Miss Thomas is in my custody, and as such, she's under my protection," Cord told him coldly.

"I wasn't taking anything she wasn't giving away already. She ain't nothing but Martin's slut."

Autumn gasped at his words.

Cord stepped protectively forward to shield her from him. "Get out of Sagebrush. I don't want to see you anywhere around."

Miles looked over at him, his expression hate-filled. He'd always resented Mike hiring Cord on as a deputy, and when Cord had gotten the sheriff's job instead of him after Mike's death, he'd been furious. Rage ate at him. He cursed Cord and the woman loudly and walked unsteadily from the cell.

Cord followed Miles out. He didn't trust the other man. Cord locked the front door behind him after he'd gone, and then started back to check on his prisoner.

Autumn had remained standing where she was, staring after Sheriff Randolph. So much had happened to her in such a short period of time that she found it all hard to believe.

She told herself it had to be a bad dream and that she would wake up now.

She even closed her eyes for a moment, hoping to find when she opened them again that she was back in her own bedroom in Philadelphia. But when she did open her eyes, she found herself staring at the broad width of Sheriff Randolph's chest. He'd returned so quietly that she hadn't heard him approach. He was standing before her in the open cell doorway, watching her intently as she lifted her gaze to his.

"Are you sure you're all right?" Cord asked, concerned.

"Yes, thanks to you. I don't know what I would have done if you hadn't shown up when you did."

"Don't even think about it," he said, not wanting to think about it himself. "Miles is gone, and he won't be back. And I won't leave you again. I'll be right here if you need me."

At that moment, all Autumn wanted to do was go back into the protective circle of his arms and draw on his strength, for she had felt safe there before. She knew that what she was feeling was ridiculous—he was the sheriff and she was his prisoner—but it didn't change what was in her heart.

Cord felt suddenly awkward standing there with her, although he wasn't sure why. He told himself this was Grace Thomas. Certainly, she didn't deserve what had just happened to her, but she was a part of an outlaw gang, and he had to keep her locked up. Cord closed and locked her cell door, taking the keys with him. He locked the back door to the building again, so that no one would bother them again that night.

"Do you need anything?" he asked, ready to return to his desk.

"Only my freedom."

He had no answer for her. Turning away, he went into the outer office.

It was over an hour later when Thatch reported in to Cord, and Cord told him the news.

"You fired Miles?" Thatch was shocked.

Cord quickly explained what had happened.

"I thought he was a good man," the deputy said in disgust.

"So did I or I wouldn't have trusted him alone with her. Did you see anything going on around town?"

"No. Dodson and the woman with him returned to the hotel. Everything seems normal. Will you need any help here overnight?"

"No."

"I'll check back with you first thing in the morning, then. It's going to be interesting to see what happens. I wonder where Martin is."

"So do I." The thought was troubling, but Cord knew there was nothing they could do but wait for the outlaw to make his move.

When Thatch had gone, Cord went to sit at his desk. He was glad he had one deputy he could rely on.

Cord's thoughts turned to Dodson, and he found himself thinking about the authenticity of the letter the man had presented to him. It had looked legal enough, but he didn't believe it was. Though the woman he'd left just now had seemed fragile, he knew from when he'd arrested her earlier what a fighter she was. He was still certain that if she'd been able to get to her gun, she would have tried to use it.

Thoughts of her connection to Rod Martin returned, and Cord got up to pace the office. He wondered anew why the outlaw had sent his woman into town ahead of him. Cord hoped he had foiled his plan by locking Grace up, but he couldn't be sure. He wanted to question her further, but because of her encounter with Miles, he decided to wait until the next day. Determined to be ready in case there was any more trouble that night, Cord got a shotgun out of the gun case and loaded it. He set it within easy reach of his desk chair.

Cord hadn't heard any sounds coming from his prisoner in a while, so he decided to look in on her. He opened the door to the cell area to discover that Grace had fallen asleep on the narrow cot, with a single blanket covering her.

It startled him to realize that, asleep, she looked the innocent angel. Her fair complexion was flawless, and the golden mass of hair spread out around her was highlighted by the glow from the flickering lamplight.

As quickly as he allowed himself to think she was angelic-looking, he denied the description. He knew that impression was wrong. Looks were often deceiving, and there was nothing innocent or angelic about Grace Thomas.

The realization saddened him a bit, for her life seemed like such a tragic waste. He wondered what had happened to cause her to end up this way.

Cord stood there in silence for a moment longer, then returned to his vigil at his desk.

It was going to be a long night.

Chapter Six

Ralph Baxter stared at James Dodson in disbelief. "You say Sheriff Randolph arrested her?"

"That's right. He stopped the stagecoach on its way into town and took her into custody," James replied angrily. He and Muriel had been waiting outside the office door for the lawyer first thing the next morning and had followed him inside as soon as he'd arrived. "I want you to see that she is released immediately. It's bad enough she had to spend the night in jail! I even took your letter over and showed it to the sheriff, but he refused to let her go. For some reason, he kept calling her 'Grace Thomas.' "

Ralph went pale at the news. "I see." He suddenly grew a bit agitated. "I'll go speak with him right now."

"Do you have any idea why all this has happened to our poor Autumn?" Muriel asked, still at a loss to explain the events of the previous day.

Ralph cleared his throat a bit guiltily and avoided answering her question. He stood up nervously and started to hurry around his desk. "Let me talk to Sheriff Randolph. I'm sure this is a terrible misunderstanding that can be straightened out."

"I hope you're right, but the sheriff didn't seem to think so yesterday," she went on. She'd noticed that the lawyer hadn't really answered her question, but freeing Autumn was most important, so she let the matter drop for now.

James had also noticed the strange, sudden change in the lawyer's demeanor. He wondered at it, but he, too, let it go. He just wanted Autumn out of jail as quickly as possible.

In fact, he wanted Autumn safely back home in Philadelphia. He was ready to head east today. He hoped there was a stagecoach coming through, for it would take no time at all for the three of them to be packed up and waiting at the station. He had convinced himself overnight that he wouldn't have too much trouble talking Autumn into leaving Sagebrush.

"We're going with you," James told Baxter.

"No, I want you both to wait here for me. I'll bring Miss Thomas back to be reunited with you."

James and Muriel exchanged worried looks.

James in particular wanted to be there when the sheriff found out the truth.

"We prefer to go along," he insisted.

"It will be handled more smoothly if I speak with Sheriff Randolph alone," Ralph explained. Paul Thomas had sworn him to secrecy about his private affairs, and he intended to keep that promise. "Please have a seat in the outer office and make yourselves comfortable. I hope this won't take too long. I'll be back as quickly as possible."

James and Muriel did as he'd directed, but they didn't like it.

Ralph quickly unlocked the file where he kept his most important papers and drew out the documents he knew would secure Autumn Thomas's release from jail. Then he left James and Muriel waiting in his office while he made the two-block walk to the jail.

Cord had passed a restless night. Troubled by all that had happened and worried that Martin might show up at any moment, he'd gotten little sleep. The tension he was feeling eased when the new day dawned, but he still knew he was going to have to deal with Ralph Baxter.

"Morning, Ralph," Cord greeted the lawyer as he entered his office. "I've been expecting you."

"Sheriff Randolph," Ralph said respectfully, knowing the news he had to impart was going to be hard to believe. "I came over the moment I got word from Mr. Dodson and Miss Williams about what's happened with Miss Thomas. I'm afraid a terrible mistake has been made."

"What kind of mistake?"

"You've arrested an innocent woman."

"I've heard this story before." Cord eyed the attorney skeptically. "The woman I arrested is Grace Thomas, Paul Thomas's daughter. She's part of the Martin gang and wanted in connection with Sheriff Gallagher's murder."

"It's true, the woman you arrested is Paul Thomas's daughter—"

Cord smiled at this confirmation.

Then the lawyer finished, "But your prisoner's name is Autumn, not Grace. Paul Thomas had two daughters."

"Two?"

"Yes. Would you allow me to speak privately with Miss Thomas for a moment, please? I promise I will explain everything to you in detail after I've spoken with her. She's unaware of some of this information, and I believe it would be best if I talked with her first."

Cord was tempted to refuse him, but he knew the attorney to be an honest man. He begrudgingly led him back to the cell area.

Autumn looked up as they came toward her. She didn't recognize the man with Sheriff Randolph, but she was hoping against hope he was the lawyer.

"Miss Thomas?" Ralph said. "I'm Ralph Baxter, your father's attorney."

"Thank heaven!" She stood up, eager to be released.

"I need to talk with you first, before we go." He looked at Cord. "If you could give us a few minutes alone, please?"

Cord nodded and went back to his desk, closing the hall door behind him to give them the privacy the lawyer seemed so desperately to want.

"Why aren't we leaving now? Haven't you told him who I am?" Autumn demanded. She could see no reason to stay locked up a minute longer. Surely, Baxter had proven her innocence to the lawman.

"I wanted to explain everything to you before I talk to the sheriff."

She frowned, suddenly wary of what he was about to tell her. "Explain what to me?"

"Miss Thomas—I know this must have been a very difficult time for you, getting the news about your father this way."

Autumn looked up at him. "Yes, it has been. I didn't even know my father was alive until I got your letter. My mother had told me he was dead—that he'd died when I was a baby."

Ralph nodded in understanding. "There were many troubling aspects to dealing with your parents' situation. Your father left a letter for you." He took an envelope out of the papers he'd brought with him and presented it to her. "I believe this will explain everything."

Autumn stared down at the sealed envelope,

seeing her father's script for the very first time.

"I'll read it later." She wanted to be alone when she read his words to her.

"It would be best if you opened it now. The information contained in the letter is essential to obtaining your release."

"But I'm not who the sheriff thinks I am! You know that! How could he make such a stupid mistake and be the sheriff here in town?"

Ralph said nothing. He only waited for her to read her father's letter.

Impatiently, Autumn tore the envelope open. She started reading the enclosed pages in silence:

Autumn—

If you are reading this letter, then I am dead and buried.

I do not know how much your mother told you about me. She left me when you were just a baby. I tried to keep her from going, but she wouldn't listen to reason. Her family had money, and she missed the fancy lifestyle she'd been living back East. She wanted to take both you and your twin sister, Grace.

Autumn stopped reading. She stared down at the letter she held in trembling hands, shocked to the depths of her soul by the revelation.

She had a sister, a twin, named Grace.

Autumn looked up, her gaze meeting and holding the lawyer's.

"I have a twin?" Her voice was choked with emotion.

"Yes," he answered quietly. He could see the torment in her eyes. "An identical twin."

"I never knew." A myriad of conflicting thoughts and feelings raged within her as she read on.

> *Your mother and I finally agreed that we would each take one of you, and that there would be no further contact between us.*
>
> *I took Grace, but she grew up to be just like your mother. I've disowned her.*
>
> *I have not tried to get in touch with you in all these years because I am a man of my word. Do not think that I don't love you. I have thought about you and missed you every day. I am leaving everything to you.*
>
> *Mr. Baxter will explain.*
>
> > *Your father,*
> > *Paul Thomas*

Autumn was taken aback by this new discovery. She sat down on the side of the cot, letter still in hand, trying to come to grips with the knowledge that she had a sister—a twin named Grace. Deep in her heart, Autumn was torn between rejoicing at the news that she had a twin, and fury over all the lies she'd been told.

Grace.

As she thought of her sister's name, she glanced up at the lawyer.

"Grace is the name Sheriff Randolph kept calling me." Her voice faltered.

"Yes—it is," he said quietly.

Autumn frowned as everything Sheriff Randolph had been saying suddenly began to make sense. "Is my sister in trouble with the law?"

Baxter cleared his throat a bit nervously as he prepared himself to give her the bad news. "The last time we heard anything about Grace was nearly a year ago, and she had taken up with Rod Martin."

"He's the outlaw the sheriff was talking about."

"Martin's notorious—and deadly. How your sister ended up with him, we never knew for sure. He and his men have been robbing and killing for years, and no one's been able to stop him. Martin and his gang killed our sheriff, Mike Gallagher, not too long ago. Sheriff Gallagher had arrested one of Martin's men and was taking him in for trial when they ambushed him and shot him in the back. That's why Cord Randolph has been so adamant about keeping you locked up. Sheriff Gallagher was his friend. Cord took the sheriff's job after his murder."

Autumn realized now how condemning her actions had been on the stagecoach—fighting him and trying to draw her gun.

The lawyer went on with a slight shake of his head as he stared at her. "I have to admit the resemblance between you and Grace is amazing. It's no wonder Cord was so positive that you were your sister."

Her sister—It troubled Autumn that her twin

was involved with such evil people. She didn't know how Grace had come to that, but somehow she was going to find out.

Autumn realized how lucky she had been that Sheriff Randolph hadn't shot her when he'd stopped the stagecoach. For a moment, she allowed herself to feel a bit of sympathy for the lawman, but it was quickly replaced by anger.

"He could have allowed me the chance to prove my true identity."

"He did—this morning," Baxter said. "Sheriff Randolph has been extra careful with this case. I'm sure that's why he intercepted the stage outside of town. He was probably afraid there might be a gunfight, and he didn't want to risk anyone in Sagebrush getting hurt. But that's over and done with. I'm going to straighten this all out for you right now. I just need to speak with him for a moment, then I'm sure you'll be free to go."

Autumn hated to spend another minute in jail, but there was nothing else she could do. She watched the lawyer disappear into the outer office and hoped the sheriff wouldn't prove too stubborn or hardheaded about letting her go. She wanted to get as far away from this jail as she could.

"What I couldn't tell you before but am now at liberty to explain is that Paul Thomas had not only one daughter. He had two, identical twin daughters, Grace and Autumn," Ralph began.

Cord stared at him in disbelief.

"I know it's hard to believe, and I only know a portion of the whole sad story. Paul's wife, Lori, divorced him when the girls were infants. I don't know exactly how it came to pass, but they reached an agreement that each of them would take a daughter. Lori Thomas took Autumn and went back to Philadelphia. Autumn is the woman you now have locked up in back. Paul kept Grace and raised her himself. As you know, he threw her out, and that's when she got mixed up with Rod Martin."

"And Autumn knows nothing about her sister's activities." Cord concluded flatly.

"Nothing. She didn't even know Grace existed until now, and she only learned of her father when I contacted her about inheriting his estate. Her mother had told her that her father died when she was a baby, and she never mentioned that she had a twin. I just gave her the letter Paul wrote to her before he died, explaining everything."

Cord was completely frustrated by this turn of events.

"I'll get her for you."

Cord stood and got the keys out of his desk drawer. He had believed he was finally closing in on the gang after her arrest, but he'd been wrong. He was back to where he'd begun—empty-handed with no clues to go on, and now he was even short a deputy.

At the thought of Miles, anger flared in Cord. He had trusted the man. Since Mike had hired him on, he had believed Miles was a good and honorable lawman. It was a mistake in judgment he would never make again. He would always be thankful that he'd gotten back in time to stop Miles from harming the woman he now knew was Autumn Thomas.

Cord went back to her cell to release her.

As soon as she saw him approaching she came to stand at the door.

Cord knew he owed her an apology. "Sorry about the inconvenience." He held the door wide for her.

"I told you you were making a mistake," she said as she hurried past him, eager to be gone.

"I was just trying to do my job."

She paused and looked back at the lawman as he stood before the empty cell. He was a proud, strong man, but he was also a very moral person who'd protected her from harm even when he'd believed her to be her sister. "Sheriff Randolph—I'm sorry about my sister's involvement with the outlaws. I didn't know about any of this until today."

"Baxter explained everything to me," he said.

She stood there a moment longer, then went into the office.

Ralph smiled at her in greeting. "Your friends are waiting for you at my law office. Shall we go?"

"I do need to get my reticule." She looked at Sheriff Randolph, who'd followed her out.

"It's right here." Cord got her bag out of his

bottom desk drawer and handed it to her.

Autumn opened the purse and looked inside.

"There is one thing missing, Sheriff," she challenged, "my derringer. I'd like it back, please."

Cord knew he had no legal right to hold on to it. He went to the gun case and took out the small weapon. "Be careful with this, Miss Thomas. It may be small, but it is a lethal weapon. Guns can be dangerous—in the wrong hands."

"I know. I brought it along to protect myself in dangerous situations," she countered, her gaze locking with his as she finally had a chance to explain her actions to him. "The only reason I tried to draw it when you stopped the stagecoach was because I thought you and your deputies were outlaws. I thought you were going to rob us."

"Sometimes first impressions can be deceiving." He found himself smiling slightly, in spite of his dark mood.

Autumn was amazed by how that small smile transformed him. When Cord reached out to give her the gun, their hands accidentally touched. It was a single, simple touch, but it sent a shock of physical awareness through Autumn. She was careful not to let her reaction to him show. She quickly turned her attention to stowing the gun in her purse.

"Good bye, Sheriff Randolph." She turned to the lawyer, ready to leave.

"Goodbye, Autumn Thomas," Cord said.

Autumn and the lawyer turned to leave. Autumn hoped she would never have to see the inside of a sheriff's office or jail cell again.

It was at that very moment that the office door flew open and Beth Gallagher came rushing in.

Chapter Seven

"Cord! I'm so glad you're here. I just heard you arrested the Thomas woman," Beth Gallagher began, then stopped in mid-sentence. Her expression altered as they watched. Her look of hope turned to one of pure loathing as she came face to face with the woman she thought was partially responsible for her husband's death. "You!" She spat out the word.

"Beth—" Cord was surprised to see the widow so early this morning. Since learning the truth about Autumn, he'd been glad that he hadn't spoken to Beth the night before but his relief was short-lived. He moved quickly to her side.

"What is *she* doing out of the jail cell? She should be behind bars!"

"Excuse me?" Autumn had no idea who this

woman was, and she was chilled by the vehemence of her words.

"Why is she out walking around free?" Beth demanded. She stopped and looked at Cord in anger and confusion.

"Beth, it's all right," Cord tried to reassure her.

"What do you mean, it's all right? This woman is one of them! You've got to keep her locked up, or, better yet, take her out and hang her right now!"

"Mrs. Gallagher," Ralph interrupted in a calming voice, "this young woman isn't Grace Thomas."

The widow looked at him in disbelief. "Of course she is. I used to see her around town!"

"Ralph is right, Beth. This isn't Grace Thomas. This is her twin sister, Autumn," Cord added.

"Paul Thomas only had the one daughter! We all know that!"

"That's what we were led to believe for all these years," Ralph went on.

"I just found out today that there were twins. This young lady—" Cord began.

"Lady? You call her a lady?" Beth turned on Autumn and grabbed her by the arm. "She's no lady."

Both men moved to protect Autumn.

Cord took Beth's arm to draw her away from Autumn. "I give you my word, Beth. She isn't Grace Thomas."

Cord nodded to Ralph to leave with Autumn. The lawyer shepherded her toward the door. Autumn had gone pale, but she did not cower before the widow's open hatred.

"You're going to let her go? Just walk out of here?" Beth asked incredulously.

"She's innocent. She hasn't done anything wrong," Cord explained.

"How can you be so sure?"

"Ralph has proof of her identity, and he has no reason to lie about it. You know I want to catch the Martin gang, but not at the expense of an innocent woman."

"I hope you're right about her being innocent," Beth charged in an ugly tone. "It could all be a trick. I hope you don't end up regretting your decision to let her go."

Without another word, the widow walked out on him.

Anger and frustration ate at Cord, but there was nothing he could do about it.

He could only start hunting for the outlaw gang all over again.

Autumn was deeply shaken by the encounter with the former sheriff's widow. She stayed close by Ralph's side as he walked with her down the street at a rapid pace.

"Are you all right?" he asked, concerned.

"I am now that we're away from there."

"I'm sorry you had to see Beth Gallagher that

way. She really is a lovely, gentle woman, but since Mike's murder—"

"I can understand why she's so distraught, but I find it hard to believe my sister could have had anything to do with her husband's murder."

"If I were you, I wouldn't let anybody else in town hear you talk that way. You don't know anything about your sister," Ralph warned her.

"But I intend to find out. She's my twin—" Autumn began, still awed by the knowledge.

"And she's chosen to associate herself with a gang of killers. Be glad your father disowned her. She's gone, and with luck she'll stay gone, so you won't ever have to deal with her."

"Why did he disown her? What could she have done that was so bad?"

"Your father never confided that in me."

"And Grace never tried to see our father again?"

"To the best of my knowledge, no."

"I truly don't understand how my mother could have gone away, knowing she never planned to come back, and left one of her babies behind." The revelation was completely at odds with the mother she'd known and loved. Autumn longed to know more about the mystery that was her family's past. She hoped there might be someone at her father's ranch who could help her.

"My office is just ahead," Ralph said. "I didn't tell Mr. Dodson or Miss Williams any of this. I thought it best to leave it to you to tell them at your discretion."

"Thank you. I appreciate that."

When they reached the office, James and Muriel leaped up.

"You're all right." James sounded relieved.

"I'm fine."

"Thank heaven Mr. Baxter was able to free you." Muriel hugged her. The sheriff had been so obstinate, she'd worried that he wouldn't believe the lawyer either, and would continue to refuse to let Autumn go.

"Is everything all straightened out now?" James asked.

"Yes. Let's go in and have a seat. Miss Thomas can explain to you what happened before we go over the will."

Ralph directed them to sit in the chairs before his desk, and Autumn quickly told James and Muriel all that had transpired. They were as shocked as Autumn had been by the news about Grace.

Muriel's expression saddened as she faced Autumn. "This explains so many things about your mother that I never understood at the time—"

"None of that matters now," James interrupted, not wanting the conversation to turn maudlin. "What matters is that you're out of that filthy jail, and we can finish taking care of your business here with Mr. Baxter, and go home." James had had enough of Texas. The sooner they made the return trip to Philadelphia, the better.

Autumn found his attitude troubling, but said nothing. "It is good to be out of jail."

"Oh, darling, no lady should ever have to suffer such indignity," Muriel sympathized. "The sheriff did treat you properly, didn't he?"

The memory of her terrible encounter with the deputy returned, but she ignored it. There was no reason to speak of it. Sheriff Randolph had saved her, and she hadn't been harmed in any way, only frightened.

"Yes," Autumn reassured her. "I've often imagined doing exciting things with my life, but being a prisoner in jail was never one of them."

Muriel smiled at Autumn's attempt at humor. "It's all over now. Things can only get better from here on."

"That's right," Autumn agreed.

"I have your father's will right here, if you're ready for the reading?" Ralph began spreading out the document before him.

"Please," Autumn said.

Ralph read the last will and testament out loud. All Paul Thomas's worldly possessions were left to Autumn. She was now the sole owner of the Lazy T Ranch, which, according to the lawyer, was a successful cattle ranch.

"Will we be making the trip to the Lazy T this afternoon?" Autumn asked.

"It will be better if we wait and make a fresh start in the morning. I do want to mention that one of the neighboring ranchers, Pete Miller, is interested in buying the ranch if you're of a mind to sell. He spoke with me about it not too long ago."

"Sell?" The idea startled Autumn. She hadn't even considered selling.

"You have a buyer already? That's wonderful," James put in. He was ready to have the lawyer handle the sale immediately. "How soon can you start the negotiations? What would be a fair asking price?"

"James!" Autumn objected. "I don't want to sell the ranch—at least, not yet."

He controlled his irritation with an effort. "I was only trying to make things easier for you, my dear. It's only natural that you'd want to go to the Lazy T and take a look around first."

"We'll be ready to go in the morning, Mr. Baxter," Autumn told the lawyer.

"You're staying at the Sagebrush Hotel?" he confirmed.

"Yes," James answered for them.

"I'll meet you in the lobby at nine o'clock."

"We'll be ready," Autumn promised.

When Thatch reported in to Cord a short time later, he was surprised to see the cell empty and the prisoner gone.

"What happened? Where is she?"

Cord quickly told him of the meeting with the lawyer and the truth about Autumn's identity. Thatch was amazed.

"I'm going to take a couple of hours off. I need some sleep," Cord said.

"After a night like you just had, I'd need a drink."

Cord gave him a tired smile. "That's not a bad idea. I'll be back later this afternoon. Keep things quiet here."

Thatch chuckled. "After yesterday, that'll be easy. Enjoy your time off."

Leaving Thatch in charge, Cord headed for the small house he rented in town. As he walked past the Sundown Saloon, he thought of Thatch's remark and realized his deputy had been right. He did need a drink. Even though it wasn't quite noon yet, he went in.

The saloon was quiet, and Sam looked up when Cord came through the swinging doors.

"Well, good morning, Sheriff. This is a surprise," Sam said as Cord went to stand at the bar.

"Whiskey," Cord ordered.

"I take it you're having a bad morning?" Sam was surprised. It wasn't like the sheriff to drink this early in the day.

"Some days are better than others."

"I thought things were going good for you. Last night, everyone was talking and celebrating because you'd arrested Grace Thomas." Sam set a glass of whiskey before him.

Cord took a deep drink, then told the bartender about the woman's mistaken identity.

Sam's expression was one of disbelief. "So it wasn't her after all? Damn—who would have guessed?" Sam understood the sheriff's dark mood now. "We were all thinking it wouldn't be long before you'd have Rod Martin and his men locked up right along with her."

"That's what I was hoping for, too, but I'm going to have to start all over again."

It angered Cord that the outlaws' trail was cold. He wanted to go after them. He wanted to track them down and bring them in, to see them pay for their crimes, but for the time being he was helpless.

And Cord Randolph didn't like being helpless.

"I hope you catch up with them before anybody else gets hurt," Sam said.

"Me, too." He took another drink and enjoyed the whiskey's power as it burned all the way down.

"So, do you think this mystery daughter from back East is here to take over the Thomas ranch?"

"It looks that way."

"Running a spread that big is a hard job for a man who knows what he's doing. How's a woman like this one going to be able to handle it?"

"I don't know, and we didn't have much of an opportunity to talk to her about her plans." For the first time since coming in the saloon, Cord managed to grin at Sam.

"I can't imagine why," Sam chuckled as he pictured the arrest. "I heard tell you dragged her right off the stagecoach, brought her into town and locked her up."

"I was just doing my job," Cord said with a shrug, still smiling, "trying to keep the town of Sagebrush safe."

"And you're doing a fine job," Sam complimented him.

Cord's smile faded. "If I was so damned good, I'd have Rod Martin behind bars right now."

"Don't be so hard on yourself. He knows you're after him, and he's lying low. He'll show up eventually, and when he does, I know you'll be ready."

"You're right. I will," Cord said, turning serious again.

"Maybe the arrival of Paul's estranged daughter isn't such a bad thing."

"She's a complication I didn't need."

"Yes, but it might work out in your favor. If Grace Thomas hears about her father's death and discovers she's got a sister she didn't know about, she'll probably want to come around and get a look at her."

"You're right."

"I think you need to try to win over this Autumn," Sam said slyly. "Find a way to spend some time with her. Make nice."

"Unless it's official business, Autumn Thomas isn't going to give me the time of day."

"Go after her, like you'd go after the gang," Sam challenged. "Spend some time courting her. The closer you get to her, the better. That way if Grace shows up, you'll know about it."

"She's engaged. Her fiancé made the trip with her."

"Why should that stop you? I never knew you to be one to give up without trying when you wanted something—and you do want Martin, don't you?" Sam urged. "Go on. Make nice with her. She can't be ugly. I've seen Grace Thomas around town, and she was a good-looking woman."

Cord smiled at that. "Autumn Thomas is not ugly."

"So she is attractive," Sam confirmed.

"Very." Cord thought of how beautiful and innocent she'd looked when he'd watched her sleeping. He also remembered how it had felt to hold her after Miles's attack.

"Then that just makes this all the easier for you. It's not too painful courting a pretty woman. What's stopping you?"

"I don't think she's too fond of me."

"So change her mind. It can't hurt to try. What have you got to lose?"

Cord frowned thoughtfully. "You're right about Grace. If she finds out what's happened, she might come around." He finished his drink. "I think I'll ride out to the Lazy T and check on things in a few days."

"Want another whiskey?" Sam offered.

"No, but thanks. I'll see you later tonight."

"I'll be looking for you."

Cord was in a considerably better mood when he left the saloon. Sam's suggestion was a good one. He didn't know if anything would come of it, but at least it was a place to a start.

Chapter Eight

"Cord let you out of jail?" Gail was shocked to see Autumn enter the restaurant late that afternoon with James and Muriel.

"I beg your pardon?" James stiffened, offended.

Autumn quickly spoke up. "Yes. Sheriff Randolph realized that a mistake had been made about my identity. Everything's fine now."

"Oh." Gail looked doubtful, but she knew Cord wouldn't have let the woman go unless it was true. "Well, come on in. There's a table over here."

Gail seated them toward the back of the restaurant, and Autumn appreciated what little privacy the location gave them. She wanted to relax and enjoy the meal. They placed their order and were glad when the food was served quickly.

"I really am anxious to get out to the Lazy T. It's a shame we couldn't go today," Autumn said as she was finishing her dinner.

"I think a quiet night here in town will do us good." James had never thought he would hear himself say that. "The ranch isn't going anywhere."

"That's true," Muriel put in.

"I do find it promising that a neighbor is interested in buying the place," James said, broaching the topic he wanted to discuss. He was ready for her to make a deal and get rid of the ranch.

"We'll see," Autumn said, being deliberately evasive. "I'm not so sure I want to sell."

James gave her a look of disbelief. "Why wouldn't you? You don't know anything about ranching."

"I can learn how to run the ranch," she returned, feeling a need to develop some connection with her deceased father. The Lazy T had obviously meant a lot to him.

"Why would you want to?" James asked sarcastically. He dismissed her interest out of hand, for he was still determined to leave Texas as quickly as possible.

"You mean you don't want to stay here and be a rancher, James?" Muriel asked him in a teasing manner, hoping to lighten his mood.

He, however, found nothing the least bit humorous in her question. "No, Muriel, I don't," he bit out. "Our lives are back in Philadelphia,

Autumn—not in this godforsaken wilderness."

"James is right about that," Muriel agreed looking at Autumn. "And from what your mother told me, she did hate living on the ranch."

"So my father stayed here, and Mother left—with me." Autumn had so many unanswered questions about the past; she feared most would never be answered.

"I can't imagine why he wanted to stay," James said. "Philadelphia is civilized. I can't say the same for Sagebrush."

"I'm sure once you settle in, it grows on you," Autumn countered, defending the town she still knew very little about.

"You have to admit, it has been an adventure coming here," Muriel said.

"Where else would we get that kind of welcome?" Autumn added. "It was exciting—if nothing else."

"Are you ready for some dessert?" Gail asked, coming to the table and interrupting their conversation.

They quickly placed an order for pie. Gail returned with their food and had just finished serving them when James glanced over and saw the restaurant door open and Sheriff Randolph walk in. He watched as the waitress rushed over to welcome him.

"I guess there's no escaping him," James muttered in irritation. The less he was reminded of Autumn's time in jail, the better.

Autumn heard his remark and looked up to see Sheriff Randolph standing near the entrance, his hat in hand, talking with the waitress. Autumn remembered the reaction she'd had to his touch earlier that day, and she stared at him now, all too aware of his presence. She realized he was a very handsome man.

The thought surprised her, and her gaze remained on him. She had been around good-looking men—sophisticated men with money and power. But there was something about Sheriff Randolph. He had the look of a man in complete control, a man of authority who commanded respect from those around him. The white shirt he wore fit his broad shoulders perfectly, and his dark pants hugged long, lean legs. His gun rode low on his hip.

The realization that she was even having such thoughts about the lawman surprised Autumn. She forced herself to look away, to look back at James and try to concentrate on what he was saying.

And then she heard Sheriff Randolph laugh.

It was a deep, resonant sound that touched a chord within her. Against her will, Autumn found her gaze drawn back to him.

Sheriff Randolph was laughing good-naturedly at something the waitress had said, and he was smiling down at her. He looked relaxed and at ease, and very different from the man she'd been forced to deal with at the jail.

Then, as if sensing her gaze upon him, Cord glanced her way.

Across the room, their gazes met.

In that moment, it seemed to Autumn that all time was suspended.

"Don't you agree, Autumn?" Muriel asked for the second time.

Her question interrupted Autumn's straying thoughts and dragged her back to reality. "I'm sorry, Muriel. What were you saying?"

"James and I were discussing how long it will take you to straighten out your father's estate. I was saying a week, maybe two at the most. What do you think?"

"I can't make that decision yet. I really won't know until we get to the ranch and I've had a chance to look over everything," she answered.

James was furious with her. He had seen that her attention had been focused on the sheriff, while she'd ignored them, and he didn't like it one bit.

"We need to figure out how soon we'll be going home," James pointed out.

"Why?" Autumn looked from one to the other.

"I'll have to buy our return tickets and arrange our travel schedule."

Autumn was irritated that he was trying to take charge of her life. "I realize you didn't want me to make this trip, James, but I had to come. Now that I'm here, I can't even consider leaving until

I've learned the whole truth about my past—and the truth about my sister."

"*Your sister?*" James repeated, horrified. "Don't even consider trying to contact her in any way. I forbid it!"

Autumn stared at him, wondering what right he had to forbid her to do anything. He wasn't her husband yet. "There is no way for me to contact her, but I hardly think it's any of your concern, James."

"It is very much my concern," he argued. "You will soon be my wife. I refuse to allow you to put yourself in danger."

"I wouldn't be in any danger."

"Your sister is a wanted criminal! Look what you've already suffered because of her. You were arrested and forced to spend a night in jail. The best thing for us to do is to finish taking care of your business here as quickly as we can and then return to Philadelphia so we can put all this ugliness behind us." He spoke sternly, and his expression was completely serious. He was dictating what he expected to happen, and he meant for her to obey him without question.

"As you just said, James, this is *my* business," Autumn said defiantly, "and I will take care of it myself—in my own time."

"Of course you will, dear," Muriel said, sensing the growing tension between them. "That's why we accompanied you—to help you in any way we can. We had no idea things would turn out to be so complicated, but that doesn't matter.

What matters is that James and I will do everything in our power to get you through this very trying time."

Autumn smiled at her. "I appreciate your help more than you'll ever know. It has been hard for me—learning about my father and sister this way. But it would have been far worse to have gone through my whole life never knowing about them. I may not find out what caused all the unhappiness, but I have to try to learn the truth. I'm just hopeful someone at the ranch will know and be able to tell me."

"What will you do if no one does?" Muriel asked.

"I'll deal with that when it happens. For now, I'm just glad to be here."

James kept his expression carefully blank. He didn't know how Autumn could possibly be glad to be in a town like Sagebrush. Only bad things had happened to them since they'd arrived. The place was so uncivilized, James wasn't sure what to expect from one minute to the next. The time he was going to be forced to spend in this area was going to be tedious for him. As dreadful as traveling west had been, though, he was actually looking forward to making the return trip. At least, once they were heading back east, the worst would finally be behind them.

"Evening," Cord said, nodding to them after Gail had seated him at a table nearby.

They returned his greeting as they prepared to leave.

Gail regretfully excused herself from waiting on Cord to settle up with James. Though the tip he gave her was a nice one, she was glad his party was gone. The fewer customers she had to take care of right now, the better. She didn't care about making money; she wanted time to spend with Cord.

James escorted Autumn and Muriel to their rooms at the hotel. They bade good night to Muriel first, and, once she'd disappeared inside, James walked Autumn to her room a little farther down the hallway. When she started to unlock the door, he took the key from her and opened it, then gave her back the key.

"You'll be all right tonight? Is there anything you need?" James asked attentively as he gazed down at her in the dimly lighted hallway. In spite of her headstrong ways, he thought she was a vision of loveliness.

"No, I'm fine."

For some reason, Autumn found she was very tired of his company. She needed some time alone to think and sort out her feelings.

"Well, good night," James said in a quieter voice.

Before she could turn away, he gathered her gently into his arms and kissed her. She hadn't been expecting his kiss, and she went still in his embrace. When the kiss ended and he stepped back, she was surprised to find she was almost actually relieved to be free of him.

107

"Good night, James."

Autumn went quickly into the room and locked the door behind her.

Several hours later, she lay in her bed, tossing and turning. Thoughts of James and the way he had been acting troubled her. She told herself that she loved him—that was why she had agreed to marry him. He was certainly everything she'd ever wanted in a man: he was handsome and well-educated and wealthy. They would have a good life together in Philadelphia once they were wed.

In her mind, Autumn relived the kiss he'd given her for what seemed like the hundredth time. She'd experienced little emotional reaction to it, and she had honestly been glad when he'd left her. Autumn told herself she'd only reacted that way tonight because she was still angry with him for trying to force her to sell the ranch and leave Sagebrush right away, but there was a part of her that wondered.

Restless, Autumn gave up trying to sleep and rose from the bed to go to the window. She brushed the curtain aside and looked out. High above in the star-studded night sky the moon shone brightly, bathing the town in its pale soft glow. The night was quiet. The streets were deserted except for a solitary figure she could see walking slowly down the darkly shadowed sidewalk toward the hotel. For a moment, she wondered if the man was dangerous since he was out so late at night.

And then she recognized him.

It was Sheriff Randolph.

Autumn stepped back from her window a bit, but she did not let the curtain fall. Entranced by some need she couldn't explain, she remained where she was, watching the lawman continue on. Only when he had completely disappeared from sight did she return to her bed.

Cord's mood was watchful as he made his way through town. For a moment, earlier, he'd sensed that someone was watching him. His instincts were seldom wrong, so he was being extra careful, but there was no one else on the streets and nothing unusual happening. All was quiet, and that was good. Satisfied that his town was safe, Cord called it a night.

Chapter Nine

Ralph drove Autumn, James and Muriel to the ranch in his carriage. He'd hired a stable hand to bring their luggage, and the man trailed behind them now in a buckboard. The day started out cool enough, but the sun was beating down on them, and the heat grew more and more oppressive.

"We're almost there," Ralph announced as they drove up a slight incline.

"Thank God," James said under his breath. The trip over the rough roads in the heat and dust had seemed endless.

"There's the Lazy T," the lawyer announced as they topped the rise. He reined in so they could see the ranch buildings spread out below them.

"So this was my father's home," Autumn said, awed by the scene.

Autumn wasn't sure what she'd been expecting, but she was impressed by her first look at the Lazy T. The sprawling ranch house was bigger than she'd imagined, and there were several outbuildings along with a stable and corral. A stream ran nearby, and though the landscape was nothing like the lush greenery she was accustomed to in Pennsylvania, the rugged terrain and the mesquite trees appealed to something deep within her.

"It doesn't look like much," James remarked. He was thoroughly unimpressed and more than a little disgusted that they had traveled so far for so little.

"You've been on Lazy T land for the last half hour," Ralph pointed out. "Paul built the house at this location for the water."

"How many hired hands still work here?" James asked. Ever concerned about money, he was already wondering how the payroll was being met. He hoped the cost of keeping the ranch going wasn't draining Autumn's inheritance.

"Jake and Sherry Jenkins have worked for your father for as long as I can remember," Ralph told Autumn. "Sherry kept the house for him and did the cooking. Jake's the foreman. Jake's never mentioned that any of the men quit, so things are probably still running smoothly."

"Are they expecting us?" Autumn asked, anxious to meet the couple.

"Yes, I sent word yesterday that we'd be out today," Ralph answered. He urged the team on.

Autumn grew more excited as the carriage neared the ranch house. She saw a dark-haired, pretty woman come outside to stand on the porch.

"That's Sherry," Ralph told them as they drove up.

"You're here." Sherry hurried from the porch to greet them as they all descended from the carriage.

When Autumn turned to Sherry, she was startled to find there were tears in the woman's eyes.

"I can't believe it," Sherry said in an emotional voice as she gazed at her in awe.

"Sherry, this is Autumn." Ralph made the introductions.

"You truly are the image of Grace."

"So I understand," Autumn said, smiling slightly but feeling a bit uncomfortable under the other woman's scrutiny.

"Welcome home, dear," Sherry said.

"Home," Autumn repeated, testing the word. She looked up at the house.

"Yes. This was your father's home, and now it's yours," Sherry told her, her voice filled with warmth.

Ralph quickly introduced Sherry to James and Muriel.

"I'm sure Mr. Baxter has already told you all about me and Jake."

"Yes, he did," Autumn said. "It's nice to meet you. Is your husband here, too?"

"Jake will be back later. He and some of the men rode out to check on the herd earlier this morning. Come on inside, and I'll show you around."

Sherry's manner was so warm and friendly that Autumn liked her immediately. She accompanied her indoors, leaving the others to follow.

James remained standing by the carriage, in no hurry to go inside. He looked around, his displeasure with the whole situation obvious.

"I hope Autumn doesn't plan on staying here too long," he muttered to Muriel after Ralph had gone in the house.

"Be patient with her," Muriel encouraged. "This is all so new to her. You have to give her some time."

"I will. I just hope she doesn't need too much," he snarled.

Muriel went on in, leaving him alone. James lingered there for a moment, and only followed the others indoors when the buckboard bringing their trunks pulled up and the hired hand started to unload them.

Autumn hadn't been sure what to expect as she entered her father's house. After all the negative comments James had made during the ride, she'd prepared herself to find that it was little more than a hovel. She was pleasantly surprised to discover that the main room was large and comfortably furnished. A large gun case dominated one wall, and a fireplace another. A massive desk was in an alcove off to the side, and on the wall behind the desk hung an oil portrait of her father.

Autumn was startled by the painting, for it seemed very realistic. The only picture she'd ever seen of her father before had been the small one her mother had had from when they were first married. It had been difficult to tell much about him from that, but now she found herself mesmerized by the imperious-looking, silver-haired man who seemed to be staring down at her. She was drawn to stand before it.

"That's a good likeness of your pa," Sherry said as she came to her side.

"He was a handsome man, wasn't he?"

"Yes, he was."

"Sherry—Mr. Baxter's told me a lot, but he never told me exactly how my father died."

The other woman's smile faltered a bit as she recalled the tragic accident. "It was an accident and so sad."

"What happened?"

"Jake and some of the hands were breaking a new stallion in the corral. It was a beautiful horse, but it was stubborn. Your pa was here at the house, but he heard all the shouting and went to see what they were doing. He decided to try to ride the stallion himself." Sherry ended the story there, not wanting to tell her the rest of what had happened.

"Oh."

Muriel had joined them, and she touched Autumn's arm in a supportive gesture.

"We miss him," Sherry said.

Autumn looked back up at his portrait and then tore her gaze away. "I'm just sorry I never got to know him."

In an attempt to lighten their suddenly somber mood, Sherry suggested, "Let me show you around the house."

Autumn and Muriel turned to go with her, and it was then that Autumn noticed the framed map on the wall.

"Is this the Lazy T?" She studied it intently, realizing just how big the ranch really was.

"Your pa was so proud of this place. He worked hard to make it a success. The ranch was all that mattered to him."

"My pa," she repeated slowly. "It still seems strange to say that."

"We can talk more later, if you like," Sherry offered.

"I'd like that. Thank you."

"The kitchen is in the back, and there are four bedrooms down the hall." Sherry led the way.

"I had no idea the house would be this nice."

"Well, let me show you the bedrooms first, and then we can figure out where you want to put your trunks," she said as Ralph took charge of directing the hired hand to bring their things inside. Leading the way down the hall, Sherry

115

opened the first door. "This was your pa's bedroom."

Autumn stepped to the doorway and looked in. A heavy, iron-framed bed and a chest of drawers dominated the room. Everything looked as though her father would be returning at any moment.

"I didn't go through his personal things," Sherry explained. "When Mr. Baxter told me you were coming, I thought it was best to leave that for you to do."

Autumn didn't know if she was looking forward to the task or not. A sense of disappointment grew within her. For some reason, deep in her heart she had hoped that there might be a portrait of her sister displayed there—or maybe even a likeness of her mother. But there was nothing. There was no evidence to prove that she truly did belong here. There was only the last will and testament that told her this was the man who had given her life.

Autumn turned away and moved on down the hall.

"This room was"—Sherry opened another door and pushed it wide for her—"Grace's."

Autumn was surprised to see that it was still decorated in a feminine way. "I thought my father had disowned Grace."

The older woman smiled sadly. "He did, but he could never bring himself to throw her things out."

Autumn was puzzled by her father's actions,

but she felt, somehow, instinctively drawn to this bedroom. "I'll take this room while I'm here."

"You will be staying for a while, won't you?"

"Yes—" Autumn began.

James had been trailing along behind them, listening with little interest to their conversation. As the discussion turned to the length of their visit, he interrupted before she could say anything more. "We'll be here for a few days at least. We're not sure how long yet."

"I see." Sherry noticed that Autumn's posture stiffened a bit at her fiancé's abrupt manner.

She led the way to show them the rest of the house. Afterward they returned to the main room and found Ralph waiting for them with the hired hand. Muriel and Sherry told the man where to put the trunks, while Autumn and James spoke with the lawyer.

"If you're all settled in with Sherry, I'll be leaving you for now."

"Thank you for everything," Autumn said as she walked outside with him.

James went along and stayed by her side as the lawyer climbed into his carriage.

"I'll be in touch with you if I hear any more from Pete Miller about wanting to buy the place," Ralph said, taking up the reins.

Autumn started to tell him not to bother, but James spoke up too quickly for her.

"That will be fine."

Ralph looked around for Muriel, wanting to say goodbye to her, too, but she hadn't come outside to see him off. He bade Autumn and James farewell and headed back to Sagebrush.

While Sherry prepared the midday meal, Autumn and Muriel went to their rooms to unpack and freshen up.

Autumn closed the bedroom door behind her and stared around at the room that had been her sister's. Sherry had mentioned that some of Grace's things were still there because her father had refused to get rid of them. Curious, she looked through the dresser and found several drawers filled with her sister's personal items.

With utmost care, Autumn went through the garments. She unfolded each blouse and each skirt, wanting to learn more about her missing twin from them. When Autumn found a pair of breeches among the clothes, she was honestly surprised. She hadn't even considered that a woman living on a ranch might wear pants. The idea of it intrigued her and made her smile as she tried to imagine her sister wearing the garment. In a moment of pure curiosity, she undressed and slipped the pants on. They fit her perfectly, and made her realize that not only did her sister and she look alike, but they were also the same size. She was amazed at how comfortable the pants were and the freedom of movement they allowed her.

Autumn decided that there were definitely some good things about living in the West. Back in Philadelphia, a lady might wear a split riding skirt on rare occasions, but pants were never accepted as proper attire. Autumn donned a blouse, then ventured from the room to find Sherry.

"Sherry, I was wondering—"

Autumn didn't get any further as Sherry turned around and gasped out loud.

"Oh!" When her surprise faded, she managed a sweet-sad smile. "You are her twin—there is no doubt."

"Did Grace wear pants here on the ranch?" she asked.

"Yes, she wore them a lot."

"Dear God, Autumn! What have you got on!" James had come into the room and was completely taken aback by her attire.

Autumn turned to him, smiling. "My sister's pants. Do you like them?"

"No! You need to change clothes right now! You can't allow anyone to see you wearing those . . . those . . ."

"Pants," she finished for him.

"Yes! Go change," he demanded, his gaze condemning. "No decent woman would dare be seen wearing anything so outrageous in public."

"James, my sister wore them all the time," she began to explain.

"And that explains everything, doesn't it? We know all about your sister, don't we?" he sneered.

Autumn felt a sudden need to defend Grace. She grew angry at his judgmental attitude. "We don't know a thing about my sister," she challenged. "We only know what other people have told us about her. You shouldn't judge Grace so harshly."

"I shouldn't have an opinion about a woman who runs off with an outlaw? You're a lady, Autumn. You're nothing like your sister, thank heaven."

She hadn't intended to wear the pants for very long. She had only meant to try them on, but his attitude changed all that. She looked at Sherry.

"Is it almost time to eat?"

Sherry answered quickly, "Yes, it is. Go ahead and sit down."

James was furious with Autumn for ignoring him, but he knew this wasn't the time or place to continue the discussion. He would straighten this out with her later—when the hired help wasn't around to listen.

Sherry served the food she'd prepared, and Muriel joined them to eat. She, too, was surprised by Autumn's choice of attire.

"It is rather scandalous by our standards back home," Muriel began.

"Exactly," James agreed.

"But we're not back home. I can see why a woman would want to wear pants living here," Autumn said, deliberately being defiant. She didn't know what had come over her, but she suddenly had had enough of James's critical remarks.

They fell silent as they ate.

Sherry left the ranch house to give them some privacy until it was time to start preparing the evening meal. She promised to get her husband and the hands up to the house that evening.

"I'd better go through my father's things first," Autumn declared, girding herself emotionally for the task to come.

"You go on. I'll take care of cleaning up the kitchen," Muriel told her.

James had remained quiet throughout the meal. He realized he wasn't accomplishing anything by arguing with Autumn. He didn't want to fight with her continually, so he decided to try a different approach. When Autumn disappeared into her father's room, he followed her, glad to have a moment alone with her.

"Autumn—" He kept his voice low because he didn't want Muriel to overhear him.

Autumn had just started going through the top drawer and had found a locked box that looked like it might be important. She set it aside to look to James. He had come up behind her, trying not to let himself stare at the curve of her hips so clearly defined. When she turned to him to see what he wanted, he took her in his arms and tried to kiss her.

"James—don't—" she said, resisting. He had her cornered, and she felt awkward and uncomfortable with the bed so close beside them.

"Don't?" He'd thought she would be pleased by his display of affection.

"This isn't appropriate."

His intention to woo her over to his way of thinking died as his anger returned. He wanted to rage at her that she was hardly one to judge what was or was not appropriate. But he held his tongue, merely stiffening at her rebuff. He moved away from her.

"Do you need any help?" he asked coolly. "Shall I carry the drawer out to the living room so you can sort through things more easily?"

"Thank you." Autumn realized that if she didn't agree, he would probably stay there in the bedroom with her while she worked, and she wasn't in the mood for that kind of togetherness with him.

Chapter Ten

Autumn opened the box and stared down at the small framed picture that had been locked away there. Her breath caught in her throat.

It was a family portrait.

A tremor ran through her as she stared down at the only picture she'd ever seen of her whole family. Her father stood tall and proud behind her mother, who was seated and holding two babies, one nestled in the curve of each arm.

"It really is true, all of it," she said softly. "I wonder which one was me."

James shifted closer to see what she was looking at. "Maybe Sherry can tell you."

Autumn hoped Sherry would be able to, but it didn't really matter. All that mattered was that she'd found this picture, and any lingering doubt she'd had that this had all been a dream was gone forever. She went to her father's desk and positioned the portrait prominently there.

Filled with a sweet ache of belonging that she had never known before, she returned to sorting through more of her father's belongings.

When Sherry returned several hours later, Autumn stopped her before she could begin working in the kitchen. Autumn drew her to the desk.

"You found it," Sherry said, immediately noticing the picture.

"It was in the locked box."

"I hadn't seen it in years. I thought he'd destroyed it so Grace wouldn't see it." Sherry picked up the portrait to look at it. "They seem so happy here. You're the baby on the right. And that's Grace."

"I was going to ask if you knew," Autumn remarked, pleased.

"You were beautiful babies, and you grew up to be beautiful young women."

They shared a smile, and then Sherry went on to prepare the evening meal. Later, after they'd just finished eating, Sherry's husband Jake came up to the house with the ranch hands.

Autumn went outside to meet everyone. She spoke with the men at length, but noticed that several of them eyed her with open interest.

"Do any of you know my sister?" Autumn asked.

"Most of us have worked for your pa for quite

a while. We knew Grace," one of the men answered a bit cautiously.

"Grace was real pretty, and you look just like her," another one added.

Autumn took his remark as a compliment. "Thank you."

They spoke for a while longer. Jake and the hands regaled her with stories about how hard her father had worked to make the Lazy T a success. None of them spoke of his death or mentioned her sister again. Autumn did not know that Jake had insisted the men not talk about those things.

After James and Muriel retired, Autumn and Sherry were finally by themselves.

"Do you have time to talk now?" Autumn asked as she helped Sherry finish cleaning up after dinner.

"Of course," Sherry answered. She had known this moment was coming, and she was as ready as she would ever be.

"I'd appreciate anything more you can tell me about my father and sister. There's still so much I don't know."

"It had to be hard for you—growing up without a pa," Sherry sympathized. "I know what a rough time Grace had without your mother's influence."

"What did my father tell her about us?"

"The same thing your mother told you, I guess—that she was dead."

"So Grace didn't know about me either?"

"No. We weren't allowed to mention either one of you. Your pa threatened to fire anyone who did."

"How long have you worked here?"

"Years. Your pa hired me and Jake right after you were born."

"So you knew my parents when they were happy."

"Well, by the time I was helping out, your ma was already miserable. She was used to a better way of life, and she hated it here. I know she tried real hard to talk your pa into leaving. They had quite a few fights about it, but he wouldn't even think about giving up on his dream to make the Lazy T a success. I know your ma's family had money. I remember your pa talking about it, but he refused to live off her. He loved your mother and didn't want her to go."

"If he loved her so much, why didn't he go back to Philadelphia with her?"

"He loved ranching, and he loved Texas. He wasn't happy anywhere but here. Your pa thought if he built up the ranch and made a lot of money, she'd stay, but she wasn't willing to give him the time he needed to build his own fortune. She didn't understand why it was so important to him. When they parted, it was not on good terms. The divorce was vicious. He fought hard to get custody of one of you girls. He believed it would keep your mother from going, but she couldn't bear this life any longer. She packed everything up and left with you one day while he was out on the range. He came home to find the two of you gone."

"It's so hard to believe my mother could have left my sister behind like that."

"She had no other choice. If she'd tried to take you both, your pa would have hunted her down and dragged her back."

Autumn still couldn't understand the terrible choice her mother had been forced to make.

"Why did he get so angry with Grace that he disowned her? What could she have done that was so terrible?"

Sherry looked even more saddened. "Your pa was a gentle man in the beginning, but after he lost your mother the way he did . . . well, he changed. He couldn't deal with the truth—that she didn't love him as much as he loved her. He started drinking. He didn't get drunk very often at first, but as the months and years passed and your mother didn't return, he grew more and more angry."

"That must have been terrible for Grace."

"It was difficult. Especially as your sister got older. She began to remind him too much of your mother—in her looks and in her actions. The resemblance drove him to drink even more heavily."

"What did Grace do?"

"At first, Grace didn't understand. She was young and innocent, and just tried to stay out of his way whenever he started drinking. As she got a little older, she got wilder. I guess she wanted attention, I don't know. Your pa caught her sneaking in late one night."

"Where had she been?" Autumn was aghast.

"I don't know, and I'm not sure exactly what happened between them. I only know your father thought she was locked in her bedroom, and when I went to check on her in the morning, she was gone. She just ran off."

"Did he go looking for her?"

Sherry looked ashamed. "Not right away. He got drunk and swore that he didn't care if he ever saw her again. He told us never to mention her name around him."

Autumn could only imagine the pain and rejection Grace had faced, knowing their father resented everything about her. Autumn's own life with her mother had been so sheltered and filled with love compared to what her sister had experienced.

"If he was that miserable without my mother, why didn't he admit he was wrong and go after her?"

"If there's one thing your pa had, it was his pride. He could never let himself go after your mother, no matter how much he missed her and wanted her back. I know he missed you, too."

"He did?"

"Oh, yes, but he was a man of his word. He had promised your mother that there would be no further contact, and he kept his word."

"How did you find out what happened to Grace?"

"One of the hired hands heard she was work-ing in a saloon in Eagle's Nest. Your pa finally swallowed his pride then and went to check on her, but she'd already gone. The bartender told him she'd taken up with Rod Martin. I'd never seen him as angry as he was when he got back. That was when he gave up and washed his hands of her. He wrote her completely out of the will."

"I wish things could have been different."

"I do, too. It was so sad, the way everything happened. But you're here now. You're home, and I hope you stay," Sherry said, smiling warmly at her. "I'm going to go on now. I'll see you first thing in the morning."

"Good night."

Autumn walked outside with Sherry and stood on the porch. She stayed there long after the other woman had gone, gazing up at the clear night sky. It was a beautiful night, and she sa-vored the peace of the moment.

I hope you stay.

Autumn considered Sherry's words and won-dered what the future held for her. She won-dered if she would ever get to meet her sister. Now that she understood how painful Grace's life had been on the ranch, Autumn doubted that her sister would ever willingly come back. She offered up a silent prayer and waited for an an-swer, but none came. Her mood was quiet as she went inside to retire for the night.

* * *

"You should never have killed that sheriff from Sagebrush," Charley Bowen told Rod Martin when the outlaws showed up at his small ranch. Charles had known Rod for years and had let him stay at his spread whenever he needed a place to hide out, but murdering the lawman had changed all that.

"What else was I going to do? Sheriff Gallagher was taking Joe, here, to stand trial." Rod motioned toward one of his men. "We had to free him."

"The law is after you, Rod."

"Has been for years."

"Well, this time you've gone too far, and I don't want to be anywhere around when a posse catches up with you."

"They ain't gonna get me," Rod said with confidence as he started to dismount. "Sheriff Gallagher was the best lawman around, and he couldn't stop us."

"Don't bother to get down," Charley insisted. "I want you gone. Leave now."

"We won't be staying long—just a couple of weeks," Rod assured the rancher. "We just pulled off a job in Snyder, and we need to rest up for a while."

"I don't care. I don't want this kind of trouble anymore!"

"That ain't very neighborly of you," Rod said, his voice turning cold as he realized Charley was serious.

"This don't have anything to do with being

neighborly," Charley retorted. He knew that if that new sheriff in Sagebrush, Sheriff Randolph, heard the Martin gang was at his place, he'd be arrested and hanged right along with the others. "This has to do with staying alive!"

Without warning, Rod drew his sidearm and fired point-blank at the unarmed man. The shot killed Bowen instantly.

"Guess he don't have to worry about staying alive anymore," Rod said with a cold grin.

Grace bit back a scream of pain and outrage at the carnage, while the men in the gang only laughed at Rod's remark.

At the sound of the shot, one of Charley's ranch hands came running out of the stable. Rod saw him coming and shot him down, too, without a second thought.

"Looks like we got us a place to hide out for a while," Joe Simons chuckled.

"I don't think any of Charley's other hands are going to give us much trouble about staying," Frank Gordon added, glad that Rod had taken care of things so simply.

"Get rid of the bodies while I take a look around and have a few words with his other men," Rod directed. "It should be safe to lay low here until we figure out what we're going to do next."

Joe, Frank, and Lou Carter, the other gunman who rode with Rod, quickly moved to do as he'd ordered.

Rod looked at Grace. "See what you can find inside to eat."

"You killed the sheriff from Sagebrush?" Grace repeated. She was shocked by the news.

"It was the only way to get Joe free," Rod said, paying little attention to her comment. He'd deliberately left her behind at their campsite when they'd ridden out to ambush the sheriff. There were times when she slowed him down, and they had needed to strike quickly when they'd rescued Joe. "What Charley said don't matter none. The law's been after me for years. That ain't nothing new. I ain't afraid."

She was completely amazed that Rod had no concern other than for his own interests. Charley had stood in his way, so he'd gotten rid of him, just shot him down. And he didn't care. She'd thought the two men were friends. She realized now that she had been wrong. Rod had no friends.

Although the knowledge that Rod was capable of such ruthlessness came as a revelation to Grace, she realized it shouldn't have. It was an insight she'd avoided facing in all the time she'd been with him. She'd hidden from it, wanting to believe she was with Rod because she cared about him, but now she faced the truth. She had taken up with Rod only to escape the life she'd been leading working in the saloon. She'd felt trapped, and running away with Rod had seemed like a way out. Grace knew now, at long last, that she had made a terrible mistake.

Rod went on, "I'm hungry. Go fix me some food."

"All right."

Grace was glad to have the excuse to get away from him for a while. She managed to keep her turbulent emotions hidden as she dismounted and went into the house.

Grace had always known Rod was a dangerous man, and in the beginning it had been that dangerous element that had excited her and drawn her to him. Now, though, she had come to understand that he wasn't just dangerous—he was deadly. He was completely amoral, a man without a conscience. He only cared about himself, and he would do whatever was necessary to get what he wanted.

Fear grew within Grace. Until now, she had convinced herself that she enjoyed being known as Rod Martin's woman, but not anymore.

She had to get away from him.

Somehow, tonight, she would find a way to do it.

It was after midnight, and Grace still lay awake beside Rod in the ranch house, too tense to sleep. Rod had thought nothing of claiming Charley's bed for his own, and he slept beside her completely unaware of her turmoil, snoring loudly.

Charley had kept a lot of liquor in the house, and Rod and the other men had done their best to drink it all in one sitting. Rod had been falling-down drunk when he'd come to bed, and

Grace had been glad. She'd pretended to be asleep, unable to bear the thought of him touching her, and she'd been relieved when he'd quickly passed out without trying to take her.

Memories of Charley's murder haunted Grace. She realized she was putting her own life in danger by planning to run away, but she had no other choice. Until now she had always been able to find a way to justify what they'd done—the robberies and the occasional shoot-out that followed. But she could find no way to forgive these savage killings.

Grace struggled as she tried to decide where she could go. She was wanted by the law for taking part in the gang's robberies, but that was the least of her worries. Rod's temper was her main concern—and her main fear. She wanted to get as far away from him as she could, as quickly as she could. She had to make sure he never found her, because she knew there would be hell to pay if he did.

Grace thought about going home to the Lazy T and her pa. She missed her home and the safe haven she'd known there. Certainly, her pa could save her from Rod's vengeance—if he would do it. Remembering the last time she'd seen her pa, though, she believed in her heart that he wouldn't help her.

Knowing she couldn't go home again, Grace lay staring at the ceiling. Her thoughts were in turmoil as she tried to decide what to do—where to go—whom to turn to.

And then the memory came back to her.

If I can ever help you, just let me know.

Pete had said those words to her.

Pete—the man she'd loved so long ago.

He had managed to track her down at the job she had taken, the Last Chance saloon in Eagle's Nest. She could still remember how shocked she had been to see him. For a moment, she'd hoped that he had come to tell her he loved her and was sorry for what had come of their night together.

But it hadn't happened.

Pete had only told her that if she ever needed anything to let him know.

Grace realized now how foolish she'd been not to take him up on his offer, but at the time, she'd been too proud to go with him, and too desperate to escape from her pa.

But now, everything had changed.

She'd learned her lesson, but she feared it might be too late to save herself. Even so, she had to try. She wondered if Pete's offer still held. She hoped he'd meant it, for she was going to go to him now. He was her only hope, her only haven.

Grace looked over at the sleeping outlaw beside her. Rod did not look so fearsome asleep, but she knew the truth about him. He could murder innocent men and laugh about it.

She knew she would never feel safe again—not until she was far, far away from Rod Martin.

Grace waited another hour to be certain that

the other men were sleeping, too. Ever so cautiously, she shifted farther away from Rod until she could climb out of bed without disturbing him. She stood unmoving at the bedside, waiting to see if he roused.

All remained quiet.

Relieved, Grace crept from the bedroom. She held her breath as she made her way out of the house. She was fearful that someone might hear her at any moment. But her luck held, and she made her escape without incident.

Until now, Grace had never fully appreciated the numbing effects of liquor. She was glad Rod and the others were so drunk.

Grace reached the stable and quickly saddled her horse. Taking her mount's bridle, she led him from the stable. When she was far enough away so no one would hear her, she mounted up and disappeared into the night. She knew she had to move quickly, and she had to do everything in her power to hide her trail.

It wouldn't be easy, but she would manage.

Her very survival depended on it.

It was late morning when Rod woke. He was hung over and in a black mood as he came out of the bedroom.

"Where the hell is Grace?" he shouted, then grimaced as pain pounded through his head.

The other men were still asleep, having passed the night in the main room. Joe was stretched out on the sofa, while Frank and Lou slept in chairs. They stirred at Rod's shout and looked up at him bleary-eyed.

"What's wrong?"

"I was looking for Grace," he answered, annoyed that she wasn't available to wait on him.

"Maybe she's outside," Joe suggested. "You want to go look, or should I?"

"You go," Rod ordered, not ready to face the brightness of the day.

Joe didn't argue. He got to his feet and made his way painfully out of the house to look around. He'd thought it would be easy to find her, that she would be close by the house, but there was no sign of Grace. He went back in to tell Rod.

"What do you mean she ain't out there?" Rod asked. He had lain back down on the bed and opened one eye to glare at Joe.

"I'm telling you I looked around and didn't see her. I don't know where she is."

Rod cursed under his breath and got up. He was angry as he stormed from the house intending to teach Grace a lesson. He expected her to be there when he wanted her.

"Grace!" he bellowed as he strode about looking for her, but there was no answering call.

Frowning against the pain of his headache and the glare of the sun, Rod went to the stable to see if she was there.

There he discovered her horse was gone.

He returned to the house and burst inside. "Where did she go?"

137

"Go? What do you mean?" The other men looked at him in confusion.

"Her horse is gone and so is she," he snarled. "When did she ride out?"

"We don't know. We didn't hear anything last night," Joe and the others insisted.

"The bitch has run off!" Rod swore. A murderous rage filled him. No woman ever ran out on him.

"You think she might go to the law?" Frank asked.

"I don't think so, but I don't want to take the chance. I'm going after her."

"You need help?"

"No. I'll find her myself," he said, his tone ugly with the unspoken promise of what he would do when he found her. "Wait for me here. I'll be back."

Chapter Eleven

"I'll be back late," Cord told Thatch as he mounted up to ride out to the Lazy T.

"Good luck," the deputy told him.

"I'm going to need it. I doubt Miss Thomas is going to be very cooperative, but I'll try to convince her to contact us if she hears anything from her sister." Sam's idea of using her to get information had been a good one. Cord knew it was a long shot, but it was all he had to work with.

"I've always heard you were a smooth talker with the ladies," Thatch said, grinning at him.

"I'm afraid it's going to take more than smooth talking to get Autumn Thomas to work with me, but I guess we'll find out just how good a talker I really am." He smiled back at his deputy, but the expression was forced. There wasn't much to smile about right now. "I'll be back as fast as I can."

Cord rode for the Lazy T at a brisk pace. Even as he kept his thoughts focused on his reason for going, a part of him realized he was actually looking forward to seeing Autumn again. He wondered how she was faring, living on the ranch. It had to be quite a change for her to take up residence in West Texas. He wondered, too, how her fiancé was adjusting to life on the Lazy T, and he smiled again. This time his smile was real.

"Why, isn't that Sheriff Randolph?" Sherry asked in surprise as she glanced out the window to see a lone man riding in.

"The sheriff is here?" James asked, rising from the sofa to accompany her outside. "I wonder what he wants. Maybe he's come to let us know he's arrested the right people this time." His tone was snide.

Sherry ignored James's sarcasm as she welcomed the lawman. "Afternoon, Sheriff. What brings you out to the Lazy T?"

"Hello, Sherry—Mr. Dodson. I want to speak with Miss Thomas," Cord replied. He dismounted and tied up his horse, expecting Autumn to come out of the house at any moment. "Is she here?"

"She's down at the stable," Sherry told him.

"Thanks. I'll go find her there."

"Is there anything I can help you with?" James

asked. He was not at all pleased to see the lawman, and he was certainly not pleased that the fellow wanted to talk to Autumn again.

"I need to see Miss Thomas." Cord dismissed James's offer and strode toward the stable.

James wanted to know the reason for Sheriff Randolph's visit to his fiancée. Certainly, the trip to the ranch was no whim on the sheriff's part. James decided to follow him.

Autumn was in the stable with George, one of the ranch hands. George had just saddled horses for them and was planning to take her for a ride around the ranch. She was an accomplished horsewoman and was eager to explore the Lazy T.

Autumn had discovered in the few days since she'd arrived just why her sister had worn pants around the ranch. The long skirts of day gowns were totally impractical. This morning, knowing she would be riding with George, she had forgone the riding habit she would have worn back home and had donned Grace's pants. She knew her mother would have been outraged, and she correctly anticipated James's reaction. She had ignored his protest, though, for she was coming to realize the benefit of dressing more sensibly here in Texas.

"Miss Thomas?"

Autumn recognized Sheriff Randolph's voice immediately. She turned, surprised by his presence. He was standing in the stable's wide doorway with the sun shining behind him, a tall, broad-shouldered, dominant figure silhouetted against the brightness of the day.

"Sheriff Randolph—Is something wrong? Why are you here?"

Cord couldn't believe his eyes. There before him stood Autumn Thomas—and she was wearing pants. He stared at her for a moment, his gaze taking in the way the pants revealed the curves of her hips and legs. He frowned at the direction of his thoughts and denied any attraction he felt for her. He strode forward, telling himself he was there on business, nothing more.

"There's nothing wrong," he assured her. "I wanted to speak with you privately for a few moments."

Autumn knew the topic must be important if the lawman had come all that way to speak to her.

"Of course."

She told George that they'd go for their ride when she'd finished with the sheriff, then walked outside with the lawman.

Cord stopped to look down at her when they were alone. "First, I wanted to apologize again for what happened in town and make sure you were all right."

"I'm fine, thank you," she assured him. She would never forget how Sheriff Randolph had saved her from the deputy even when he'd believed her to be an outlaw. Though she couldn't say she liked the arrogant lawman, she knew he was an honorable man.

"Good."

"Sheriff Randolph, I'm certain this isn't a social call on your part."

"You're right. I came because I wanted to ask for your help."

"You want my help?" She was incredulous.

"*Our* help," James put in as he joined them, uninvited.

Cord was annoyed by his intrusion, but did not object. He went on, speaking to them both. "Yes. There's been no new word yet on the Martin gang—"

"Maybe they've decided to go straight," Autumn said hopefully, lifting her gaze to his.

Cord gave a harsh laugh. "That's not going to happen. Rod Martin is ruthless, and I'm worried about what he might be planning next."

"So what can we do to help *you* do your job?" James asked with more than a hint of derision.

"Miss Thomas," Cord said, "I want you to let me know if your sister tries to contact you."

"Sherry says Grace doesn't know anything about me."

"Word can get around. If Grace hears about you or about what happened with your father, she may show up at the ranch, and if she does, that will mean Rod Martin isn't far behind."

"So, what you really want me to do is to betray my own sister to you." Autumn stared at him.

James said nothing as he listened to them. He thought the idea of turning Grace in to the law was a wonderful one, but he was nervous at the thought that Martin might come to the Lazy T with her. He believed, as the sheriff said, that Martin was a dangerous outlaw.

"No, this isn't about betrayal," Cord responded, trying to explain his position to her. "With your help, I can stop a gang of outlaws before they have the chance to hurt anyone else."

Autumn and Cord glared at each other, at a standoff.

"If you should hear from your sister, try to convince her to work with me. The law will go easier on Grace if she cooperates. I can help her."

Anger flared in Autumn's eyes. "You'll help her, all right—just like you helped me that day on the stage."

"I didn't know who you were then. I had no idea Paul Thomas had twin daughters, and neither did you. You might as well accept it—I was just doing my job," he pointed out with maddening logic.

"And you'll just be doing your job when you arrest my sister and lock her up."

"That's right. She is wanted by the law."

"If we hear anything at all, Sheriff, we'll contact you," James answered for Autumn, not wanting to discuss the matter any further.

"I'd appreciate it."

"But we may not be here long enough to concern ourselves with the problem. Mr. Baxter told us he has someone interested in buying the ranch, and he sent word out earlier today that he's arranged a meeting for us with the buyer at his office on Saturday," James went on before Autumn could say anything.

Autumn had been angry to begin with, but she grew even more furious when James took it upon himself to answer for her. As soon as Sheriff Randolph had gone, she intended to let her fiancé know what she thought about his controlling ways.

Cord was surprised by the news, although he realized he shouldn't have been. It was only logical that Autumn would want to sell the Lazy T. She'd been raised back East by her mother and knew nothing about ranching.

"I see. Well, I hope things work out the way you want them to, but if you do learn anything, let me know." He sensed by the stormy look on Autumn's face that his welcome there had worn thin. "I'll be going now. Miss Thomas, Mr. Dodson."

Cord tipped his hat to Autumn. He knew when to cut his losses.

Autumn watched the lawman as he mounted up and rode away, so confident, so sure of himself. His words about her sister echoed in her mind. *She is wanted by the law.* Only when he'd ridden from sight did she turn on James.

"What did you mean, telling him we'd contact him right away if we heard anything from Grace?"

"I meant just that," James said brusquely. "As the sheriff said, she's an outlaw. If she shows up here, we are obligated to turn her in."

"There's no way of knowing if she ever will contact me, but if she does, I won't give her up to the sheriff."

"Are you out of your mind?" he argued. "Sheriff Randolph told you the men she rides with are murderers and thieves,"

"I couldn't betray her."

"You're defending a woman who's been involved in God only knows what kind of terrible—*illegal*—activities!"

"That woman is my twin sister. If I get the chance, I have to help her."

"You would be helping her by turning her in," James argued. "You'd be stopping her from committing any more crimes and getting herself into even deeper trouble with the law."

Autumn's fury didn't abate as she gave James a cold look. She had heard from Sherry why Grace had run away, and, although the knowledge didn't justify the things her sister had done while with the Martin gang, it made her desperate actions more understandable.

James knew she was angry with him, and he decided to try a different tack. "Autumn, you know I love you. I'm only thinking about what's best for you. This really isn't worth arguing about it. There's no reason for Grace to show up now, and we're not going to be in Sagebrush long enough for her to hear about you."

"What if I decide I want to stay?"

"Stay? Here? Why would you?" He dismissed

the notion as preposterous. "The message you got today about the meeting with the potential buyer is the best news we've had since we got here. We'll meet with the man and take whatever amount he wants to pay, then we can catch the next stagecoach heading back to Philadelphia."

Autumn drew herself up. "It sounds like you have my whole life planned out for me, but I don't remembering asking you to."

"What?"

"I'm not sure I want to sell the ranch."

"Why wouldn't you?" James was dumbfounded by her statement. "Living here is hell-ish. Your mother knew that. Why do you suppose she went through such horror to go back to Philadelphia?"

His words only added fuel to the fire of her fury. She realized suddenly that she must have turned out more like her father than her mother. She liked being on the ranch.

"You may find living here hellish, but the Lazy T is my father's legacy to me. The ranch is a successful operation. It's a money-maker. Why would I want to sell out?"

James's anger was growing to match hers. "Because, my dear, you are not a rancher. You are a lady. Philadelphia is our home, and always will be."

"I'll go through with the meeting," she told James. "I'll listen to what the man has to say, but I'm not promising you I'll take his offer."

"That's fair enough." At least she'd agreed to

attend the meeting, James thought. With any luck, she would regain her senses by Saturday. He would talk to Muriel about it and enlist her help in convincing Autumn that they needed to sell the ranch and return to Philadelphia.

Autumn considered their discussion at an end. She turned away from James and started back into the stable.

"Where are you going?" he asked.

"For a ride, just like I'd planned before the sheriff showed up," came her answer and she disappeared into the stable.

Chapter Twelve

Autumn was glad George had left her saddled horse tied up and waiting for her. George was nowhere to be seen, though, and she was glad. She was going for a ride, all right, but not the one he'd had planned for them.

She had talked to James. Now she meant to have a few words with Sheriff Randolph.

Autumn untied the reins, then swung up into the saddle and rode from the stable.

The sheriff had disappeared from sight, but that didn't matter. She was going after him, and she wasn't going to stop until she caught up with him.

As Cord made his way toward town, he wasn't sure that his strategy to convince Autumn to help him had worked. Her fiancé had taken over the conversation and promised to contact him if they heard anything, but the strong-willed Autumn hadn't said a word. Cord wasn't so sure she was going to cooperate.

At the sound of a rider coming up behind him, Cord slowed his pace and looked back. He was surprised to find it was Autumn. He stopped to wait for her to catch up.

Cord kept his gaze upon Autumn as she covered the distance between them. She was handling her horse with an expertise that impressed him. Eastern lady that she was, he hadn't expected her to be such a good horsewoman, and he found himself wondering how many other hidden talents she had. She certainly hadn't ceased to amaze him since their first encounter. Cord had thought she seemed angelic when she'd been asleep in the jail cell, but now she resembled an avenging angel—beautiful yet determined—as she galloped toward him.

"Sheriff Randolph—I'm glad I caught up with you." Autumn reined in beside him.

"Is something wrong?" he asked.

"Yes," she stated emphatically, still angry. "This whole situation with my sister."

"What about it?"

"I want to talk to you about her."

He was not sure what was left to be said, but he agreed. "Let's go over in the shade."

He directed her to a small grove of trees that would afford them a little protection from the scorching heat of the midday sun. They dismounted, and Autumn came to stand before him. Her manner was tense as she looked up at him.

"You really can't expect me to turn my sister in if I hear from her. She's my own flesh and blood. I couldn't betray her that way, no matter what she's done!"

Now it was Cord's turn to grow angry. "Miss Thomas, your sister is part of a gang that murdered my best friend. You know about Mike Gallagher. You met his wife—no, you met his widow. Rod Martin and those who ride with him belong behind bars for all the suffering they've caused."

For a fleeting moment, Autumn saw in Cord's expression all the pain he was feeling over his friend's death, but he quickly masked it.

"I suppose none of this really matters, since I haven't heard from her," she began.

Cord was glaring down at Autumn. "It does matter. You're defending a woman who is your blood relative, but whom you've never met."

"She's my sister. I want to help her."

"By turning her in, you would be helping her. You'd be keeping her safe, and you'd be helping me keep the people of Sagebrush safe. I don't want anyone else to be hurt or killed."

"And you think I do?"

"I didn't say you wanted people to be hurt."

"Well, that's what it sounds like to me. If I don't turn my sister in, it will look like it's my fault if anything happens," she argued.

"I didn't say it would be your fault. I just think you should maybe think of others."

"Instead of thinking of myself?" She was outraged.

"Yes," Cord answered.

Autumn had had it. Without thought, she raised her hand to slap him, angry that he would even think she could be so selfish and unfeeling.

Cord reacted instantly, grabbing her wrist before she could hit him.

The air was charged with emotion as they stared at each other.

The last thing Cord had meant to do was insult Autumn. He'd made the trip to the ranch to try to win her over.

He wanted her on his side.

He wanted her to help him.

He wanted her.

The truth was powerful.

In that moment, as they stood there alone in the wilds of the West Texas countryside, Cord acknowledged for the first time what he had tried to deny to himself. He was attracted to Autumn, to her beauty, her spirit, her intelligence.

He wanted her.

Cord didn't say a word. He pulled her to him, his mouth seeking hers in a dominating, hungry kiss that startled them both with its intensity.

Autumn's breath caught in her throat at the touch of Cord's lips on hers. Her heartbeat quickened. She knew she should resist his embrace, but she had never known a more exciting kiss. His lips were a firebrand upon hers, evoking feelings deep within. She remained still, fearful that any movement on her part would cause him to break away.

Cord lost himself for a moment in the fiery heat of the exchange. The kiss had been instinctive, and his reaction to having Autumn in his arms was one of pure desire. The realization seared him, and it took all the strength he could muster to finally put her from him.

"I know you're engaged to Dodson, but I'm not going to apologize for kissing you."

"You're not?" she repeated, still stunned by what had just passed between them.

"No, because I'm not sorry I did it, Autumn." He smiled gently as he spoke her name.

"Sheriff Randolph," she began awkwardly, fumbling for something to say. A moment before, she'd been ready to slap him, and now she only wanted him to take her back in his arms and kiss her again.

"My name is Cord."

"Cord." She liked the sound of it.

Autumn knew she should be feeling guilty for having kissed him, and for having enjoyed it. She told herself she was promised to James, but she also knew that she had never reacted this way to any of the kisses James had given her. A sense of wonder filled her at the hunger Cord's embrace had evoked within her. The attraction between them was elemental and exciting—and forbidden.

"I don't think you're selfish, Autumn," he said more gently. "I just want Martin stopped. I don't know what drove your sister to join up with him, but there is no denying how dangerous he is. He's a danger to you, as well as to the people of my town—and your town, too. I want him to pay for his crimes."

The anger and resentment she'd felt earlier faded as she accepted the truth of what Cord was saying. His motives were pure. He was just trying to protect his town.

"Think about what I said."

"I will." She looked up at him, seeing him in a whole new light.

Cord met her gaze and found he couldn't look away. He knew it was wrong to want to kiss her again. He knew he shouldn't do it. He even thought she might resist him this time, but he couldn't stop himself. He took Autumn in his arms again.

She did not resist. Their first kiss had begun in anger. This kiss was pure desire.

Cord held her close as his lips moved over hers with demanding mastery.

Autumn told herself this was Cord, not James, but it didn't matter. She met him willingly in that exchange.

He deepened the kiss. They clung together, caught up in the wonder of their embrace.

Only the stirring of the horses nearby jarred them back to reality and forced them apart.

"You'd better be getting back. I'll ride with

you to make sure you get there safe," he offered.

"There's no need," Autumn said nervously. She was shocked by her own wanton behavior, and not ready to put herself in a situation where she'd be dealing with both James and Cord. A solitary ride to the ranch would give her time to gather her thoughts. "I'll be fine."

She went quickly to mount up. She looked down at Cord as he came to stand beside her.

"Be careful," he said.

Still a bit stunned by all that had transpired between them, she simply nodded in response, then wheeled her horse around and rode away.

Cord watched her go. Only after Autumn had gone out of sight did he mount up himself.

The trip back to town was a long one for Cord as he relived Autumn's kisses in his thoughts. She was a beautiful, desirable woman. There was no denying that he wanted her, no matter how hard he might try. But he knew that Autumn's loyalty to a sister she'd never met was misguided. He could only hope she would listen to him and ultimately choose to do the right thing.

Rod Martin was out there somewhere. Though Cord hadn't had much luck so far, he was confident it was just a matter of time until he tracked him down.

The outlaw's days were numbered.

Cord only hoped Autumn wouldn't get hurt when the time came for the final showdown.

* * *

Autumn slowed her pace as she drew closer to the ranch, for she wasn't ready to face James just yet. She wanted to be calm when she saw him again, not feeling confused and a bit guilty as she was now. Her thoughts were chaotic as she tried to make sense of her wayward emotions.

It had been wonderful to kiss Sheriff—she stopped—to kiss Cord. She'd thought him arrogant and high-handed, and maybe he was, but, she understood now, in a good way. Cord was a strong man, a powerful man, a man in control. Everything he'd said to her made sense. He was only trying to keep everyone safe from harm.

Autumn found herself smiling as she thought of their first encounter, of how he had grabbed her right off the stagecoach. It had only been a short time ago, but so much had happened in the days since that it seemed like weeks.

Her thoughts turned to James, and her smile faded.

They were engaged. She had believed she loved him when she'd accepted his engagement ring. They were to be married.

Autumn looked down at the ring on her finger. She wondered now if she did love James. She didn't understand how she could have reacted so strongly to Cord if James was the man who held her heart—the man she was to spend the rest of her life with.

Autumn grew tense as she tried to sort out her feelings. Mentally, she compared the two men. James was handsome, sophisticated and successful. He had money and was influential back in Philadelphia society. They had known each other socially before he'd proposed, and Autumn had accepted because he was a good match—and she'd thought she loved him. But she now realized that they had spent little time getting to know one another on a more personal, intimate level. That had happened on this trip to Texas, and she wasn't sure she liked what she'd learned about his dictatorial ways.

Cord might be a dominant, powerful man, but he used his power to make life better for the people of his town.

James wanted only to control Autumn, so he could get her back to Philadelphia as quickly as possible. He wanted to simply pick up where they'd left off, to resume their lives as if nothing had happened. He had no interest in her needs or wants. He only cared about his own.

And yet they were to marry and spend the rest of their lives together.

Autumn grew even more troubled. As she returned to the ranch, she decided to avoid James for as long as she could. She had some serious thinking to do about her future.

Chapter Thirteen

Saturday morning couldn't come soon enough for James. He was up before dawn. He had never thought he would be this excited about going to Sagebrush, but he was. He was eagerly anticipating the moment when they would meet with the lawyer and arrange the sale of the ranch.

Since their discussion the previous day, James had known that Autumn was reticent about selling and angry with him for pushing the idea. She'd been distant with him and cool to any attempts he made to discuss the matter further. James was certain, though, that with the lawyer's help, he could convince her that selling out was the right—and smart—thing to do. Then, as soon as the papers were signed, he intended to head straight to the stage office and book their return trip to Philadelphia. His only fear was how long they would have to wait for the next stagecoach out of town.

James's spirits soared as he realized it was no longer a matter of weeks until they returned home, it was now only a matter of days. He could hardly wait to put all the heat and dust and misery behind him.

After dressing, he left his bedroom. It was still dark outside, and he was surprised to find the front door standing open. He crossed the room to close it, wondering who'd left it open, and was startled to find Autumn standing alone on the porch.

"You're up early," he remarked quietly. He went to stand with her.

Autumn was staring off at the sunrise where the edge of dawn had begun to brighten the eastern horizon. The rising sun was transforming the night sky into a canopy of pink, orange and gold that was breathtaking in its beauty. She had been standing there for some time, enjoying the freshness of the early morning and savoring the peace of the moment. She was falling in love with this place. By finally acknowledging that to herself, she came to understand that she truly was her father's daughter.

"Isn't it beautiful?" Autumn said. "If an artist painted a picture of it, no one would believe it was real."

"It is beautiful," James agreed, "but not as beautiful as you are."

He had gotten up that morning determined to work at making things better between them today. Soon they would be back home and all the ugliness of this trip would be behind them. He wanted to smooth things over and get back to where they had been before they'd received the lawyer's first telegram.

Autumn was surprised by his words and glanced up at him, wondering at this sudden change in him. They'd been circling around each other since their confrontation the other day. She had deliberately stayed away from him as much as she could because of her uncertain and troubled feelings. No matter how she'd tried, she hadn't been able to put the memory of Cord's kisses out of her mind.

James knew nothing of her thoughts about the lawman. He only knew that they were alone for a moment, and he wanted to take advantage of the situation. He moved closer and took Autumn into his arms, drawing her to him. With Muriel still asleep and none of the ranch hands stirring, he knew it was safe to kiss her.

Since their arrival in Texas, James believed that Autumn had been too caught up in the tragedy of her parents' past to take the time they needed for each other. He meant to have some private time with her now.

His bold move startled Autumn. She told herself this was the man she was engaged to, the man she planned to marry. But when he deepened the kiss, her instinct was to resist, and she had to force herself to relax in his arms and accept his attentions. Something within her whispered that she should be enjoying his kiss, not merely tolerating it, but she pushed the taunting thought away. When at last James released her, she managed to smile up at him.

"Good morning," Autumn said.

"Yes, it is a good morning," James agreed, feeling quite confident of himself. He was certain she wanted him. "How early did you want to leave for town?"

"Sherry said if we left by mid-morning we'd arrive in plenty of time for the meeting." Her misgivings about the meeting were real, but she wasn't going to mention them to James. He had made his thoughts on the matter very clear, and she wasn't in the mood to argue with him any further. She would wait until they were in the meeting and make her final decision then.

"Do you want to stay in town for the dance Mr. Baxter mentioned in the letter?" James had yet to decide how he felt about the occasion. Since attending the dance would mean he would have to spend less time at the Lazy T, he supposed he was all for it.

"Yes. Muriel and I talked about it, and we both agree it should be fun. We'll plan on spending the night in town." Autumn hadn't said a word to anyone, but she was secretly looking forward to the dance. She was hoping she might see Cord again.

"All right." *Fun* hardly described James's feelings about the dance, but he was happy to do whatever was necessary to win Autumn's favor. He wanted her amenable to his way of thinking, and if suffering through the dance would help to speed them on their way back home, he would do it gladly.

They heard Muriel in the house and went inside to finish getting ready for the trip.

"Here they are now," Ralph Baxter announced to Pete Miller as Autumn and James entered his office later that morning. He got up from behind his desk and went to greet them.

Pete stood up, too. He had been trying to gird himself for this moment. No matter how much time had passed, the ache of missing Grace was still with him.

Pete turned slowly to watch Grace's identical twin come into the room. The resemblance between the two women was extraordinary, and a turmoil of emotions tore through Pete at the sight of her. He had to remind himself that this wasn't Grace. It was painful for him, but he managed a cordial smile.

"Hello, Miss Thomas. I'm Pete Miller," he said.

"Mr. Miller." She smiled in greeting.

"Pete, please," he insisted, offering her a chair.

"And I'm Autumn." Autumn moved to sit down as Ralph introduced Pete to James.

"My pleasure," Pete said, shaking hands with James.

Pete fought against his desire to stare at Autumn as he took the chair beside her.

"You certainly do resemble Grace," he remarked.

"Did you know my sister?"

"Yes. I did." Pete said no more. He knew there was no point in talking about the past. It was over. He couldn't change it. He had come today only to make an offer for the ranch.

"So, Pete, I understand you're interested in buying the Lazy T?" James barged right in, not hesitating to bring up the reason for their meeting. The last thing James wanted was to be forced to sit there and listen to stories about Grace. The less said about her the better, as far as he was concerned.

"That's right," Pete responded. "I've spoken with Ralph at length, and I think you'll find the offer I'm prepared to make most reasonable."

"Good." James was ready to talk money. He looked at the lawyer expectantly. "How long do you think it will take to conclude the sale?"

"We should be able to get all the paperwork done in a few days," Ralph answered.

"That's wonderful."

Pete spoke up again, telling them the dollar amount he was willing to pay.

James was quite satisfied with the offer. He was ready to take charge of closing the deal when Autumn decided she had heard enough.

"Pete, thank you for your offer. I appreciate your fairness. It's most generous, and I'm sure

163

it's a good price for the Lazy T, but I'm not certain I want to sell the ranch just yet."

There was silence in the room.

"Autumn—" James was humiliated that she'd dared to interfere with his negotiations. He wanted her to shut up so he could get things signed and sealed.

Autumn, however, was not about to be cowed by him. She was not going to let him take control of her business.

"I made the trip here to the Lazy T to learn more about my father, only to discover—to my surprise—that I have a sister I didn't know about. Until I've come to understand everything that happened with my family, I need to stay here. I want to stay here. I'm just not ready to walk away from everything—to leave before I know all the answers, and in all honesty, I'm not sure when I will be."

Ralph was confused and irritated. He'd worked with Pete to try to make the sale a simple transaction. "I thought you wanted to sell the ranch."

"Eventually I may sell," Autumn began.

May sell! James couldn't believe what he was hearing.

"And if or when I do—" Autumn was saying

"*When!*" James repeated the word with strong emphasis. She was balking at this strategic moment, and it infuriated him.

Autumn refused to be cowed by his warning tone. She ignored James as she went on, speaking to Pete, "I'm not sure if or when I'm going to sell, Pete. It may be a month from now or it may be ten years from now. I don't know. I do promise you, though, that when I am ready, I'll come to you first."

"Autumn, are you sure about this?" James ground out. He didn't understand why she'd bothered to make the trip into town for the meeting if she'd had no intention of concluding the deal. He'd thought things would go smoothly, that the only haggling might be over the price. He'd been wrong. James didn't like being wrong. He also didn't like being made a fool of in public.

"I'm very sure," Autumn answered. Then she turned to the lawyer. "Mr. Baxter, I thank you for your help. I'm sorry things turned out this way, but for right now, this is what I have to do."

"Well, I thank you for coming," Ralph said. "I'm just sorry we weren't able to work everything out."

Autumn stood to leave. James rose, ready to accompany her.

Pete and Ralph stood up as gentlemen to watch them go.

"I'm sorry, Pete," Ralph said.

"So am I. I was hoping to take over the Lazy T with Paul gone, but I guess it'll have to wait." He was thoughtful for a moment as he stared after Autumn and James. "She sure looks like Grace, doesn't she?"

"Yes, she does."

Pete had been hoping that when he met Autumn, he would discover that his feelings for Grace had faded. Seeing Autumn, though, had only reminded him all the more of how much he still cared for her sister.

As he started from the lawyer's office, Pete again found himself deeply regretting what had happened between him and Grace. He should have told her that he loved her the night she'd come to him. Everything would have turned out differently if he had. It had been too late by the time he'd tracked her down at the saloon in Eagle's Nest. He would live with that regret the rest of his life.

To this day, Pete's frustration was great. As he left Ralph's office, he couldn't help wondering what his life would have been like if only he'd told Grace sooner of his love. Sadly, he realized he would never know.

James managed to hold his tongue until he and Autumn were far enough away from the law office so no one else could hear what he was about to say.

"I can't believe what you just did in there!" he raged at her in a low, barely controlled voice as they continued to walk down the street.

"I beg your pardon." Autumn looked at James, startled by the sound of his fury.

"You had a man sitting there with cash practically in hand, ready to buy your damned ranch, and you refused to sell it to him!"

"I am not ready to sell the Lazy T," she told him with icy calmness.

"You'd better get ready," James said in a tone that brooked no argument. "I've had about all I can stand of West Texas. It's time for us to go home."

Autumn could not believe what he was saying. She glanced around the busy street and knew this was not the place for such an emotional discussion.

"This is not the time to discuss this," she told him, keeping her voice down.

"Why not?" he demanded. "When is the right time? How many more endless days and nights do we have to spend in this hell hole before you're ready to admit you made a mistake by coming here?"

"Coming here wasn't a mistake for me!" she insisted, her anger with him growing even more. "I'm sorry you don't agree with me, but I've made my decision."

"You've made your decision," James repeated as he looked at her, thoroughly disgusted. His fury knew no bounds. He'd thought they'd been in agreement when they'd made the trip to Texas. He'd thought it was understood that they would sell the ranch and return home.

"That's right. I've decided I'm going to stay."

"We are engaged, Autumn. You are soon to become my wife. We can hardly be married if you're living here and I'm in Philadelphia. A good wife is submissive to her husband. She's obedient and—"

"James, we shouldn't be talking about this while we're standing in the middle of the sidewalk in broad daylight."

"Then how about I take you back in this alley where no one will hear us?" he snapped.

James grabbed Autumn by the arm and half-dragged her down the nearby alley. He didn't stop until they were out of sight of anyone on the street. The narrow alley afforded them a little more privacy than they'd had, and now he could continue his tirade.

"I want to know by what right you came to the decision to stay here without speaking of it to me first? As your future husband, don't I deserve some consideration?"

"We are not married yet, James," she countered.

He muttered something unintelligible.

"Put yourself in my place—if you can," Autumn continued defiantly. "The Lazy T is my only connection to a part of my family I didn't even know existed until a short time ago."

"You were better off before," he asserted. "Did you really want to know you had a sister who's wanted by the law?"

Autumn looked at James as if seeing him for the first time. "Yes. I never dreamed I had a father still alive and well in Texas, let alone a sister. I can't just walk away from the Lazy T and pretend it isn't important to me. I want to spend some time at the ranch. I want to learn everything I can about my father, and my sister, so what happened will make more sense to me."

"You can worry about the past all you want, but what about our future? Isn't that important to you?" he demanded, his fury not abating in spite of her arguments. "My life and my work are in Philadelphia. I do not intend to spend the rest of my days here in Texas, and as my wife, neither will you. I can see no reason to hold on to a ranch the size of the Lazy T when it can be sold for a very respectable sum of money. Financially, you're comfortably well off now. The money from the sale of the ranch would only make things that much better for you."

"Is that all you ever think about? Money?" Autumn challenged. Nothing James had said had had any effect on her decision. If anything, his continued arguments only made her realize how different they truly were.

"I'm merely trying to look out for your interests, my dear."

"If you were concerned with my interests at all, you'd understand why I want to stay."

Her logic was lost on James. He was ready to grab her and shake some sense into her, to forcefully convince her that she was making a big mistake. His expression turned thunderous, almost threatening, as he took a step closer to her.

"Is something wrong here?"

Sheriff Randolph's question startled them both to stillness.

Chapter Fourteen

"There's nothing wrong, Sheriff Randolph," James ground out, struggling to adopt a more relaxed demeanor as he stepped away from Autumn to face the lawman.

"Do you mind if I interrupt?" Cord said, confronting James.

Cord had been across the street when he'd seen James grab Autumn by the arm and force her down the alleyway. Cord didn't know what was going on, but he didn't want anyone putting his hands on Autumn in anger.

"Not at all."

"Are you all right, Autumn?" Cord's gaze went over her critically, making sure she was unharmed.

"Everything is fine," she assured him. As she answered, their gazes met and locked. The memory of his embrace returned in a rush, and a shiver of sensual awareness swept through her. Autumn wondered how many more times Cord could appear at just the right moment to save her. He had rescued her from the deputy, and now, by his mere presence, he had distracted James. She was beginning to think Cord was her guardian angel.

"Are you sure?"

"I'm sure," she told him.

"If you'll excuse us, Sheriff?" James said coldly, dismissing him. He did not like the intimacy he sensed between these two, and he wanted to get Autumn away from the other man. "We'll be going now."

James took Autumn by the arm and escorted her past the lawman back to the street.

Cord watched James draw her away and found the sight objectionable. Logically, he told himself he had no rights to her—she was James's fiancée. He had no claim on her. But all the logic in the world didn't change how he felt.

If Autumn had balked or resisted the man's touch in any way, Cord would have immediately gone to her aid, but she accompanied James without protest. Cord felt the sting of some strange emotion as he watched them go. He realized in annoyance that the emotion was jealousy.

The discovery troubled him, and he scowled. He told himself he should concentrate only on what was important—catching Martin. He told himself he had no time for women right now, and especially not a woman who was engaged to another man.

Autumn and James started down the street toward the hotel. Only then did she pull her arm free of his touch.

"We are not done discussing your decision yet," James said, his tone insistent and imperious.

"I am," she returned.

"I don't think so." He stopped, ready to confront her again.

Autumn kept walking, her head held high, uncaring that he was still upset with her. It didn't matter. What mattered was that she had made her decision, and she was going to stay with it.

"Autumn—" He sounded threatening.

"I'll see you later, James." She did not look back.

James was seething as he watched her walk away from him. He knew it would be best if he didn't follow her and force a confrontation. It would be pointless to try to reason with her in his current mood.

James stared after Autumn for a moment longer, then turned and stalked off in the opposite direction, needing to put some distance between them. He entered the first saloon he came to. He definitely believed he deserved a drink. It had been a long day, and it wasn't over yet. There was still the exciting Sagebrush dance coming up that night. James knew he really needed a drink.

Cord emerged from the alley to see Autumn making her way toward the hotel alone. There was no sign of James anywhere around, and that puzzled him.

From what they'd told him out at the Lazy T, Cord had expected Autumn to sell the ranch today at the meeting with the lawyer and leave Sagebrush as quickly as she could arrange it. Judging from what he'd just overheard her saying to James, though, he had been wrong. *You'd understand why I want to stay*—It sounded as if she planned to hold on to the Lazy T and remain in the area, and, obviously, her fiancé was not happy with that choice.

As Cord considered the possibility of Autumn remaining in town, he smiled. He quickly told himself he was smiling only because her presence there might draw Grace back to town and ultimately lead him to Rod Martin. But a quiet part of him acknowledged that he was glad Autumn was not going to leave. He wanted her to stay.

Cord returned to the sheriff's office, thinking of the dance coming up that night and hoping Autumn would attend.

Rod Martin was in a foul mood. He had spent several days hunting for Grace without success. He'd lost her trail the first day out. He'd expected it to be simple to pick up her tracks again.

After endless searching, though, he'd finally given up and headed back to the hideout. He still couldn't believe that she'd dared to leave. No one ever ran out on him—no one.

"You didn't find Grace?" Joe asked as Rod rode up to the ranch house, alone.

"You see her riding with me?" Rod snarled.

"No." Joe thought it was funny that Grace had managed to get away. She must have done a damned good job of hiding her trail if she'd lost an old tracker like Rod, but he kept his amusement to himself. He didn't want to make Martin any madder than he was.

"It's just as well she's gone. I ain't got time to be dealing with women right now."

"You ain't worried about her?"

"Hell, no. There's a price on her head, too. She can't cause us any trouble."

"You ain't gonna miss her?"

"One woman's as good as any other. Let's go inside. I need a drink."

Autumn stared at her reflection in the mirror of her hotel room. She was as ready as she would ever be for the dance. Earlier in the day, she'd been excited about attending, but after her fight with James, the last thing she felt like doing was spending any more time with him. There would be no backing out, though. Muriel would be dressed and ready to go in just a few minutes, and she supposed James would be, too, although she hadn't spoken with him since they'd parted so abruptly on the street.

Autumn was definitely not in the mood to listen to any more of James's dictates that night. Short of declaring herself deathly ill and unable to attend, she supposed there was no way to avoid him, though. They would be going to the dance as planned, and it was almost time to leave.

A knock came at her door.

Autumn tensed, believing it was James. She went to answer it and was relieved to find Muriel standing outside.

"You look pretty tonight," Autumn said as she came into the room.

"Thank you," Muriel answered. The blue dress was one of her favorites, and she hoped Ralph Baxter would notice. "I see you're about ready to go, too. I do love that gown on you."

The gown Autumn had chosen was dark green and fit her perfectly. The bodice was modestly cut, revealing just enough cleavage to be tempting without seeming too daring. With her hair pinned up in a sophisticated style, Autumn looked absolutely beautiful and the perfect lady.

Muriel approved wholeheartedly. "The way you look in that gown is certainly a far cry from the way you looked wearing your sister's pants."

Autumn laughed. "Yes, it is, but I have to tell you, the pants are much more comfortable and definitely easier to move around in."

Muriel gave her a secret smile. "I would love

to be daring enough to wear pants, but I fear I'm too old to be so unconventional."

"Out here I don't think convention has anything to do with it. We can always go to the store in Sagebrush and try to find you a pair," Autumn teased.

"One of these days I may be feeling daring enough to take you up on your offer. Have you heard from James yet? Wasn't he supposed to meet us here in your room ten minutes ago?"

"I haven't seen or heard from him since I left him on the street." When Autumn had returned to the hotel after her argument with James, she had confided in Muriel what had happened between them.

"I wonder where he is." Muriel said. "If he doesn't show up soon, I suppose we should go on to the dance without him."

"Are you sure you want to bother?"

"Why not? We're already dressed up, so we might as well enjoy ourselves while we have the opportunity. Let me go knock on his door and see if he's in his room," Muriel offered. "Wait here. I'll be right back."

The older woman hurried down the hall, leaving Autumn to complete her toilette.

As Autumn put the finishing touches on her hair, she found her attitude about attending the dance changing. The prospect of going without James pleased her, as did the thought of seeing Cord again. Surely, as sheriff he would have to stay around and keep an eye on things tonight.

Autumn found herself smiling at her own reflection.

Muriel was quick to return.

"James didn't answer his door. I don't want to miss the dance because of him. Let's go."

Autumn was relieved that James hadn't shown up. The evening was certainly going to be more enjoyable without him.

Autumn's and Muriel's hearts were light as they left the hotel on their way to a big night in Sagebrush.

The dance was being held on the grounds of the church, and the sounds of music drew them there. Lamps had been lighted all around the dance floor that had been set up, and couples were already circling the floor. Tables with refreshments were arranged near the church itself, and the area was crowded with townspeople intent on having a good time. Autumn and Muriel were eager to join in.

Cord, Thatch and Jared, the new deputy, had come to the dance early to make sure everything went smoothly. On occasion a drunken brawl had been known to break out, so they made their presence known to keep the peace among the cowboys, who could get a bit rowdy sometimes.

Cord deliberately stayed in the background, keeping watch and visiting with folks when he had the opportunity. He'd told himself that he wasn't deliberately watching for Autumn, but he did find himself on several occasions scanning faces in the crowd to see if she had come. He had seen no sign of her yet. He hoped she planned to attend, but he couldn't be sure after the scene he'd witnessed between her and her fiancé.

Cord was talking with the pastor of the church and several other townsfolk when he finally caught sight of Autumn arriving with Muriel. His gaze lingered on her, taking in how breathtakingly lovely she was. She appeared every bit the elegant lady, and he found he couldn't look away. He didn't understand James's absence. He'd expected the man to be at her side all evening. He certainly would have been if Autumn was his fiancée.

"Look—is that Miss Thomas?" asked one of the women who'd been speaking with the pastor.

"It has to be. She looks just like Grace," another responded.

Everyone gathered there with Cord turned to stare at Autumn.

Even the pastor remarked, "It's no wonder you arrested her by mistake, Cord. The resemblance is amazing."

"That's all they have in common," Cord said. "Miss Thomas is a lady."

Cord excused himself and went to speak with Autumn and Muriel. As he made his way to them, he was aware of the murmur going through the crowd as the townspeople saw her for the first time. Many were staring openly at her. He felt almost protective of Autumn, for he was certain the gossips in town were going to spread ugly rumors.

"Good evening, ladies," he said cordially.

"Hello, Sheriff Randolph." Autumn hesitated to call him Cord in front of Muriel.

"I'm glad you were able to attend tonight."

"So are we," she replied.

"We wouldn't have missed it," Muriel said.

"Would you care to dance?" Cord turned to Autumn.

"Why, yes, thank you."

Cord had been prepared for her to refuse him, but he didn't question his good fortune. He swept her into his arms and out onto the dance floor.

The music had a smooth, sensual rhythm, and they moved as one among the other couples.

"You look very lovely tonight, Autumn," he told her.

"Thank you. It worked out nicely that the dance was tonight while we were in town."

"I don't see Dodson. Did he come with you?"

"He's been detained. He may join us later," she answered quickly. It wasn't a lie, for James had obviously been detained somewhere. She just didn't know where, and she honestly didn't care. If he wanted to, she was sure he would catch up with them later.

Cord was hoping it would be much later. He enjoyed having her in his arms, and if he could have found a way to make this dance last the whole night, he would have done it.

"You're a fine dancer," Autumn remarked, impressed by his ability.

"Why, thank you, ma'am." Cord found himself chuckling. "My mother would have been glad to know you think so. She worked hard on me when I was young to make sure I was skilled enough not to injure any young lady who was brave enough to dance with me."

"So you think I'm brave, do you?" Autumn asked as she looked up at him and smiled.

"I know you are," he answered, his tone becoming more intimate as their gazes met.

Autumn knew she had to break the spell Cord was trying to weave around her, so she deliberately changed the subject back to his mother. "Well, your mother did a good job teaching you. You'll have to thank her for me."

"I'd like to, but she's dead. Both my parents died some years back."

"I'm sorry. It's difficult losing one's parents."

"It was hard, but at least I had the privilege of knowing both of them."

"You were blessed. I feel that I missed so much by not getting to know my father or Grace."

"Have you made any decisions about what you're going to do now?"

"For the time being, I plan to stay."

"I'm glad."

"So am I," she answered.

They fell silent as they continued to dance.

* * *

Pete stood with his longtime friend Dan Barry at the side of the dance floor. He had been caught up in watching Autumn dance with Sheriff Randolph.

"I can't believe how much she looks like Grace." Dan gave a shake of his head in disbelief.

"Neither can I." Pete's words were almost a sigh.

Dan had long known how Pete felt about Grace. "Why aren't you out there asking her for the next dance?"

"She's engaged."

"Who's she engaged to? Sheriff Randolph isn't her fiancé, and he didn't hesitate to ask her to dance. Being engaged isn't the same as being married. Ask her for a dance. Go on," Dan encouraged.

His words were all it took to send Pete out to Autumn's side as soon as the music ended.

"May I have the next dance, Autumn?" Pete invited.

"Of course." She looked up at Cord even as she took Pete's arm. "Thank you, Cord."

"My pleasure." Cord started to walk away, but he didn't get far.

"There you are, Cord Randolph. I've been looking for you," Gail said appearing at his side.

"Good evening, Gail," he said cordially.

"I love this tune. Will you dance with me?"

"Of course," he replied, ever the gentleman.

Gail knew she was being brazen, but she didn't care. This was her chance to corner Cord and dance with him, and she was going to take full advantage of the opportunity. She'd been furious as she'd stood at the side of the dance floor watching him dance with Autumn Thomas. Jealousy had eaten at her and left her more determined than ever to go after him.

As Cord took her in his arms and began to dance with her, she was in heaven. She thought that perhaps the night would turn out wonderfully after all.

In the meantime, Pete was squiring Autumn around the dance floor. He remembered another time when he'd danced this way with Grace, but he fought down the memory. He told himself to just enjoy the dance.

"Did you know my sister very well, Pete?" Autumn asked.

"Yes, I did. I was . . . fond of her," he responded, not sure how his answer would sound to Autumn.

"You were? What happened?" She was curious at the way he'd phrased his answer to her.

Pete wasn't sure exactly how much to reveal to Autumn, but he knew she'd probably hear some talk around town eventually, so he decided to be honest. "I cared about her, but it didn't work out between us."

"Oh, that's too bad." She was a bit taken aback by his forthright answer. She was curious, too, as to why her sister hadn't returned his affection. Pete seemed like a very nice man. "I'm sorry. I'd really like to talk to you about her sometime, if you wouldn't mind. I've been trying to learn more about her."

"That would be fine."

"I'll look forward to it."

The dance came to an end, and he escorted her to where Muriel was standing near the refreshment tables. He thanked her, then went back to where Dan was waiting for him.

"Well? How did it go?" Dan asked.

"Autumn's very nice."

"And?"

"No 'and.' "

"Why not? She's blond and beautiful. She looks just like Grace."

"But she's not Grace," Pete answered simply.

Chapter Fifteen

James didn't get drunk often, but after his argument with Autumn, he'd made a point of doing just that. He had passed the rest of the afternoon and early evening drinking and gambling at the saloon. Only when he finally noticed that it had gotten dark outside did he remember he was supposed to have met Autumn and Muriel to escort them to the dance. Excusing himself from the poker table, he scooped up his winnings—a considerable sum for one so inebriated—and headed back to the hotel.

James made it to his room and got cleaned up a bit before going to Autumn's room.

He expected Autumn and Muriel to be waiting for him, dressed and ready to go. He had thought they would be glad to see him, especially

Autumn, since he believed she owed him an apology.

It never occurred to him that since he was over an hour late in coming for them, they might have grown tired of waiting and gone off on their own.

James knocked on Autumn's door, then took a step back to wait for her to open it.

And he waited.

Then he frowned. He had expected her to be eagerly anticipating his arrival, to throw the door open and welcome him. It did his ego and his temper little good to believe she was deliberately ignoring him.

He knocked once more, and waited again.

When, again, there was no response and no sound coming from within the room, he decided to ask the clerk at the front desk if he knew of Miss Thomas's whereabouts.

A bit unsteady on his feet, James managed to make his way down to the lobby. The young man working there looked up at his approach.

"Is something wrong, Mr. Dodson?"

"It's Miss Thomas. She isn't answering her door," he answered. His words were a bit slurred from all the whiskey he'd drunk, but his manner was still arrogant.

"Miss Thomas and Miss Williams are gone, sir. They went to the dance down at the church," he explained, expecting him to be relieved at this news. He was shocked when the look on the man's face turned ugly and vicious.

185

"They went to the dance?" James was furious that the two women had not waited for him. He had had about all he could take of Autumn's continued defiance of him.

"Yes, sir. They left some time ago," the clerk said nervously.

James didn't say another word. He stalked out of the hotel with only one thing on his mind—finding his fiancée.

"Are you having a good time?" Muriel asked Autumn as they stood together at the side of the dance floor.

"Yes, I am," she replied, smiling. "What about you? I noticed you dancing with Mr. Baxter."

"Ralph." Muriel slipped and called him by his first name, then blushed slightly. "Oh, well, yes, he did ask me for a dance or two."

"And you enjoyed every one of them."

She smiled at Autumn. "As a matter of fact, I did. He's a very nice man."

"Here you are, ladies," Ralph said as he joined them, carrying two glasses of punch.

"Thank you, Mr. Baxter," Autumn said.

"Please, call me Ralph. Muriel does."

Autumn agreed as she accepted a glass of punch and took a sip.

"I noticed you dancing with Pete Miller. He's a good man. It's a shame we couldn't work out the sale for you, but I understand why you want to stay."

"I think Pete does, too. He's a gentleman. He

told me that he cared for my sister."

"Yes, he did. When Grace ran away, Pete was worried about her and went to look for her. He wanted to bring her home."

"He did?" she asked. "Did he find her?"

"Yes—but it was rather sad the way it turned out."

"What happened?"

"Grace was working at the saloon in Eagle's Nest. He offered to help her, but I guess by then it was too late. She was already mixed up with Martin and too caught up in that world."

"Thank you for telling me." She glanced toward Pete, who stood across the dance floor talking with another man near the refreshment tables. Pete was a nice-looking man, and she wondered why her sister hadn't accepted his offer. He seemed to be a genuinely good person. "It's a shame she didn't come back with Pete. Things would have been very different right now if she had."

"They certainly would have," Ralph agreed.

"May I have the next dance, Autumn?" Cord asked as he came to stand with them.

Autumn accepted Cord's offer graciously. Muriel took Autumn's punch glass and watched as the sheriff guided Autumn out onto the dance floor.

"That's their second dance tonight," Muriel remarked with a slight smile. "Although I'm not counting."

"But Autumn is engaged to James." Ralph was shocked at her unspoken suggestion.

"Yes, she is, isn't she?" Muriel said. She was troubled by the whole situation. The more time she spent with Autumn and James, the more doubts she had about the wisdom of their upcoming marriage. Marriage was forever, and she feared they were so different that they would find little happiness together.

Ralph found her remark strange, but said nothing more.

Autumn relaxed and allowed herself to just enjoy being in Cord's arms, moving as one with him. It seemed so right, so natural somehow, for her to be there. She had seen him dancing with the waitress from the restaurant and had actually known a moment of jealousy. It had surprised her and forced her to examine her feelings for him.

"Are you having a good time?" Cord asked.

"Yes. Everyone here in town has been very friendly."

"Sagebrush is a friendly town," he said, glad that no one had given her any trouble tonight about her sister. "Just look at the warm welcome you got from the greeting party that met your stagecoach."

Autumn couldn't help herself. She laughed out loud at his remark.

Cord had never heard her laugh before, and

he decided he liked the sound. He smiled down at her.

James had reached the dance and was looking for Autumn. He finally saw her on the dance floor, laughing and carrying on with the sheriff. He was growing more furious with each passing moment.

Drunk as he was, James wasn't about to let Autumn get away with her reprehensible behavior. First, she'd refused to accept his judgment about selling the ranch; then she hadn't waited for him to escort her to the dance. And now she was dancing with the very lawman who, not so very long ago, had thought she was an outlaw and had locked her up! James was determined to put an end to this ridiculous behavior of hers once and for all. He strode out onto the dance floor, weaving his way between the dancing couples until he reached Autumn and the lawman.

"I believe this is my dance." His expression was black as he spoke. He was almost hoping the sheriff would try to cause some trouble with him.

Cord stopped dancing.

"James—where have you been?" Autumn was startled by his sudden appearance.

"Why, I've been looking for you, my dear," he replied, emphasizing the endearment as he glared down at her. He stepped forward and held out his hand to her. "If I may?"

Autumn moved away from Cord and went into James's arms.

James felt triumphant as he began to dance with her. He said nothing more, though, for his fury hadn't lessened.

Drunk as he was, he didn't notice that his steps were unsteady or that he was lacking his usual dancing expertise. Autumn, however, noticed immediately.

"Perhaps we should sit this dance out," she suggested.

"No. I want to dance with you," he insisted.

James pulled her even more tightly against him. He pawed at her a little, and he even leaned forward and tried to kiss her. Autumn managed to dodge his effort, and the kiss landed awkwardly on her cheek near her ear.

"James, what are you doing?" she asked, troubled by his behavior.

"I was trying to kiss my fiancée," he answered with a sodden grin.

"Not here." She didn't want to become a spectacle.

"Why not?"

"This isn't the time."

"When is the time?" He leered at her.

Autumn had never really dealt with anyone so drunk before. She kept her smile in place as she tried to avoid his groping hands and his cloddish footwork.

When at last the music ended, James looked at Autumn smugly. "There, we've had our dance. Now we can call it a night and go back to the hotel."

"I'm not ready to leave," she objected, not wanting to be alone with him in this condition.

His gaze narrowed as she dared to defy him again. He stopped walking to regard her coldly.

"Oh, yes, my dear, you are," he told her with confidence. "You're ready to leave this dance and this town."

"What are you talking about?"

"I'll tell you," he said. "I see that Mr. Baxter is here and so is Pete Miller. We're going over to speak with them and tell them you've changed your mind, and you're ready to sell the ranch. We can finish up the legalities of the sale tomorrow, and then we'll leave Sagebrush on the first stagecoach out of here Monday afternoon."

"You don't give up, do you?" Autumn returned hotly.

"You need a strong man to guide you, my dear, for it's quite obvious you need help making intelligent decisions."

"And that's why I have you?" she said, amazed at the conceit he'd revealed.

"Exactly. You wanted me to come with you to help you, and I am doing just that. Come on," he said, ready to take her arm and guide her over to where the lawyer was talking with Muriel. "Let's go tell Mr. Baxter right now about your change in plans."

"I will not."

"Yes, you will." He grabbed her arm.

"You're drunk, James!" Autumn jerked free of his hold and walked off in the opposite direction.

Annoyed, James went after her. He was determined to get rid of the ranch that very night. "Autumn! Where do you think you're going?"

Autumn kept walking. She wanted to get as far away from him as she could. She hadn't been around many drunks before, and she wondered if they were all as obnoxious as James was.

James was dogged in his pursuit, not letting her out of his sight. He didn't speak again until they had moved beyond the crowd of townspeople. He was going to have the last word with Autumn, and he was going to do it now. He just didn't want an audience when it happened.

"Autumn, did you hear what I said? The lawyer is right over there on the other side of the dance floor. Let's go over and talk to him," he urged, so drunk he was oblivious to her growing fury.

"No."

"What do you mean 'no'?"

"Exactly that, James. I told you before, I'm not going to sell the ranch. I'm staying in Sagebrush."

"And I told you we are going back to Philadelphia."

Autumn wished he'd never left Philadelphia. James had proven to be a stubborn man when he was sober; drunk, he was impossible to reason with. She knew there was no point in even trying to have a conversation with him.

"I think it would be best if we called it a night, James. I'll see you tomorrow."

"I'll walk you to the hotel."

"No, thank you," she said, dismissing him as coldly and as abruptly as she could. "I came without you, I can return without you." She turned away from him and disappeared back into the crowd.

At her deliberate snub, James was livid. He stood there, looking around at the people of Sagebrush in a judgmental, condemning way. He thought they were all as stupid as Autumn's father had obviously been. There was absolutely no reason for anyone in his right mind to want to live in Sagebrush. He didn't know what had happened to Autumn since they'd arrived, but she was turning into a woman of little class and even less intelligence, and he was finding dealing with her absolutely maddening. Too proud to chase after her any more tonight, James remained where he was, seething in silence.

·

Chapter Sixteen

Cord had had no choice but to walk away after James had cut in on him and Autumn. He sought out Thatch and Jared, to see how things were going. All had been quiet so far. They'd been keeping an eye out for Martin, just in case he decided to show up in town to cause some trouble tonight. There had been no sign of him, and they were glad. The deputies went off to make their rounds, while Cord remained at the dance.

Cord looked out on the dance floor, wanting to catch a glimpse of Autumn. He saw her walking off with James, and noticed that James appeared angry about something. Cord remembered how the man had treated her earlier that day, and he decided to make sure she was all right.

By the time Cord circled the dance floor, Autumn had left James and disappeared into the crowd. Cord was glad that she'd gotten away from her fiancé, but he found himself still worrying about her. He made his way in the direction she'd gone, and he thought he saw her in the shadows not too far off.

"Autumn." Cord said her name softly as he found her in a darkened corner.

"Oh—Cord—you surprised me."

"Why are you hiding back here?" he asked.

"Hiding is the right word, I think," she answered.

"Is there trouble?" He was ready to defend her if need be.

"It's just James—"

"What happened?"

"He's drunk, and I've never seen him drunk before. I don't even know him when he acts like this."

"You did the smart thing getting away from him."

Cord's words soothed Autumn, and she found herself comparing the two men.

Cord accepted her for who she was.

James didn't.

Cord had just told her that she was smart.

James obviously believed she was too dullwitted to take care of her own life.

"Thank you, Cord. My life is so confusing right now, it's hard to know if I'm doing the right thing."

"Follow your heart," Cord said. "What is your heart telling you to do right now?"

Autumn lifted her gaze to him. Standing over her, he looked so handsome that her reaction to him was immediate and powerful. Her breath caught in her throat, and her heartbeat quickened. Her eyes widened as excitement pulsed through her.

She warned herself that this was the sheriff of Sagebrush, the man who was after her sister—not James—not her fiancé.

But all the logic in the world couldn't stop what she was feeling.

Cord saw the change in her expression, and he let his gaze drop to her lips. He remembered how sweet her kiss had been and he knew he needed to taste of her again. Unable to deny himself, Cord closed the distance between them.

Autumn found herself engulfed in his embrace, his lips upon hers in a fiery brand that left no doubt about the heat of his desire for her. Instinctively she moved closer, molding herself to the lean, hard strength of him. His arms closed around her. Autumn felt protected, yet aroused.

Her conscience screamed a warning for her to stop—to draw away. It cautioned her that kissing Cord wasn't right.

But in her heart she recognized that nothing in her life had ever been so right before.

A low, soft moan escaped Autumn as she surrendered fully to his kiss. She lifted her arms and looped them around his neck, drawing him even closer.

Cord stifled a groan of pure passion as Autumn moved willingly against him. She was beauty and excitement, and he wanted her as he'd never wanted another woman. Heat settled low within him.

And then he heard the vague sound of shouts coming from a distance.

Reality returned with a vengeance.

Cord ended the kiss and dropped his hands away from Autumn. He took a step back, needing to break off all physical contact with her. If there was trouble, he needed to be able to think straight, and he definitely couldn't do that with her in his arms.

"What's wrong?" Autumn asked, gazing up at Cord in confusion. Still caught up in the glory of his kiss, she didn't know why he'd broken away from her.

"It sounds like a fight." He looked around, trying to see where the trouble was. "I have to go."

Autumn stared after Cord as he rushed off in the direction of the commotion. She hadn't wanted him to leave her. She wanted him to come back to her and kiss her again. It took a moment for her to bring her runaway emotions under control. When she finally started to follow Cord, she wondered what on earth could be going on.

* * *

James glared at Thatch as he declared in a loud voice, "You may be a deputy, but you're just as stupid as your sheriff!"

"Mr. Dodson, there's no need for any trouble tonight. Why don't you come with me?" Thatch could tell the man was drunk and looking for a fight.

"I'm not going anywhere with you." James declared. "The only place I'm going is back to Philadelphia."

Thatch thought that was a great idea. If there had been a stagecoach leaving right that minute, he would have put Dodson on it. But there wouldn't be another stage heading east for two more days; the next best option was to get Dodson away from the dance. "There are ladies in attendance here tonight, so why don't we—"

"Ladies? In this town? Hardly." He snorted in derision.

One of the men from Sagebrush who'd been listening to the exchange with some amusement heard this remark and grew angry. He confronted James.

"Watch who you're talking about, *friend*," the man said in a quiet but unyielding tone.

"I'm not your friend," James sneered. "And I'm only speaking the truth."

Thatch was trying to move James along, to get him out of harm's way before anything happened, but his last remark ended any hope of his escaping unscathed.

At James's insult, the other man came at him, swinging.

James had looked away for a moment and was caught unaware by the attack. The man's blow struck him forcefully. James staggered, but did not lose his footing. He turned surprisingly quickly, ready for a fight.

The two men were grappling violently when Cord came rushing up. He and Thatch shared a look of understanding as they both made a grab for the combatants, wanting to separate them before anybody got hurt. Thatch managed to get hold of the man from town, while Cord physically dragged James away.

James was mindless in his drunken fury, and the fact that someone was trying to manhandle him only made him madder.

Cord released James after a moment, thinking he had finally calmed down.

James was far from calm, though. When he realized it was the sheriff who'd grabbed him, he turned and attacked Cord.

Used to dealing with drunks, Cord was ready. He grabbed James's arm and twisted it up behind him, almost forcing him to his knees.

"Maybe next time you'll listen to my deputy," Cord ground out. "I think a night in jail will do you good."

"You can't arrest me, Sheriff Randolph. I've done nothing wrong," James declared confidently as he struggled to look Cord in the face. He fought futilely against his hold. "That man attacked me! He hit me first! I was only defending myself!"

Cord did not ease his grip.

"You're right, Mr. Dodson. I'm not going to arrest you," Cord responded.

James looked smug and superior, but only for a moment.

"I'm just going to lock you up until you're sober. It's only to keep you safe."

James's expression changed to one of shock and outrage. "You can't put me in jail!"

"Oh, yes, I can, Mr. Dodson. In case you've forgotten, I'm the law here in Sagebrush."

Cord nodded to Thatch to release the man he was holding and told him, "You go on and get out of here." Then he told his deputy, "Let's go, Thatch."

Cord, with Thatch's help, half-dragged, half-led the drunken, protesting, still-fighting James off to jail.

Autumn had come after Cord to see what the trouble was. The sight of James being so wildly disruptive shocked her deeply.

"I can't believe James could act that like," Muriel said as she came to Autumn's side.

"He's drunk," Autumn offered as an explanation.

"Well, Cord certainly knew how to handle him."

"Yes, he did." Autumn had to admit that Cord and his deputy had done a fine job of controlling James. She could just imagine how angry her fiancé was going to be in the morning once he'd sobered up. "And he may have done me a favor."

"Why? Was James causing you trouble tonight?"

"Oh, yes," she said resignedly. "He was still pressuring me to sell the ranch to Pete Miller. It seems he just can't take no for an answer from me."

"I'm sorry, dear," Muriel said. She had always liked James, but she'd expected him to be more understanding of Autumn's situation.

"There was some excitement, I see," Ralph said as he sought them out. Being from Sagebrush, he was accustomed to the occasional drunken brawl at their social gatherings. The sight of the lawmen hauling James away had startled him, though. "It was James?"

"I'm afraid so," Muriel remarked.

"Would you like me to escort you back to the hotel?" he offered.

"That would be wonderful, Ralph. Thank you," Muriel told him, appreciating his thoughtfulness.

Autumn took one last look after her fiancé. He was still trying to fight Cord's hold on him, but Cord appeared to be handling him with little trouble. Disgusted and disillusioned, she turned away. She was more than ready to return to the hotel.

James never gave up his struggle against the lawmen all the way to the jail.

"I want to see the lawyer! Get Mr. Baxter for me now!" he demanded, still fighting as they brought him inside.

Cord and Thatch had to all but physically throw him into the jail cell.

"You're not seeing any lawyer," Cord informed him as he slammed and locked the cell door behind him.

"I have my rights! You have no grounds to hold me!" James charged, his fury unabated.

Cord gave him a cold smile. "I wasn't planning on charging you with any crimes, Mr. Dodson. You'll be free to go in the morning, but if you keep causing trouble, I could change my mind. I could charge you with an assault on officers of the law, not to mention disturbing the peace."

The deadly serious tone of his voice finally made an impression on James. He stood there glaring at the sheriff through the bars of the cell.

"That's better," Cord said, appreciating James's momentary silence. He started back toward the office.

"You'll pay for this," James muttered.

Cord heard him and looked back. He smiled tightly. "I don't think so, Mr. Dodson."

Then Cord shut the door to the office.

James remained standing there alone in the darkened cell. He stared around himself in disbelief that he could have ended up in jail.

Anger grew within him at his circumstances, and he blamed Autumn for what had happened.

This was all her fault. He should never have let her convince him that they needed to make the trip to Texas. He swore under his breath, cursing her for her headstrong ways. He was humiliated to have ended up in this situation, and thankful that none of his friends in Philadelphia would ever learn about his incarceration. He vowed to himself, then and there, that he would never accede to her wishes again. She would follow his direction from this day on—or else.

Satisfied that he knew what he was going to do, James sat down on the cot. He hoped the long hours of the night would pass quickly, but he doubted they would—not trapped in a jail cell like he was.

Autumn was troubled as she settled in her hotel room for the night. Her life had been so much simpler just a short time before. Now everything she'd always believed to be true had changed, and life had suddenly become terribly complicated—especially where James was concerned.

She had donned her nightgown and was about ready to get in bed when a knock came at her door. Tugging on her robe, she went to answer it, believing it was Muriel.

Autumn opened the door to find Cord standing before her.

Chapter Seventeen

"Cord—" Autumn clutched her robe even more closely around her as she looked up at him.

Cord swallowed tightly as he stared down at the sight of her clad only in her nightgown and wrapper. There in the doorway of the softly lighted room, she was a vision to behold. Her hair was down and brushed out, loose around her shoulders in a cascade of soft golden curls.

He wanted to reach out to her.

He ached to hold her.

Desire, pure and stark, pounded through him, and he had to force the need away. He had come only to check on her and for no other reason— or at least that was what he was telling himself.

"I went back to the dance and found that you and Muriel had left," he said quietly. "I wanted to make sure you'd gotten back here all right, and let you know that I'll be keeping Dodson locked up until tomorrow morning. He'll be sober by then."

"Do you think keeping him all night is really necessary?" she asked, knowing how upset James would be to spend the night in jail.

"Some men can handle their liquor, and some men can't."

"I understand," she told him. She'd seen how belligerent James had been. "Thanks for letting me know."

He nodded, ready to leave, knowing he had to get away from her quickly.

"Well . . . good night, Cord."

"Has it been a good night, Autumn?" he asked. The heat of his need for her flamed to a fever pitch even though he was trying to control it, fighting to deny it. He told himself he was simply a lawman doing his job, but he realized there was far more to his coming to see her than simply giving her the news about James.

Autumn lifted her gaze to Cord's. Mesmerized, she remembered his kiss as they'd clung together in the darkness. She found herself answering him in a voice just barely above a breathless whisper, "Yes."

Caught up in a whirlwind of turbulent emotions that threatened to sweep her away, Autumn was unable to resist the magnetism of her attraction to Cord. She took a step back into the room, her gaze never leaving his as she issued the un-spoken invitation.

It was all Cord needed. He came into the room and closed the door silently behind him.

They didn't speak.

There was no need for words between them.

He reached out to her.

Autumn went into Cord's embrace willingly, lifting her lips to his in an offering he couldn't refuse.

His mouth claimed hers hungrily, and the power of his kiss took her breath away. She clung to him, reveling in being close to him.

"Oh, Cord—"

His forbidden desire drove him.

He wanted her.

He needed her.

Emboldened, he began to caress Autumn. His hands explored the soft curves of her lush body through the silken material, as his lips continued to plunder the sweetness of hers.

Autumn had never been touched so intimately before. She gasped at the feelings that Cord's bold caresses aroused within her. When his lips left hers to trail hot kisses down the side of her neck, a shiver of pure erotic pleasure trembled through her. Cord felt her response and drew back long enough to brush away the barrier of her robe and gown from her shoulders, revealing the glory of her bared breasts to him for the first time.

Startled by his daring move, Autumn was

tempted to cover herself, but the look in Cord's eyes stopped her.

His gaze was upon her, and he thought her the most beautiful woman he had ever seen. Ever so gently he reached out to her. His fingers skimmed over her silken flesh, caressing, arousing. Autumn trembled before the power of the passion his touch created within her. When his lips traced the same sensual path, she gasped in rapturous delight and gave herself over to the wonder of his love.

Cord sensed her surrender. He swept her up into his arms and carried her to the waiting bed. He laid her upon the welcoming softness, then followed her down, his passion for her driving him.

Autumn was enraptured. The ecstasy of Cord's heated caresses left her senses reeling. She was mindless in her need for him, reality erased by the passion he had awakened within her.

Cord moved over her, and Autumn raised her arms in welcome. She wanted to touch him as he had touched her. She wanted to be as close to him as she could. She lifted one hand to caress his cheek.

It was then he saw it.

The ring—another man's claim to her. She was engaged to James.

Cord went still.

Autumn had been caught up in the pleasure of his loving, and she didn't understand this sudden change in him. She looked up at Cord to find that his expression had hardened. He looked so cold and distant that he seemed almost unapproachable.

"Cord?"

He did not respond. He only shifted stiffly away from her and rose from the bed.

"What is it? What's wrong?" Autumn asked, feeling lost and so very alone as he stood over her.

"I have to go," Cord said flatly, struggling for control. His need for her was still powerful within him, but he knew he couldn't go back to her or he would risk losing what little control he had over his forbidden desire.

Autumn was chilled by the tone of his voice. Reality returned in a painful rush of humiliation as she realized what had almost happened between them.

She watched in silence as Cord turned and walked away. He looked back as he reached the door.

"Lock this behind me," he ordered.

And then he was gone, quietly closing the door behind him, without another word to her.

Autumn stared at the closed portal, embarrassed to the depths of her being. She looked down at James's ring on her finger and was shamed by her actions. She had acted the wanton with Cord. All Cord had to do was touch her or kiss her, and she was lost to the power of her attraction to him.

Getting up from the bed, she covered herself

as she went to the door. She was tempted to throw it open and race after him, to find Cord and tell him that her engagement to James was a mistake and that she was going to end it when she saw him next. Autumn knew now that she could not remain engaged to James, feeling as she did about Cord. She stood there at the door for a moment, her hand on the knob, before she finally locked it as he had told her to do.

Autumn went to her bedside and turned out the lamp. Darkness surrounded her, but that was what she wanted. She went to the window to watch for Cord on the streets below. It seemed a long time, but finally she saw him walking away from the hotel, heading to the sheriff's office. She longed for him to look back her way, but he didn't. He moved on and disappeared into the night.

Autumn went to lie down, but her restlessness left her tossing and turning as she tried to calm her runaway heart.

She never knew that Cord had remained in the hall outside her room until he had heard her lock the door. Only then, when he was certain she was safe, had he left her.

Just before she drifted off to sleep, Autumn realized that Cord had saved her again tonight.

This time he had saved her from herself.

James passed out for a few hours on the hard, miserable cot, but he got little real rest. By dawn, he was awake and pacing around the cell. He had sobered up, and he was thinking as clearly as he could considering the pounding in his head. It wasn't often that he drank to excess, but yesterday had been a very difficult day.

Yesterday was over now, though. A new day had dawned, and he was ready to take advantage of it. He wanted to get out of jail—now. He felt filthy from spending the night there and couldn't wait to get back to the hotel and bathe.

Then he thought about seeing Autumn again. He wasn't sure exactly what the morning would bring, but he was certain it wouldn't be pleasant. She had walked away from him last night without a backward glance, and he was beginning to wonder if she was prepared to walk away from the future they had planned together. If she couldn't abide by his wishes, then there would be no future for them. He meant to be the man of the house, the head of the family. His word would rule, and she would have to accept that if she planned to be Mrs. James Dodson.

At the sound of the door to the office opening, James looked up to see the deputy coming with the keys to the cell in hand.

"It's about time," James said coldly.

"I can always leave and come back about noon," Thatch returned with little sympathy or respect. He had no use for stupid drunks, and this man qualified.

"Thank you for coming, Deputy," James amended, managing to keep sarcasm out of his tone.

"That's better. Try not to get so rowdy next time you're drinking, Mr. Dodson."

"There won't be a next time."

"Glad to hear that. That's good news. Real good news." Thatch unlocked the cell door and held it wide for him.

James wasted no time leaving. He didn't bother exchanging any further pleasantries with the deputy, but left the sheriff's office and marched straight back to the hotel. He had only one regret. It was Sunday and there was no stagecoach out of town until the following afternoon.

Autumn had awakened early. Her sleep had been uneasy, for troubling thoughts of James had disturbed her rest off and on all night. She was up and dressed when the knock came at her door. She was hoping it would be Muriel, coming to see if she was ready for breakfast, but she had a feeling it was James.

Her instincts were proven correct when she opened the door and saw James standing there before her. He was still dressed as he had been the night before, and she realized he hadn't even gone back to his own room yet.

"I think we need to have a serious talk," James announced, striding into her room without waiting to be asked. At that moment, he cared little for etiquette. They needed to discuss their future, and they needed to do it in private.

Autumn was taken aback by his abrupt manner. "Are you all right?"

"I'm just fine—after spending the night in the renowned Sagebrush jail," he snarled. "But that isn't what I came to talk to you about. I plan to leave for Philadelphia tomorrow, and I expect you and Muriel to be making the trip with me."

She met his gaze straight on. "James, I have no plans to return to Philadelphia anytime soon. I want to stay here on my ranch."

"Our future is in Philadelphia. Our home is in Philadelphia."

"I'm not sure where my home is anymore," she told him, firm in her conviction that she was not ready to leave the Lazy T. "If you want to go back East tomorrow, you're free to do so, but I won't be going with you."

"You dare to . . ." He couldn't believe that she would dare to continue to defy him.

"I am doing what I have to do," Autumn said, cutting him off. She looked down at the engagement ring on her hand that branded her as his woman. She thought of the ranch, of her possible future there—and she thought of Cord's kiss. There was no regret in her heart as she slipped the ring off. After all that had happened, she could no longer remain engaged to James. "Considering how we both feel, I think it would be best if we end our engagement now."

She held out the diamond ring to him.

James stared at her for a moment as the meaning of her words sank in. *She was breaking off their engagement!* Fury replaced his shock. He snatched the ring from her.

His voice was cold and his tone one of undisguised loathing as he told her, "I won't be returning to the ranch with you. Have my things sent to me here in town."

"All right."

"What about Muriel? Will she be traveling with me or staying with you?"

"I'll ask her as soon as I see her and let you know."

He nodded tersely, and without another word, left the room. He shut the door silently behind him, just as he was shutting her out of his life from that moment on.

Autumn sat down on the edge of the bed, wondering how she had come to this moment. She had a sister she'd never met, who was a wanted outlaw. She owned a ranch, but knew nothing about ranching. And she had just broken off her engagement to James, a man who just a short time before she'd planned to spend the rest of her life with.

Autumn wondered if she had done the right thing.

And then she remembered Cord's kiss. Any doubts she'd had were erased by the memory of the ecstasy she had found in his arms.

Chapter Eighteen

"You're up and about awfully early today," Muriel said when she went to Autumn's room. She was surprised to find her young friend dressed for the day and already packed for the trip back to the ranch.

"I didn't sleep much last night, and James came by about an hour ago."

"They let him out early, didn't they?"

"They only planned to keep him until he sobered up."

"How was he?"

"Well, he was sober," Autumn admitted.

"And not very happy, I'm sure," Muriel added.

"That goes without saying. Muriel—" She paused for a moment to gather her thoughts. "I broke our engagement this morning. I gave James his ring back."

The older woman glanced quickly at Autumn's hand and saw that the ring really was gone. "It couldn't have been easy for you."

"No, it wasn't, but it was the right thing to do."

"You're sure?"

"Yes, I'm sure. He was planning to take the first stage out of here tomorrow, and he was insisting I leave with him. He doesn't understand my feelings about the ranch, and he had no interest in wanting to understand. He only wants to go back to Philadelphia."

"It's a whole different way of life out here," Muriel said.

"Yes, it is. It's completely different from what we're used to, but I intend to stay."

"I see."

"James wants to know if you will make the trip back to Philadelphia with him. We have to let him know today."

Muriel went to Autumn and gave her a supportive hug. "I'm not going anywhere. I'm staying right here with you for as long as you want me."

Autumn hugged her back. "Thank you."

"Your mother wanted me to keep watch over you, and I intend to do just that."

"I wonder if Mother ever thought you'd be doing it here in Sagebrush."

"Probably not, but you know what?" At Autumn's curious look, Muriel went on with a secret smile, "If I hadn't come with you on this adventure, I would never have met Ralph. He's wonderful."

"I am so glad you're happy."

They shared a gentle laugh.

"Do you want to speak with James again, or shall we just leave word for him at the front desk?" Autumn asked.

"Let's just leave him word. I doubt he has anything more to say to me, and I know it can't be easy for you."

"No, it wasn't, but I had to do it."

They heard the sound of the church bells, and Autumn looked at Muriel.

"Would you like to go to church? We've got time to make the service."

"That's a wonderful idea. We have a lot to be thankful for."

"Yes, we do."

They left word about Muriel's plans for James at the desk and hurried off to attend the church service.

The church was crowded, and they were welcomed warmly by the people there. They found room in a pew near the back and settled in for the minister's sermon.

"Love." Reverend Woods called the word out as he came to stand before his flock. "That is what God expects of us. That is our sole reason for being. We are called to love and to be loved.

If mankind followed this belief, there would be peace in the world. There would be joy on Earth. If we loved and were loved, all our days would be filled with God's glory. Say amen!" he exhorted the congregation.

"Amen," they echoed.

"But we are not perfect. Over and over again, we have shown God just how weak we are by the choices we make in our daily lives. We must strive to change our ways, but to do that we must first change what is in our hearts. Think about it—What do you seek from life? What is it you want?" He paused for effect. "Do you want power? Wealth? Why? For the pleasure those things can bring while we're here on Earth? Friends, we only spend a few years here. We spend eternity with God! So prepare yourselves. Be ready."

"Amen!" one of the congregants called out.

The preacher smiled. "Start this moment. Remember to 'love one another as I have loved you.' Live your lives this way always. Paul has told us that there are three gifts—faith, hope and love, and the greatest of these is love. It is not always easy to love everyone, but we must try." He paused again, then went on, "Now, when I say 'love' to you, I am not talking about carnal desire. Do not be fooled into thinking that fornication is love. Fornication is lust, and lust is one of the deadly sins."

Autumn fought to keep her expression carefully blank as she listened to the minister. *Love*—

Lust—She swallowed tightly as the memory of being in Cord's arms the night before played in her mind. His embrace had been heavenly, and she had been caught up in the ecstasy she had found in his kiss. Autumn felt a little guilty knowing she had kissed Cord before she'd returned James's ring. She certainly hoped God understood. She turned her attention back to the minister's sermon as he began speaking of the prodigal son.

"Do not mistake lust for love. True love must rule your life. Start with your family. Remember the story of the prodigal son—the son who was lost and was found. The son who had walked away from his family was welcomed back by his loving father with open arms. So it is for us with God. God loves us and wants us to be with Him. It is our choice to make. It is your choice to make. Will you choose the right way? Will you choose God's way?" The minister let the question hang as he concluded his sermon.

Autumn listened intently to the preacher's inspiring words, thinking it a bit eerie that his topic was so central to her life at that moment. She only wished her father had been alive so he could have heard the minister's heartfelt message, too.

Autumn thought of Grace. She wanted her sister to return home just as the prodigal son had, but their father had been harsh on her. Grace had left the Lazy T thinking he wanted nothing more to do with her. Autumn doubted that

Grace would come back, but if she did, Autumn knew she would welcome her with open arms.

"Wonderful sermon," Muriel said as they emerged from the church.

"Yes, it was, and very close to home, too. I just hope I get the chance to welcome back the prodigal daughter," she said, giving Muriel a sad smile.

"Poor Grace."

"She's out there somewhere, Muriel, and I want to know—no, I need to know she's safe."

"Well, if Grace is anything like you, she's not only beautiful, she's smart. Grace will know how to take care of herself."

"I hope you're right. I hate to think of her alone and in trouble somewhere with no family to help her."

"We'll just have to pray for her, Autumn. Right now, that's all we can do."

Autumn knew Muriel was right, but the knowledge didn't make it any easier to accept. On their way back to the hotel, Autumn found herself offering up a prayer that Grace would find safe harbor.

They made no effort to contact James before leaving for the ranch.

Ralph stopped by the hotel to see Muriel just as they were getting ready to depart. He was surprised to hear about the broken engagement and to learn that James would not be accompanying the women back to the ranch. He offered to ride with them, but Autumn was confident she and

Muriel would be fine on their own. He stayed to watch them drive off, promising to come out and pay a visit soon.

As Autumn drove the carriage from town, they passed by the sheriff's office. She found herself watching for Cord, but she saw no sign of him. The disappointment she felt surprised her, but only served to convince her all the more that she'd done the right thing about James and their engagement.

"You're quiet today," Muriel said to Autumn as they covered the miles to the Lazy T. "Are you worrying about James?"

"No. He's going to be a much happier man once he's back in Philadelphia where he belongs."

"What if you end up going back?"

"I don't know that I ever will, but if I do, it won't matter. I don't love James."

"You don't?" Muriel was taken aback by her statement.

"This trip has been quite a revelation to me. Had we stayed in Philadelphia, I would never have found out what he was really like until after we'd married. I am so glad he came out here with me. It's better to find out your differences before the wedding than after—like my parents did. They were so different, they probably should never have married."

"That may be true, but I for one am very glad they did."

"You are?"

"Yes, Autumn, dear. They had you." She reached over and patted her hand.

Autumn's heart swelled with affection for Muriel. "And Grace, too."

"Let's just hope that some day she can come home to her father's house, as well."

Grace was hot, tired, hungry, thirsty and dirtier than she'd ever been in her life, but that didn't stop her. Nothing was going to stop her. Driven by the demon that was Rod, she kept riding. She stopped only to rest her horse and get some sleep. Then after a few hours, she would be up and riding again.

All that mattered was reaching the Miller ranch. Once she was there, she would be safe— at least for a little while.

Grace had taken great care to do everything she could to hide her trail. Rod would be coming after her, she knew, and she wouldn't stand a chance of escaping him if he found her tracks. She hoped her tricks had helped her to elude him, but she could not let her guard down. She could not relax. As she continued riding toward Pete's place, Grace wondered if she would ever really feel safe again.

"What are you going to do about James's things?" Sherry asked.

Autumn and Muriel had just returned to the ranch and told her everything that had happened in town. She was delighted that Autumn had elected not to sell the ranch, and surprised that she'd broken her engagement.

"I'll take them back into town for him tomorrow," Autumn told her.

"There's no need for that. One of the men can take them in for you and save you the trip."

"I think it's important that I tell James goodbye in person. I don't want to leave things the way they were between us when we parted this morning."

"There's one thing you have to start doing, then, if you're going to be out riding around by yourself," Sherry advised.

"What's that?" Autumn was curious.

"You have to start carrying a gun. You never know when you're going to need it."

Autumn couldn't help smiling at her words. "The last time I carried a gun, it got me arrested."

"Sheriff Randolph knows who you are now. I don't think he'll be causing you any more trouble."

"I hope not," Autumn responded, but she wanted to tell Sherry that he had already caused her more trouble. Even as she thought it, she realized that Cord's involvement in her life wasn't trouble—it was a blessing. If she had never known the wonder of his kiss, she would have gone through her whole life believing that what she and James shared was true love.

Love.

Did she love Cord?

The thought surprised her.

Could she have fallen in love with the lawman so quickly? It seemed impossible. They had only known each other for a short time. Yet the feelings his kiss and touch aroused in her were unlike anything she'd ever experienced. He had only to kiss her, and she was lost in the wonder of his embrace.

With an effort, she forced her thoughts away from her heated encounter with Cord.

Autumn knew, though, that she would be counting the minutes till she could see him again.

Chapter Nineteen

It was late Monday morning when James answered the knock at his hotel room door to find Autumn standing before him.

"To what do I owe the honor of this visit?" he asked sarcastically.

"I brought your bags into town so I could say goodbye," she answered.

James was tempted to merely say "goodbye" and shut the door on her, but he controlled the impulse. He pushed the door wide and invited, "Come in."

Autumn was not worried about convention as she entered his room.

"James—"

She turned to find his gaze upon her. His expression was coolly indifferent as he regarded her.

"I wanted to thank you again for helping me get out of jail," she said.

"If your sheriff hadn't been so stupid, you wouldn't have been arrested in the first place."

"He's hardly 'my' sheriff," she corrected, finding herself coming to Cord's defense. "And he couldn't have known about me when even I didn't know about Grace."

"It's really not important."

"Well, I'm sorry everything turned out the way it did."

"Are you?" James asked shrewdly. "If you want to leave with me, there's still time to make the arrangements."

"No, I'm staying."

"You never want to go back to Philadelphia?" He still found it difficult to believe.

"I don't know about never. I only know that I can't leave yet."

"Well, good luck. You're going to need it."

There was bitterness in his tone, and Autumn knew there was no point in saying any more. She went to him and reached up to kiss him goodbye.

James accepted her kiss with little emotion. "Goodbye, Autumn."

She stepped back away from him. "Goodbye, James."

She left him without another word. As she shut the door behind her, Autumn felt as if she were closing off a part of her life. Nothing would ever be the same again. Everything had changed. She hoped the change was for the better. She thought of her reaction to James's kiss and knew she'd done the right thing, for she had felt nothing when she'd kissed him.

Stepping out into the sunshine, Autumn realized that for the first time in as long as she could remember, she felt completely and utterly free. She smiled and, as she climbed up into the buckboard, she knew where she was headed. She was going to the sheriff's office to see Cord.

Autumn entered to find Thatch sitting at the desk. She was amazed at the disappointment that swept through her. She didn't let it show in her expression, though. Instead she managed a smile.

"Hello, Thatch. I was wondering if Sheriff Randolph was around anywhere?"

"Hello, Miss Thomas. He's in back; let me get him for you," Thatch offered as he got to his feet.

"That's all right, I know the way," she told him.

Familiar as she was with the jail, she went down the hall and found Cord cleaning the cell.

"It looks different with you on that side of the bars."

Cord had seen Autumn coming, and he stopped what he was doing to watch her.

"I didn't know you were going to be in town today," he said, his gaze feasting upon her. All he'd done since he'd left her the other night was think about her. She had haunted his every waking moment and his dreams, too.

"James is leaving for Philadelphia on the stage this afternoon. I brought him the things he'd left at the ranch."

"He's going back?"

"Yes."

"What about you? Are you going with him?"

Autumn looked up at him. Just standing this close to Cord, she could feel the power of her attraction to him. She was aware of everything about him—the powerful width of his chest, the hard, lean line of his jaw, the firm contour of his lips. The attraction was both exciting and a bit unnerving for her. She was used to being in control of her emotions; being near Cord destroyed that control.

"No. I'm not going with him." She paused, then added, "I've ended our engagement. I gave James his ring back."

Cord looked down at her hand and saw the ring was gone. He raised his gaze to hers.

"I'm glad," he said softly, for only her to hear.

"So am I," she answered, remembering far too clearly how it had felt to be in his arms, lying together on the bed in her hotel room. She could see the cot behind him and fought down the blush that threatened. Autumn glanced back and could see no sign of Thatch. In a completely daring, wanton move, she went to Cord and kissed him.

He was caught off guard but only for a moment. As hungry as he was for her, he responded instantly to her nearness.

Cord deepened the kiss, tasting of her sweetness. He crushed her against him and reveled in the press of her breasts against his chest. He had been longing for this moment ever since he'd left her that night at the hotel. He had ached with his need for her and had lain awake, reliving the glory of their intimacies. Now she had come to him—and she was no longer promised to another man. He held her to his heart.

Autumn thrilled to his embrace, but she drew away from him even as he moved to hold her closer.

"Thatch is in the office," she whispered.

At her reminder of the deputy's presence nearby, Cord forced himself to release her.

"I think I like having you in this jail cell," he said as he smiled down at her.

It was a sensuous smile that stirred the already smoldering fires within her. "Maybe I could get Thatch to arrest us both and lock us up back here. What do you think?"

A devilish light shone in her eyes as she returned his smile. "I've already done my time, Sheriff."

Before Cord could react, Autumn slipped away and shut the cell door on him and locked it.

"I think it's your turn now." She gave a throaty laugh as she took the keys with her.

"Autumn—" Cord was already plotting his revenge as he watched her go.

"Thatch, I think you've got a prisoner back there who needs your help," she told the deputy with a grin as she handed him the keys.

Thatch went to check on Cord, and she heard the deputy chuckling as she left the office.

Autumn climbed up into the buckboard and took up the reins. She was about to drive away when Cord came out of his office.

"The deputy let you out already?" she teased.

"I was sober," he answered.

"So you knew what you were doing."

"Yes, I knew," Cord said, his gaze warm upon her. "I guess you locked me up for stealing."

"You can't steal something that's being freely given."

"Then what was my crime?" he asked, enjoying their banter.

"I just thought you looked like you might be the dangerous type. I've always heard it's better to be safe than sorry."

"Good advice, but only outlaws have to worry about me. If you stay on the right side of the law, I'll be there to protect you, ma'am," he drawled.

"I know."

And she did, for it seemed that he was always nearby when she needed him most.

Autumn felt a twinge of guilt over his words as she thought of her sister. She pushed the thought away, for there was no way of knowing if or when her sister would ever come home. For now, Autumn was just going to enjoy the life she'd chosen for herself.

"There's a social next Sunday afternoon," Cord began. "I'd be honored if you'd attend with me."

The thought of seeing him again delighted her. "I'd love to go with you, Cord."

"Good. Shall I come out for you?"

"There's no need. I'll meet you here."

"Until then." Cord wanted to kiss her, but it was broad daylight and they were standing right out in front of the sheriff's office.

Autumn gave him one last smile as she drove away. She would never have guessed a few months ago that she would be this excited about going to a social on a Sunday afternoon in Sagebrush, Texas. She was a woman accustomed to high society and the best things money could buy. Now, she had discovered that there were important things that money couldn't buy. Spending time with Cord at a Sunday social was one of them.

It was a dark, moonless night. All was quiet—too quiet.

Grace had reached the Miller ranch late in the afternoon and had hidden out until dark, fearful of being seen. She wanted to meet with Pete, but she had to do it secretly. There was a reward posted on her, and she didn't want to risk one of his men trying to apprehend her and take her in.

As soon as darkness claimed the land, she left

her horse tied up a goodly distance away from the ranch house and made her way on foot toward it. She had to find Pete. She hadn't done much praying lately, but now she prayed that he hadn't changed his mind about helping her. He was her only hope.

Grace reached the stable. She could hear the sound of men's voices coming from inside, so she hid and waited to see if one of them was Pete. Unmoving, barely breathing, fearful of being discovered, she listened in.

"When are Pete and the other men coming back?" one man was asking.

"Late tomorrow, I think. They're checking the herd in the south pasture. If everything goes all right, they should be back by mid-afternoon."

Disappointment filled Grace—he wasn't there. She waited until the two men had left the stable before sneaking away. There was no place for her to hide close by as she waited for Pete's return. She knew she'd have to find a place to camp out to await his return.

Grace retrieved her horse and vanished into the night, unseen by anyone on the ranch. She would bide her time and hope that Pete did return the following day. She couldn't stay in one place too long in case Rod was still searching for her.

She found a secluded spot to camp several miles from the ranch house. As she curled up in her bedroll, she told herself that it was only one more night, just one more night.

Thoughts of the last time she'd seen Pete returned as she lay there trying to sleep. With the memory came the pain and the regret that she had known ever since. She had loved him so, but when he didn't follow her on the night she'd gone to him, she'd believed he didn't care about her. Her despair at knowing what she'd done was wrong had only gotten worse when her father had confronted her that night and hit her. She'd known then that she had no alternative but to run away. The weeks that had followed had been frightening, but she'd learned she was a survivor. She'd had no one to turn to and had been forced to rely on herself. When her money had run out, she'd been desperate and had taken the job at the saloon in Dry Spring.

Looking back, Grace supposed she had become a saloon girl mostly to defy her father. When Rod had come in and taken a fancy to her, she had suffered through his attentions, seeing him as a way out. She'd never guessed that Pete would show up looking for her, wanting to take her home.

Grace had given up any hope of ever seeing Pete again. She'd been sitting on a drunken cowboy's lap that night at the saloon when she'd looked up to see Pete coming through the door. She had learned the meaning of true misery that night when he told her he had come for her. She'd insisted that she was happy with her life and sent him away.

It had all been a lie.

Grace had still loved him, and it was because of her love that she had sent him away. She had believed she was no longer worthy of him.

A traveling minister had come into the saloon a few nights later. He'd started preaching to everyone that God would forgive all sins if a person was truly sorry for them, that it wasn't too late to repent. Not many of the working girls or the drunks and gamblers had bothered to listen to his words, but Grace had.

Thinking of everything she wished she could change in her life and do over, Grace finally gave in to the tears she'd held back for so long. Silently in the night, she mourned the loss of her innocence and the end of all her dreams. She no longer dreamed of marrying Pete and living happily ever after. Now, she was only trying to stay alive for another day.

Pete was tired when he returned to the house late the following day. The cook from the bunkhouse brought him his evening meal, and after eating alone, he was ready to get cleaned up. He heated some water on the stove and fixed himself a bath. Then he stripped off his dirty clothes and sank down in the hot tub of water.

Grace had been watching the house from a distance and had seen Pete and his men ride in about an hour before sunset. Relieved that he'd returned, she'd waited until well after dark before venturing forth. She made her way to the ranch house on foot again, as she'd done the night before.

There were no lights on in the house, and she figured Pete had gone to bed. As quietly as she could, she crept up to the back of the house and tried the kitchen door. She was relieved to find it unlocked. With great care, Grace opened it, slipped inside and closed the door behind her. She moved through the house, looking for Pete.

Pete had been enjoying the bath. It felt good to scrub off the trail dust. He finished bathing and was getting ready to climb out of the tub when he heard a noise that sounded like someone moving around in the house. Suddenly wary, he got out of the tub. He fastened a towel around his waist, then reached for his gun.

There were no lamps burning in the rest of the house, so Pete turned down the lamp before he opened the door. The small room he used to bathe in was windowless and just off the kitchen. Gun in hand, he moved out cautiously, silently, unsure what to expect.

Pete walked to the doorway and looked into the living room. As he did, he saw the shadow of what looked like a man moving toward his bedroom door.

"Hold it right there," he ordered, aiming at the intruder. "I don't know what you want, but I've got a gun on you."

Chapter Twenty

Grace went still. She'd thought he was in bed, sleeping. Slowly she turned around. She was startled to see him standing before her, naked except for the towel fastened around his waist, his gun in hand and aimed straight at her. "Pete—it's me—Grace."

Pete was shocked. The last time he'd seen Grace she was dressed as a saloon girl. She'd often worn pants at home, but with her hair stuffed up under her hat, wearing a gun and holster, she was easy to mistake for a man in the darkness.

"Grace—what are you doing here?" He lowered his gun but stayed where he was.

"I came to see you because I needed to talk to you. I wanted to ask you if your offer still stood." Her gaze was riveted on the hard-muscled width of his chest. It was obvious he'd been bathing when he'd heard her in the house.

Pete was numb as he continued to stare at her. "My offer—"

"I'll understand if you want me to go. I don't want to cause you any trouble. I can leave right now. Nobody knew I was coming here."

"No! I don't want you to leave," he said, suddenly very conscious of his state of undress and the desperation of her situation. "I don't want you to go anywhere. Sit down. I'll be right back."

Pete took only a minute to go and put on his clothes. He didn't bother buttoning the shirt as he hurried back to find Grace sitting on the sofa. He took the time to light a lamp and then went to sit in the chair near her. She looked uncertain, so he wanted to reassure her.

"I'm glad you're here," he said quietly

"You are?" She was surprised. She hadn't expected a warm welcome anywhere.

"Yes. I've been worried about you all these months. The news I've heard—"

"I know."

"Is it true? Have you been with Rod Martin and his gang?"

She was ashamed, but she answered him honestly. "Yes, Pete. I took up with Rod while I was working in the saloon."

He had known it was true, but a part of him had hoped that a mistake had been made, that the law had been after the wrong woman. That hope was dashed, but he didn't allow it to trouble him too deeply. The only thing that was important was that Grace had come to him, and he had to help her.

"Why are you here? What happened?"

Grace had known the moment would come when she would have to tell him the truth. "It was terrible. I couldn't stand it anymore. I had to get away from Rod."

Pete understood what she didn't say, and a great need to protect her grew within him.

"How did you manage to get away from him?"

"It wasn't easy. I left in the middle of the night. He was drunk, so I was able to sneak off. I've been riding for days. I reached the ranch yesterday, but I heard some of your men talking. They said you wouldn't be back until today, so I waited."

"The men didn't say they'd seen you."

"They didn't. I was hiding."

"And tonight?"

"I left my horse off a ways and came in on foot."

"You're alone? No one followed you?" He was suddenly aware that Rod Martin might be somewhere nearby.

"No one. I made sure to hide my tracks." Her voice was choked as she struggled not to reveal the true extent of her fear of Rod. "I thought about going home to my pa, but I didn't think he'd take me back—not after that last night. I've always remembered what you told me when I saw you in Dry Spring."

"Grace, there's something you need to know." Pete realized she knew nothing of her father's death, and he would have to be the one to tell her.

At the change in his voice, she was suddenly wary. She went still and waited.

"Your pa died."

He heard her sharp intake of breath.

"Pa's dead?" Grace repeated. "When?"

"It's been almost a couple of months now."

"How did it happen?"

"A horse threw him."

"Oh, God." Her soul ached for the man who had loved her and raised her. She tried not to think of the ugly drunk he'd turned into—the hateful, mean man who had hit her and cursed her when they had last been together.

"I'm sorry you had to find out this way." Pete paused. He had to tell her the rest of what had happened. There was no reason to keep the news from her. "There is something else."

She studied him, trying to read his expression. The look in his eyes was sympathetic, yet guarded. "What?"

"When your father's will was read, it was learned that he'd disinherited you."

She nodded in understanding. "I thought he would after the way he acted on the last night I was home. It doesn't matter. Once I left, I knew I could never go back. Everything's changed now."

"You're right—everything has changed. But it may not be as bad as you think."

"I don't understand. How can it not be? I've disgraced myself and my family by taking up with Rod."

"There's something more you need to know. In your father's will, he left the ranch to your sister. You have a sister named Autumn—a twin—and she's here now."

Shock was too mild a word for the emotion that slammed through Grace. She immediately protested, "A sister? No, I don't have a sister."

"Yes, you do," he affirmed in a quiet tone.

"How can that be?" None of this was making sense to her.

"From what I understand, though your father told you your mother was dead, in truth your parents were divorced. Your mother left him and went back East with Autumn when you were babies, while your father stayed here and raised you."

"My mother's alive?" She had never known a mother's love, and had always felt the lack. For just a moment, hope swelled within Grace that she might be reunited with her mother. "Is she here, too?

"No, I'm sorry. She died several years ago." Grace was sitting completely still, and she had gone very pale. "I never knew her."

Pete suddenly realized just how fragile she was. He'd never thought that of Grace before, but these revelations about her past had obviously touched something deep within her heart.

"My sister—I have a twin? And she's here?"

"Yes. Autumn arrived from Philadelphia not too long ago, and she's staying at the Lazy T."

"Autumn." Grace repeated her name softly. She was nearly overwhelmed by what she'd discovered. For a moment, she allowed herself to imagine a loving reunion with her long-absent sister; then she accepted the truth of how things would be. She looked up at Pete, her shame and guilt eating at her. "How much does Autumn know about me?" she asked cautiously.

"The lawyer told her about you."

"So she knows."

"Yes." He was quiet for a moment, giving her time to think about all that he'd told her.

Grace wasn't sure what to feel. She was confused and bewildered by his revelations. She wondered if it wouldn't be best if she just rode away right now and never came back.

"I can get Autumn. I'm sure she would want to meet you," Pete offered.

"How can you be so sure?" Her father had rejected her and disowned her. She had a mother who had never cared enough to come for her. The way her parents had felt about her, Grace didn't know why her sister would care about her now, after all this time.

"I made an offer to buy the ranch from her, but she turned me down. Autumn said that until she understood more about her family and her sister, she was staying here in Texas."

Grace's gaze was troubled as she asked the question that was haunting her. "Does she really look like me?"

"Yes, Grace," Pete told her sincerely. "She's beautiful, just like you are."

She was startled by his words and unsure how to take them.

"I'll ride over to the Lazy T tomorrow and get her. I'll bring her back so you can meet."

"I know the law's looking for me. I heard Rod talking about how he'd killed Sheriff Gallagher. Won't you get in trouble if anyone finds out I'm here?" She didn't want him to be put in danger because of her.

"No one is going to find out you're here. I live alone. There won't be anyone bothering you as long as you stay inside the house and out of sight. I'll bring Autumn here, so you won't be put in any danger."

"I don't know, Pete," she said, not sure she could trust her newly discovered sister to keep her secret. "I'm not sure I'm ready to see her."

"All right. When you're ready, let me know."

Pete understood how difficult all this was for Grace. He wanted to help her in any way he could, and if that meant keeping her safe until she'd had time to come to grips with everything, he would do it. He had lost her once. He wasn't going to lose her again.

"What about Martin?" he asked. "Do you think he has any idea where you are?"

"No. I did everything I could to make sure he couldn't follow me."

He could tell how nervous she was, and he wanted to calm her and reassure her. "You'll be safe here."

"What are you going to do with me?" The fear that he might turn her over to the law wouldn't leave her.

Pete looked at Grace, his gaze holding hers. "I'm going to make sure no one ever hurts you again."

"Thank you." Her voice was barely above a whisper.

"Where did you leave your horse?"

She told him.

"I'll take care of it first thing in the morning. You can sleep in here," he said, standing and opening the door to the extra bedroom. "Would you like to take a bath or eat?"

"No, I'm too tired."

He nodded. "If you need anything, anything at all, just let me know."

"I will, Pete." She stood up and started to go to the bedroom he'd indicated.

"Grace—"

She looked back at him, still tense and worried. It had been so long since she'd felt safe.

"Good night, and sleep well."

Grace nodded and went into the bedroom. She drew the curtains and lit one of the lamps. After closing the door, she sat in a chair, trying to absorb all that had happened. For the last several nights, she'd slept outside on the ground, terrified of being discovered and fearing for her very life. Tonight, at last, she was safe with Pete.

Exhaustion—physical and mental—claimed Grace. The wide bed looked soft and inviting. Barely able to summon the necessary energy, she unbuckled her gun belt and set it aside, then took off her boots. She was too tired to worry about undressing any further. She had slept in her clothes for so long now, one more night wouldn't matter. If something happened and she had to make a run for it, at least she would be dressed. Grace lay down upon the bed and closed her eyes. Within minutes, she had fallen asleep, but not before she'd offered up a prayer of thanks for Pete and her deliverance.

Pete stayed where he was and watched Grace until she'd gone into the bedroom and closed the door. He sat there a moment longer, tempted to go open the door and look in on her just to prove to himself that she was really there—that this wasn't a dream.

And then he saw her hat on the sofa where she'd left it.

It hadn't been a dream.

Grace had returned.

She had come back to him.

Pete got up and went into the kitchen. He opened the cabinet where he kept his liquor and took out the bottle of whiskey. He wasn't much of a drinking man, but there was no doubt about it. Tonight, he needed a drink.

Sitting down at the table, Pete poured himself a shot and stared down at the amber liquid. His prayers had been answered. Grace was back. As joyous and relieved as he was at her return, he was troubled by what the future might hold for them.

Grace was wanted by the law. He could keep her hidden with him for a while, but there was no way he could keep her return a secret forever.

Pete was unsure what to do. The two of them could leave. They could run away together. He would do it if it was what she wanted. Long ago, he had realized the mistake he'd made by not declaring his love for her. He'd been too shy then, too unschooled in the ways of men and women.

Losing Grace had taught him everything he'd needed to know about life. Pete now knew that if you wanted something, you went for it. He had lived with regret all this time. He would never make that mistake again.

He loved Grace.

Pete knew she wouldn't believe him if he told her right now, so he would try to show her, rather than tell her. He would win her over and make up for all the heartache he'd caused her. It would take time. The woman she was today wasn't as trusting. She'd been through some difficult times. She'd changed. He would have to help her in any way he could.

For now, though, Pete decided he would keep

Grace out of harm's way and simply love her.

He finished his drink and went to bed. He didn't get much sleep, though. He was too excited knowing Grace was there.

Chapter Twenty-one

Muriel was humming and smiling to herself as she worked in the kitchen cleaning up after the noon meal.

"You're awfully happy today," Autumn called out from where she sat at her father's desk. She'd been working on the books since she'd returned from town at the beginning of the week, and she'd learned a lot about the financial state of the Lazy T.

"It's Friday. There's only one more day until we go back into Sagebrush for the social."

Autumn grinned. "You're looking forward to it?"

"I'm looking forward to seeing the gentleman who's escorting me to the social," she answered.

"What about you? Don't you want to see your sheriff again?"

Autumn's smile broadened. "Yes, I do."

Muriel didn't say anything, but she noticed Autumn didn't object to her calling Cord Randolph "your sheriff."

"Muriel—why is it you never married?" Autumn had often wondered why she'd remained single, but until now had never felt comfortable asking her about it.

The older woman went still. When she turned to Autumn, her expression was no longer carefree. "I was engaged once. His name was Robert. He was killed during the war."

"I never knew. Mother never spoke of it."

"It was too painful. Robert was a wonderful man. I still miss him. He had a wonderful laugh and took a great joy in living. He was young when he died—barely twenty." Muriel collected her thoughts and smiled again. "I've seen other men in the years since, but none of them was special like Robert—at least none of them until I met Ralph."

"I understand," Autumn told her. She believed there was something special about Cord, too. "It's fun to be excited and happy about something for a change."

"Yes, it is." Muriel knew how difficult these last weeks had been for Autumn. "You're proving yourself to be a very strong woman, you know."

"Sometimes I don't feel like it."

"You are. Your mother would be proud of you—and so would your father," she said and returned to her work.

Autumn remained quiet as she lifted her gaze to the small family portrait on the desk before her. She studied the man and woman, then looked at the baby who was her sister. Everyone had said how much they looked alike. Autumn hoped she and her sister were alike in other ways, too. She hoped Grace was smart enough and strong enough to take care of herself and keep herself safe.

It was near noon when Pete returned from working in the stables to check on Grace. It had been quiet in her room when he'd arisen before dawn. He hadn't disturbed her, for he'd wanted her to get her rest. He had laid out some of his own clothes for her in case she wanted to get cleaned up while he was away. The pants and shirt would be too big for her, but at least they were clean. Pete had gone out to take care of her horse and had turned it loose to run in the north pasture where no one would notice it. After completing his regular morning chores, he was ready for lunch and headed back up to the house. He couldn't deny that he was anxious to see her again.

Pete walked into the house, expecting to find Grace up and waiting for him. He frowned as he discovered that all was quiet. The clothing he'd put out for her was where he'd left it. Nothing seemed to have been disturbed.

Sudden panic seized him. He feared that she'd gone—fled in the night. Unable to stop himself, needing to know if she was there or not, he went to her bedroom and opened the door.

He was swept by a wave of relief as he stood in the doorway, staring at the sleeping woman. He started to back up and close the door, but found himself hesitating. He remained watching her for a moment longer as she slept on, unaware of his presence.

Sleeping, Grace had the same innocent beauty she had once possessed. In the haven of her dreams, she was safe. None of the darkness that had come into her life could intrude. Pete wanted her to stay in the sanctuary of sleep for as long as she could. Finally, silently, he left her to rest.

Grace was home with her father. Life was perfect. The sun was shining, and all was wonderful in her world.

And then her father began to change.

He started to ignore her, so she deliberately acted up to get his attention again. She got his attention, all right, but it was not the attention she'd wanted from him. He was angry and cruel to her now. He drank more and more heavily.

Her father's image gave way to Rod—Rod laughing in his cruelty—Rod pulling his gun and shooting down the rancher in cold-blood.

* * *

Grace sat up in bed with a start, her heart pounding, her breathing labored. She stared around, wild-eyed, for a moment, until reality slowly returned.

She was with Pete—Pete was here—everything would be all right.

The thought soothed her terror, and she lay back.

It took her a few moments to calm down. When she was finally ready to rise, she wondered at the time. The sun was shining brightly, so she guessed it was late morning. She got up and left the bedroom to look for Pete.

Grace emerged from the bedroom only to discover that Pete was gone. The small mantel clock indicated it was nearly two, and she realized with some amazement that she had slept the entire morning away. She saw that he had left out a pair of pants, a belt and a shirt for her, and she was grateful. A change of clothing was going to feel real good. It didn't matter how big the garments were; what mattered was that they were clean.

Grace took care to stay away from the windows. None of Pete's ranch hands knew she was there, and it was best to keep it that way. She was starting toward the kitchen to find something to eat when she caught sight of her reflection in a small mirror on the wall there.

She stopped to stare at herself. She had never in her life considered herself a vain woman, but today, studying her own image, she was devastated. The long months of living in Rod Martin's dangerous life-style had taken their toll on her. Her hair, unbound and loose around her shoulders, was wild, unkempt and dirty. Her skin, once pale and flawless, was now sunburned. It was obvious she'd been living on the run, for her clothes were wrinkled and filthy.

Pete had offered her a bath the night before, and she decided to take him up on it. She found the tub stored in the small room off the kitchen, along with towels and soap. Grace would have loved to soak in a hot bath, but she didn't want to risk building a fire in the stove to heat water for fear it might draw attention to the house.

She resigned herself to bathing in cold water. The prospect wasn't tempting, but it was worth any sacrifice to be clean again. She took the clothes he'd left her and locked herself in the room.

After filling the tub, Grace shed her dirty clothes and prepared to step into the cool water. If the day had been warmer, she might have appreciated the water's chill, but it wasn't. She held her breath as she sat down in the tub.

Motivated by the icy water temperature, she wasted no time scrubbing herself clean. She finished bathing quickly and rubbed herself vigorously with a towel to get warm again. Thrilled to be clean, she got dressed. She was grateful for the belt Pete had left her, for without it she would never have been able to keep the pants on. She washed her dirty things and spread them around to dry before emerging from the small room. After fixing herself something to eat, she went back to the bedroom to await Pete's return.

As Grace passed the hours alone, her thoughts turned again to all that Pete had revealed to her the night before. It was still difficult to believe that her father was dead. He had been the kind of man who'd seemed so powerful, she'd almost thought him immortal. Even now, a part of her still feared that he might show up and cause more trouble. His anger with her had been real and vindictive. She had no doubt about that at all, for he had left everything to her sister—a daughter he hadn't seen or acknowledged in years.

Autumn, her sister, her twin.

Grace wondered what Autumn's life had been like. She wondered if her sister had been happy living with their mother. She wondered, too, if Autumn liked being in Texas. Pete said she'd decided to stay on the ranch for now, but that didn't mean she wouldn't eventually leave and return to the East.

Over and over, Grace considered what Pete had said about meeting her sister. A part of her ached to know the woman who was her twin. Yet she was also frightened of what might happen to Pete if word got out that she was hiding at his ranch. She didn't want to put him in any jeopardy. He was helping her. She had to do everything she could to keep him safe, too.

It was late in the afternoon when Pete finished

his work. Grace was waiting for him as he came in.

"You're up," Pete said with a smile. A jolt of awareness went through him at the sight of her. Though she was wearing the clothes he'd left out for her, she looked more like herself. "I checked on you at midday, but you were still asleep."

"I can't believe I slept so long."

"I can. You were exhausted. I'm just glad you got some rest."

"Thank you for the clean clothes."

"I'm sorry I didn't have anything closer to your size. I'll see what else I can find for you." Pete realized he would have to be careful doing that, though, for he had to keep her presence a secret.

"I've already washed my own clothes. They should be dry by tomorrow."

"You're still going to need some other things to wear."

"I appreciate your kindness, Pete, but I'll be fine with what I have."

He knew she was right, for he couldn't do anything unusual that might draw attention to her.

He fixed them something to eat, and they sat down at the table together.

"Have you thought any more about meeting your sister?"

"Yes," she admitted. "I've thought about little else all day."

He waited for her to go on, but she didn't. "And?"

"I'm afraid, Pete. I've never been this scared before. So much has changed—I've done so many things I regret."

"I told you I'd keep you safe, Grace, and I meant it," he said quietly as he looked up at her across the table. He reached out and covered her hand with his. He had often imagined having Grace there with him, sharing his life. Things had worked out strangely, but she had come to him now, and he was going to do everything he could to make sure she never left.

"But I'm wanted by the law. I don't want anyone else to suffer because of me."

"We'll find a way," Pete told her, his gaze meeting and holding hers.

Grace nodded. Reassured by the warmth of his touch and the calm determination she saw in his eyes, she let herself believe his words were true.

Pete said no more about Autumn. He would concentrate only on keeping Grace hidden away from any danger and let her decide when she was ready for the reunion. He slowly withdrew his hand and turned his attention back to his meal.

Grace had enjoyed his touch, and she missed it when he drew away from her.

"I've been thinking about what we should do," Pete began.

She was surprised that he said "we."

He went on, "If you want, we can leave here. I can sell the ranch and we can go away."

Pete had considered many things during the course of the day. He'd thought about suggesting she turn herself in to Sheriff Randolph and try to straighten things out. Then he remembered hearing the talk about how badly the lawman wanted to find Rod Martin and his gang. Pete knew the sheriff was determined to bring in those responsible for Sheriff Gallagher's murder. He couldn't ask Grace to take that risk. He had to find another way to help her.

"But the ranch is your life. You love this place." She was shocked that he would be willing to give up so much for her.

Pete looked at her and finally said the words that had been in his heart for so long. "I love you more, Grace."

Grace was completely taken aback by his declaration. It seemed she had wanted Pete's love forever, but she didn't understand why he was telling her he loved her now. She didn't know how he could love her, after all she'd done.

"You love me?" she repeated in disbelief.

"I always have, and I want to make sure no one ever hurts you again," he said fiercely.

Grace was unsure of herself.

Pete stood up and went to her. She rose, and he took her in his arms and held her to his heart. She had longed for this moment, ached for it, but now that she was with Pete, she didn't believe she was worthy of his affection.

Pete lifted one hand to her cheek as he bent to kiss her. It was a soft, sweet exchange, one that spoke of tenderness. The gentleness of his embrace left Grace trembling as he ended the kiss and moved away from her.

"Think about what you want to do, Grace," Pete murmured.

"I will. It's just that I'm not sure," she said as she slipped into her seat.

"I understand. You've had a rough time, but that's over. You're here, and you're safe for now, but you can't hide out forever. We'll never be able to have a normal life as long as we're on the run."

"I know."

"We can leave, try to disappear, but you're always going to know that Martin is out there somewhere, maybe looking for you. If you want to stay here, I'll face the consequences with you. You can turn yourself in and offer to help Sheriff Randolph find Martin. You and I both know you won't feel safe until Martin is behind bars."

Grace knew he was right. She didn't think she could bear to live with the haunting fear that Rod might find her.

"Think about it," he urged.

Pete sat back down and they finished the meal, then passed the rest of the evening talking. He told her all that had happened in Sagebrush while she'd been away. Later, when it was time for them to retire, he disappeared into his own room for a moment.

"There's no need for you to sleep in your clothes again," he told her as he handed her another one of his shirts to use as a nightgown.

"Thank you."

"The first chance we get, we'll get you some real clothes," he promised. "Well, good night."

"Good night." She went into her room and closed the door behind her.

Her emotions were in turmoil as she tried to decide what she should do. Pete had told her he loved her and had kissed her. Her heart ached at the tenderness he'd shown her. She knew she wasn't worthy of his love, but she wanted to let him know how much she appreciated him and his help. It had been so long since anyone had cared about her. She wanted to thank him, to repay him for his kindness. There was only one way she knew to do it.

Grace waited a little longer, then changed into the makeshift gown he'd provided and quietly left her room. The house was dark. Pete had already retired. She moved silently to his bedroom door and opened it to let herself in. It was dark in his room, but she could make out his form as he lay unmoving on the bed. With utmost care, she shut the door and went to him.

Pete had been resting, but he was not asleep. He thought he heard something and opened his eyes to find Grace beside the bed looking down at him.

"Is something wrong?" he asked quickly, starting to sit up.

"No—nothing's wrong. Everything is right." Her voice was a whisper as she bent to kiss him.

Pete had thought her coming to him meant

there was trouble, but he hadn't realized what kind of trouble. The touch of her lips on his and the press of her breasts against his chest jarred him. Excitement coursed through him. His arms went around her, and he pulled her down on the bed with him. She did not resist, but deepened the kiss, wanting him to know that she desired him, too. They lay intimately together. Kiss after devouring kiss took them closer and closer to the ecstasy that awaited them. Their passions were aflame.

Pete wanted her. He needed her. He had waited for her all this time, and at last she was his for the taking.

The voice of reason stopped him as he almost gave himself over to his runaway desire. He had taken her innocence from her, and since then she had known only heartbreak. He would not be a party to her suffering anymore.

Pete broke off their kiss and took her by the upper arms to put her from him.

"Pete?"

"No, Grace. No." His words were a guttural growl as he fought to control himself as well as her.

"What?" She was confused. Why was Pete stopping? Rod had never stopped. Her only thought was that he didn't want her. She was crushed. He had claimed to love her, but those were only words.

Pete sat up and moved away from her.

Grace felt embarrassed and humiliated. He

truly didn't want her. He had rejected her. Tears welled up in her eyes. She had only wanted to come to him to thank him. She had nothing to give him but herself, and he had rejected her. She all but threw herself from the bed.

"I'm sorry—I shouldn't have—"

Pete was beside her in an instant, accurately reading her mood. "Grace—don't cry. I love you, but I'm not going to use you this way."

She looked up at him, her face tear-stained, her expression questioning and incredulous.

"I won't deny that I want you, but I won't take advantage of you." He smiled gently at her, then kissed her again, but this time it was not a passionate kiss. It was a cherishing kiss. "Not now. Not ever. Go on. Go back to your own bed before my willpower fails me."

"Oh, Pete—" The love she'd felt for him all these years grew even stronger.

"Go." He was smiling as he sent her from him. Grace was smiling as she went.

Chapter Twenty-two

"You're right," Grace announced when Pete returned to the house late the next day.

"About what?" he asked. He liked being right once in a while, but he had no idea what she was talking about.

"My sister. I want to meet Autumn."

"What changed your mind?" He had deliberately said nothing more about the idea, not wanting to pressure her in any way.

"We've already spent our whole lives apart. I don't want to go any longer not knowing her."

"I'll ride to the Lazy T tomorrow and bring her back here. It'll be tricky, but we can do it."

"How can you be so sure Autumn will come with you?"

"If she knows she's coming to see you, nothing

will keep her away. She spoke of you and your father, and how she wanted to learn more about her family during the meeting we had with Ralph Baxter."

His words left Grace feeling much better. "Do you think it will be safe?"

"For now, yes, but we're going to have to decide what you want to do. I can't keep you hidden here in the house forever. Eventually, someone will catch on. We have to make a plan before that happens."

The fact that he used "we" touched Grace's heart. "I'm sorry I'm so much trouble for you," she apologized. "I can leave—I can go—"

"Don't even think about it. I'm glad you're here with me. Now I know where you are, and I know you're safe and out of harm's way."

"I just hope Rod doesn't find me."

"We'll deal with that when or if it happens."

"He's a killer." She looked at Pete.

"Remember what I said about turning yourself in to Sheriff Randolph. From what I know about him, he's one determined lawman. I'd much rather have him on your side than working against you. Think about it. But for right now, let's just enjoy the peace we have."

"You're looking awfully cheerful this morning," Thatch remarked when he met Cord in the office.

"I am cheerful. Now that you're here, I'm off duty," Cord told his deputy as he stood up from his desk and got ready to head home and get a few hours of sleep. He'd worked Saturday night so he could take Sunday off to spend with Autumn.

"It should be a quiet day. The social this afternoon is the only excitement we've got going, and I don't think there will be too much happening there that will require vigilance."

"Let's hope not," Cord said. "I'll see you later."

He was tired, but looking forward to seeing Autumn when she came to town later that morning. He was glad he had her visit to look forward to. Certainly, nothing else was going the way he wanted it to. There had still been no news on the Martin gang.

Sherry went out on the porch when she saw the rider coming in.

"Well, Pete, it's good to see you. What brings you to the Lazy T?" she called.

"I came to see Autumn," he said as he reined in. "Is she here?"

"No, I'm sorry. Autumn and Muriel went into town for the day. There's a social this afternoon, so I don't expect them back until late."

Pete was disappointed. "Just tell her that I stopped by."

"I will."

He hated to return to the ranch and give Grace the news, for she had been so excited at the prospect of seeing her sister. Well, one more day wouldn't make a difference. They would be reunited tomorrow.

The social was being held at the same location where the dance had been staged. A temporary pavilion had been set up with tables and benches, and the townspeople started to arrive early.

Gail was excited about the day to come. At last she was going to have a chance to spend some time with Cord. She could hardly wait! He hadn't been in to eat at the restaurant for a few days, so she was really looking forward to seeing him today. She was especially looking forward to the games that were going to be played. The men always enjoyed the shooting competition and the horse race, but the ladies, particularly the single ones, enjoyed the hug-or-kiss bidding game that raised money for charity.

Gail was talking with friends when she heard someone mention that Cord had arrived. She eagerly went forward to greet him, only to find him escorting the Thomas woman and her older companion. She hoped for a moment that he had just met them on the way to the social, but after watching them together, she realized he was actually accompanying her.

Shocked and frustrated, Gail fought to stay in control. She forced a smile and decided to bide her time. Just because Cord had come with the woman didn't mean he had to leave with her.

* * *

"This is going to be such fun," Muriel said as they made their way to join the crowd.

There were organized games for the children to play. A shooting range had been set up for the men to test their prowess, and there was plenty of food for everyone.

"The socials usually are," Cord agreed.

"Oh, there's Ralph now," Muriel said excitedly as she saw the lawyer coming toward them.

"I'm glad you made it," Ralph said as he smiled down at her.

"So am I."

Autumn thought Muriel almost sounded like a flirtatious young girl. Ralph greeted her and Cord, and then escorted Muriel away.

"I think Muriel is going to have a good time today," Autumn said.

"What about you? Are you ready to have a good time?"

"Yes. What are we going to do first?"

"Let's eat."

The food was delicious, and as they were finishing their meal, some of the men called out to Cord.

"Come on, Sheriff Randolph. It's time for you to show us just how good you are."

Cord had won the shooting competition at the last social, and the men he'd beaten were looking forward to getting the chance to best him today.

"Do you want to wait here for me?" he asked Autumn.

"Absolutely not. I'm coming with you," she

said. "I want to see how good you really are. Maybe I can learn something from you on being a quick draw." There was teasing in her tone as she remembered trying to pull the derringer out of her purse. "You must be fast if you won last time."

"Accuracy is more important than speed," he told her. "Being able to outdraw someone is fine, but you've got to be able to hit your target. You can be fast and end up dead if you miss."

She stared at him, a little in awe. She had never heard him talk that way before. "You're right."

"Come on. Let's see what kind of competition I've got."

They made their way to the shooting range. A crowd gathered to watch as the men got ready to test their skill. Gail was there, making her way through the throng to get as close to Cord as she could.

"Good luck, Cord," she called out to him to get his attention.

Cord merely nodded in her direction as he kept himself focused on the competition.

Several of the men were very good, but when the shooting stopped, Cord was clearly the best marksman of them all. He had hit the target with every shot. Cheers and a round of applause came from all those gathered around.

As everyone moved away, Gail started to walk over to Cord, only to see him go straight to Autumn and give her his complete attention. Temporarily thwarted, she decided to regroup and try again later.

"You were wonderful!" Autumn exclaimed, duly impressed by his accuracy.

"Thank you, ma'am." He grinned at her.

"One of these days you're going to have to teach me how to shoot like that."

"There's no time like the present. Do you want your first lesson now?" Cord offered.

"Yes." Autumn knew how to fire her derringer, but a six-gun was new to her.

They walked back to stand before the target. After reloading, Cord handed her his gun.

"It's heavier than I thought." She was surprised as she lifted the sidearm to aim at the target.

"Just squeeze the trigger."

Autumn fired, and she missed badly.

"Let me show you how to do this." Cord moved behind her and put his arms around her to help her aim.

Cord's intentions started off purely honorable, and then he held her close. The sweet, enticing scent of her perfume was heady, and the feel of her slender body pressed ever so lightly against his was more arousing than he would ever have dreamed. He girded himself against the desire that flared to life within him. They were standing at the social in broad daylight. This was hardly the time to indulge his desire.

"Now what do I do?" Autumn asked in complete innocence, unaware of his reaction to her nearness.

What he wanted her to do and what they were going to do were two completely different things, Cord realized as he instructed, "Take careful aim. Keep your eye on the target."

She was holding the gun with two hands now, and he steadied her grip as she fired off another round.

"I almost did it!" Autumn was excited as her second shot came much closer to the target than the last one. She twisted around to smile up at Cord and found herself gazing into his dark eyes. She was mesmerized and went still for a moment as they stood there barely a breath apart.

Cord realized she'd almost done it, all right. She'd almost caused him to lose his legendary self-control. He had always prided himself on being in control, but she was sorely testing his willpower. "Let's try it again," he told her.

Autumn turned back and took careful aim one more time as Cord helped her. She pulled the trigger and was rewarded with a hit on the edge of the target.

"I hit it!" She was thrilled. "Do you think you'd have time to give me more lessons?" she asked Cord earnestly. She knew that if she was going to stay in Texas, she had better familiarize herself with using a sidearm.

"I'd be glad to. You look like you're a fast learner," Cord said, taking the gun from her and holstering it.

Muriel and Ralph saw them and came over to join them.

"Cord's going to teach me how to shoot, Muriel," Autumn said happily.

"Are you sure you want to learn?" Muriel asked.

"Oh, yes. The next time a lawman tries to arrest me, I want to be ready for him," she laughed, looking up at Cord.

He smiled back at her, thinking of their close encounter at the jail on Monday. "There won't be a next time, ma'am," he teased.

"Thank heavens," Muriel put in, not knowing about the undercurrent of their conversation.

They returned to the pavilion to discover that the hug-or-kiss game had just gotten under way.

"How do you play?" Muriel asked Ralph, curious.

"The rules are simple. All it takes is money to play. A gentleman can hug any single woman from age fifteen to twenty-five for ten cents, any woman older than that is a nickel, and all married women are fifty cents. All kisses are a dollar, no matter what the woman's age."

"I've never heard of anything like it," Muriel remarked. "How much money do you have?"

"Enough," Ralph told her, his eyes twinkling with good humor. "I planned ahead."

"What about you, Cord?" Muriel asked.

"Payday was last week, so I should have enough."

Muriel and Autumn went to join the circle of

women who were standing in the center of the pavilion, blushing and laughing in delight as their husbands and boyfriends paid the lady in charge for the right to hug or kiss them.

Gail was standing on the far side, watching and waiting for Cord. When she finally saw him, she found he was still with Autumn Thomas. She had hoped Cord would notice her, but the way he was speaking with the other woman, she was beginning to have her doubts.

Ralph hurried to stand in line with the other men, eager for his chance to kiss Muriel. Cord went along, too. A dollar was a small price to pay for one of Autumn's kisses. As they were waiting in line, Thatch sought them out.

"What are you doing here?" Cord asked, although he already knew the answer.

"I've heard the hug-and-kiss game can get pretty wild sometimes," Thatch said with a grin.

"So you're going to keep us all in line?"

"That's right. Plus I've got a little left from my paycheck and I thought I could put it to good use—seeing as how the money goes to charity and all," Thatch said. He was trying not to stare too openly at the object of his affections.

They all laughed. Ralph reached the end of the line and paid his fee for a kiss from Muriel. He hurried over to where she was standing to present her with the ticket he'd purchased as proof that he was entitled to one kiss.

"Do you want your kiss on the cheek?" Muriel asked, her eyes twinkling.

"If that's what you'd like, then I will be happy with a kiss on the cheek," he said, ever the gentleman.

"You paid for a real kiss, Ralph, and you're going to get one," she said. With that, she kissed him on the lips without further hesitation or discussion.

Ralph was smiling when they ended the exchange. "Your kiss was worth every cent, my dear."

Now Muriel found herself blushing.

Cord closed on Autumn where she stood at Muriel's side.

"I have my ticket," he said, gazing down at her and trying to keep the hunger he felt for her from showing.

"Only one?" Autumn asked, her gaze challenging his.

"I can always go back for more—until my money runs out," he said.

"I wouldn't want to leave you out of pocket for the rest of the month," she teased.

"My credit is good around town," he told her, giving her a half-smile.

Autumn's heartbeat quickened at the devilish look in his eyes and the sensuous curve of his lips. She swallowed tightly, suddenly wishing that they weren't right there in front of all the townspeople. She wished they were alone somewhere private and quiet—some place where they wouldn't be interrupted.

And then Cord kissed her, right in front of everybody.

For Autumn, his kiss was pure heaven. Her eyes closed as she met him in that cherishing, chaste exchange, and she was thrilled to the depths of her soul.

Across the circle, Gail had seen Cord buy a ticket and had waited for him to come her way. But it hadn't happened.

As she'd feared, he'd gone to Autumn. She watched now as he kissed the other woman. Gail kept smiling, knowing she had no alternative with so many eyes on her, but it wasn't easy.

"Gail—I bought a ticket for a kiss."

At the sound of the man's voice, she turned to find herself face to face with Thatch. She was surprised, for Thatch had never shown her any attention before.

"Thatch—"

Thatch had long been attracted to Gail, but until now had been too shy to act upon his feelings. Today he finally felt brave enough to venture forth, and the hug-or-kiss game gave him just the opportunity he'd been hoping for.

Thatch didn't want to risk waiting and losing his nerve. He took Gail in his arms and kissed her. There was nothing the least bit bashful about his kiss. When he ended it and let her go, he smiled, tipped his hat and walked away without saying another word. He had rounds to make.

Gail stood there, watching him go in disbelief. Of all the men in the whole town whom she might have thought would kiss her, Thatch was the last one she would have guessed. But now that he had kissed her, she thought she might be glad, especially after she glanced at Cord to see him still hovering over Autumn.

A call went up from beyond the pavilion now that the hug-or-kiss game was over, and everyone rushed to see what was going to happen next. Several of the cowboys from neighboring ranches had gotten together and decided to bring in the meanest bunch of unbroken horses they could find for a bucking-bronco competition among the men who were daring enough to try. They had made arrangements with the owner of the stable in town to use his corral for the event. The crowd migrated there now to watch the spectacle to come.

"Ralph, how good are you at breaking horses?" Muriel asked as she walked by his side holding his arm.

"I'm not good at all. I was much better at my law studies than I was at bronc riding." He hated to admit any weakness, for he didn't want her to think less of him, but there was no denying he had little talent for riding.

"Good. You're a smart man to know your limitations."

He was relieved. "Cord, here, is pretty good, from what I've heard."

"I've ridden my share," Cord agreed.

Autumn was quiet. Her happy mood of just moments before was suddenly tempered by the thought of how her father had died. She didn't know if she could bear to watch the activity if Cord was going to try. It would be too nerve-wracking. Before she had a chance to say anything, they had reached the corral.

"Who's going first?" Tom Calhoun, the stable owner, called out as he held the reins of a prancing, nervous-looking stallion.

"I'll go!" one of the cowboys volunteered. He kissed the girl by his side for luck and strutted out to the horse. He was obviously most confident of his ability.

As Tom held the horse steady, the cowboy mounted up.

"Let him go," the rider ordered.

Tom did, and ran for the fence to get out of the way.

The stallion stood still for a moment, lulling the cowboy into a false sense of security. Then in one spontaneous, violent move, the horse bucked and spun around. The man went flying from the horse's back and landed heavily in the dust and dirt. He got up, embarrassed at being so quickly thrown.

Tom got the stallion under control again, and the next daring man came forward to try to ride him. He managed to keep his seat longer than the first cowboy, to the rousing cheers of the crowd, but ultimately he, too, was thrown.

"There's got to be somebody here who can break Lightning," Tom called out.

"Sheriff Randolph! Get Sheriff Randolph to do it!" Sam called out, for he knew what a good horseman Cord was.

"Cord? You interested?" Tom called to him.

Cord knew a challenge when he heard one. He started to climb into the corral when Autumn caught his arm. He looked down at her, puzzled.

"Don't do this."

"Don't worry. Everything will be fine," he assured her, unaware of her thoughts.

He went forward, and the cheers of the townspeople left him smiling good-naturedly.

"If anybody can ride him, you can," Sam shouted to Cord. Since the saloons were closed on Sunday, Sam had the day off and could come out and join in the festivities. He'd noticed Cord with the Thomas woman and was pleased he'd taken his advice.

"You've got a lot of faith in me," Cord said.

"We all do," someone else said.

"Don't get too excited just yet," he told them, laughing. "This looks like one mean horse."

Cord prepared to mount. He cast a glance back at Autumn, who was standing quietly by the fence. Her expression was pale and strained. He swung up into the saddle and took up the reins.

"All right, I'm set," he told Tom.

Tom let go of the bridle and ran for safety yet another time.

The stallion didn't give Cord a moment to relax. He immediately began bucking and twisting in an all-out attempt to rid himself of the rider on his back.

Cord was a better horseman than the other two men had been, though. He held on tight as the powerful horse violently resisted his efforts to control him.

The stallion was determined to win the battle of wills. Charging toward the fence at full speed, the horse jerked sideways at the very last minute and spun around in a move so forceful that all who were watching gasped in shock. The momentum loosened Cord's grip, and he struggled to keep his seat as the stallion reversed direction in another violent twist. It was that final, fierce buck that dislodged Cord from the horse's back. He hit the ground hard and lay still.

"Cord!" Autumn cried out in horror.

Chapter Twenty-three

Horror flooded through Autumn. Her father had died this way.

The stallion was still loose, racing around the corral, but Autumn gave no thought to her own safety. She ran to the gate and pushed her way in. She had to get to Cord. She ran to him and knelt down.

Cord had had the wind knocked out of him. He gave a low groan as he struggled to draw a breath. He'd been thrown before, but this time it was in front of everybody and he was embarrassed. He opened his eyes, ready to get up and get right back on the horse, only to find Autumn hovering worriedly over him.

"You're all right?" she asked, relieved to find that he was conscious and could move.

"Yeah," he muttered in disgust as he sat up and looked around for the stallion.

Tom had caught the horse and was holding him across the corral from them.

"Go on. Get out of here before you get hurt," Cord told her as they stood up. He wanted her out of harm's way while he finished what he had to do with the stallion.

"You're not thinking of . . ." She didn't finish her horrified question; she recognized the look in his eyes as that of an angry, determined man.

Autumn did as she was told, but she was afraid for Cord as she returned to stand with Muriel and Ralph. He could have been seriously injured when he was thrown, and yet he was going to try to ride the horse again. She didn't know whether to be furious with him for taking the chance or worried about him because she wanted him safe.

"Cord's going to try again!" Muriel was saying excitedly. "He is one brave man."

"He is one of the best horsemen in Sagebrush," Ralph remarked, impressed with his friend's determination. "If anyone can break this horse, it's Cord."

Autumn watched nervously as Cord walked slowly back to the horse's side. He paused, then mounted the stallion in one smooth move. He took up the reins.

"Let him go, Tom," Cord directed. He was as ready as he would ever be to try again.

Tom released the bridle and ran to climb the corral fence.

The horse reared and began bucking again. He was as determined to be free as the man on his back was to break him.

Cord held on with all his might. He was prepared for the stallion's tricks this time and would not be so easily thrown. This time he would win.

The battle was fiercely waged.

The stallion refused to surrender easily to Cord's domination. He fought on, using every trick he knew to buck the rider off, but it was all to no avail. Finally, the last of his strength was gone. Only then did he stop resisting and stand in the middle of the corral, shaking from exhaustion, his sides heaving as he fought to breath.

Cord still didn't trust the stallion quite yet. He stayed firmly seated on his back, waiting to make sure the animal was truly being submissive. To test him, Cord put his knees to the mount's sides and urged him to move.

Stiffly and a bit awkwardly, the stallion took a few steps at a jerking gait. He tried to resist the commands he was given, even as he obeyed them. A rousing cheer from those watching startled him, and he bolted sideways a bit at the noise.

Cord kept his seat, though, and rode the horse around the corral in triumph. He reined in before Tom and handed him the reins when he dismounted.

"Good job," Tom said.

"Thanks." Cord was hot, sweaty and dirty after his ride, but he felt good. He had been victorious. The horse was a spirited one and would make someone a fine mount. He looked up to find Autumn watching him from where she stood near the gate with the older couple. Sam stood near them, too. Cord headed their way.

"I knew you could do it," Sam told Cord, and he clapped him on the back. His words held double meaning, and they both knew it.

"I appreciate your faith in me."

"That was some ride," Ralph said. "Well done."

"It was frightening, though," Muriel put in. "You could have been hurt."

"Everything's fine," Cord assured her, looking at Autumn. "I'm no worse for wear, just a little dirty."

"Thank heaven," Autumn said. The fear she'd experienced when she thought he'd been seriously injured only reinforced how much he meant to her. Autumn wouldn't have believed it possible that she could have come to care for him so much in such a short time, but she had.

Sam moved away, and Muriel and Ralph went with the rest of the crowd heading back to the pavilion, leaving the two of them alone.

"I'd better get cleaned up," Cord told Autumn, looking down at his sweat-stained, dirty clothes. "Do you want to go on with Muriel and Ralph or come with me?"

"I'll go with you," Autumn answered.

"My house is just a few blocks over. It shouldn't take long."

She knew there were those who would think it inappropriate for her to go to a man's home unchaperoned, but she didn't care. After the scare he'd just given her, Autumn wanted to stay as close to him as she could, for as long as she could.

"Where did you learn to ride so well?"

"I grew up on a ranch. I think I was riding before I was walking," he answered.

"How did you become a lawman?"

"My parents died when I was young. I had to find a way to take care of myself, so I used my gun. Mike Gallagher offered me a job as his deputy after saving my life one night, and I took him up on it." Even now, the pain of Mike's death was still with him. He wondered if it would ever ease.

"Sheriff Gallagher saved your life? What happened?"

Cord told her about his gunfight with Hal Sheridan, and how Mike had saved him from the ambush by Sheridan's friends later that night.

"He must have been a good man—and a good judge of character. He picked you to help him."

"I just wish I'd been with Mike that last day. If I'd ridden along with him, we might have been able to fight our way out of Martin's ambush."

Autumn heard the regret and pain in his voice. "It wasn't your fault."

"I know. He ordered me to stay behind, but I still can't help wondering . . ." He broke off as he led the way up the short walkway to his house. It was a small, one-story home on one of the quieter streets in town.

"We can't change the past, Cord," she told him sympathetically. "But I know I wish I could, too."

"What would you change?"

"I'd make sure my parents never divorced. That way my sister and I wouldn't have been separated, and she would never have run off with that outlaw and gotten into the trouble she's in."

"All we can do is learn from what's happened and try to make things better in the future."

They crossed the porch. Cord opened the door and held it for Autumn to enter.

"Are things going to be better in the future?" she asked, casting him a flirtatious glance.

"I don't know about the future, but I don't think it can get any better than being alone with you where no one can interrupt us."

Cord went to Autumn and kissed her. It was a sweet exchange. What he really wanted to do was take Autumn in his arms and give her a passionate kiss, to show her what he was feeling for her, but dirty as he was, Cord thought better of the idea.

"Go on and have a seat. Make yourself comfortable," he said. "I'll hurry to get cleaned up so we can go back and join the others."

He left her there and disappeared into his bedroom at the back of the house.

Autumn sat down on the sofa, looking around the room with interest. The home was small but neatly kept, and was quite comfortable. As far as personal things went, it was sparsely furnished, but she did notice a picture sitting on a table against the wall. Curiosity got the best of her, and she got up to look at it. Unlike her father, who hadn't put out any family portraits, Cord had his family's picture prominently displayed.

Autumn studied the picture carefully. Though Cord was young in the rendering, probably no older than ten, there was no mistaking him. Even then, his dark good looks were apparent, and she could tell he got his handsomeness from the man in the picture. She assumed the couple were his parents. They were attractive, and from the pose, they seemed like a very loving family.

Of course, Autumn knew from her own life that looks could be deceiving. Her family had appeared happy in the picture she'd found of them, too, and yet a short time after it had been made, her mother had taken her and walked out on her father. Lori Thomas had left Texas and never looked back.

Regret filled Autumn at all she had missed in her life because her family had been torn apart. She still couldn't believe how her mother had managed to conceal her father's and sister's existence from her for her whole life. She never suspected a thing.

"Cord? Are these your parents with you in the portrait?" she called out.

Cord had washed up quickly and was dressing when he heard her call. He went to see what she wanted. He had donned a pair of clean pants and a shirt, but he hadn't yet buttoned the shirt. He stood there in the doorway of his bedroom before her, his shirt hanging open, his hard-muscled chest bared to her view.

Autumn glanced toward him and was unable to look away. He was devastatingly handsome, tall, lean and powerful, and his dark good looks set her pulse racing. She realized she was attracted to him as she'd never been to any other man. Again, she was amazed that her feelings for Cord had become so intense so quickly, but there was no denying what was in her heart.

"Yes, that's my mother and father," he answered.

"They would be very proud of you, you know," she said softly, thinking of what a fine man he'd turned out to be.

Her comment caught him by surprise, and he hoped she was right. "You think so?"

She smiled at him a bit mischievously, not wanting him to get too conceited. "What's not to be proud of? You won the shooting competition at the social, and then you broke the horse. You did it all today."

"Yes, but there's still one prize I haven't won," he said, keeping their exchange light. The look in his eyes darkened as he took a step toward her.

"Which prize is that? Is there a pie-baking contest?"

"No." He laughed.

"The horse race?"

"No. The prize I'm after has nothing to do with the social." Cord came to stand over her.

"Oh?" she asked breathlessly as she looked up at him. Thoughts of the heated kisses they'd shared left her hungry to be in his arms again. His very nearness, so warm and powerful, drew her to him. "I didn't know there was another contest."

"There is. It's for your heart."

At his words, her breath caught in her throat. She lifted her arms to wrap them around his neck.

"But you've won that, too, Cord," she whispered against his lips as she offered her heart and her love to him with a simple kiss.

A shudder of pure physical desire went through Cord at her words. When she moved closer, he could not deny that he wanted her, and he crushed her to him. His mouth slanted over hers in a devouring, hungry kiss that told her without words what she wanted to know.

It was the middle of the afternoon, but that didn't matter to them. All that mattered was that they were together in the privacy of his house—and no one was going to interrupt them.

Kiss after heated kiss left them breathless with need. Autumn boldly raised her hands to his bare chest. At her brazen caress, Cord went still for a moment; then he allowed himself to relax and enjoy her touch. Her hands skimmed over him, sculpting the lean, powerful muscles of his torso. When she trailed her fingers across his stomach, a low, dangerous growl escaped him. He scooped her up in his arms and made his way into the bedroom.

Cord laid her upon his bed and stood over her, struggling to control his passion, wanting to be sure that this was what she wanted before they went any further. "Are you sure, Autumn?"

She had never been more sure of anything in her life. She smiled up at him and lifted her arms in invitation. "Yes."

At her answer, any thought of stopping was gone. Cord went to her. He was hungry to know the beauty of her love.

The fire of their passion ignited. They came together in a blaze of glory. Each touch, each caress, each kiss stoked the fiery heat of their desire.

Autumn pushed his shirt from his shoulders, and Cord drew back and sat up to strip off the offending garment. He tossed it aside as Autumn sat up, too.

"Help me," she said, trying to unfasten the buttons on her gown.

She presented her back to him, and he wasted no time on the task. He helped her slip the gown down, and she stood up only long enough to step clear of the dress. Cord's gaze went over her, lingering where the swells of her breasts were revealed to him above her chemise. He ached to touch that silken flesh, and he took her in his arms to kiss her again.

They lay back down together, desperate to be close, to caress and be caressed, to love and be loved.

Autumn gave herself over to Cord. She had never been so intimate with a man before. She gasped as he brushed the straps of her chemise down to fully bare her breasts. She marveled at the feelings that seared her at the touch of his lips upon her. His hands traced paths of fire over her as she began to move restlessly beneath him. A longing grew within her, an aching emptiness that left her feverish with desire.

Cord moved up over her to kiss her, his mouth claiming hers in a passionate possession.

Autumn welcomed him eagerly and relished the hard heat of his bare chest against her. She daringly stroked his back. She wanted to pleasure him as he was pleasuring her with his arousing caresses. Instinctively she moved her hips against him.

Cord wanted her. He needed her, but he had to be sure this was what she wanted. He had to know that she would have no regrets. He ended the kiss to look down at her.

"Autumn." He said her name in a low, love-husky voice. "If you want to stop, say so now."

She gazed up at him adoringly. She loved him even more for caring about her and trying to protect her even now. She could see the concern in his eyes and lifted one hand to tenderly touch his cheek. "I love you, Cord. Kiss me again— please."

With a groan, Cord's lips sought hers. The kiss was cherishing for a moment, but then the flames of his passion seared them.

He left her for a moment to shed the rest of his clothes. She had never seen a naked man before, and her gaze was hungry upon him. From his broad shoulders to his lean hips, he was the picture of male power and grace.

"You're beautiful," Autumn said as he returned to her.

"Men aren't beautiful," he said, a bit embarrassed by her observation.

"You are," she insisted, and she kissed him to prove that she meant it.

Cord needed no further encouragement. He stripped away the last barrier of her clothing, and they came together in a blaze of love's glory. With each touch, each kiss, each caress, the flames of their need for one another grew ever hotter.

When at last Cord moved to make her his own, Autumn opened to him. He sought the depths of her womanhood and breached her innocence. Her pain was only momentary and quickly passed. She accepted him deep within her, clinging to his strength as she came to fully understand the glory of their union. Cord held her to his heart, knowing she'd given him her greatest gift. His kiss was tender.

"I love you, Autumn," he said as he began to move.

She met him in that rhythm, thrilling to the exquisite feelings he aroused. He found her innocent ways erotic, and he quickened his pace. He wanted to please her, to show her the pure delight that could be theirs. They moved together, taking and giving—and loving.

Cord continued to caress her. He aroused her to the heights of ecstasy. His demanding touch sent her senses soaring. She reached the peak of pleasure and cried out as rapture radiated through her. She clung to him, surrendering to his masterful seduction.

Cord was lost in the ecstasy of her embrace. Their love was perfect. He shared in her glory, reaching passion's pinnacle, savoring the beauty of what they shared. They collapsed in each other's arms, sated.

It was long moments before Autumn stirred. She felt so safe, so loved in his embrace that she didn't want to move away from him.

"I didn't know it could be so wonderful," she purred, lifting her lips to his.

"You're perfect," Cord told her, kissing her on the mouth and then trailing kisses down her throat. He swept his hands over her silken limbs. She was beautiful, and he wanted her as he'd never wanted another woman.

She arched against him. Excitement shivered through her and she wrapped her arms around him, treasuring the warmth and power of him.

"We need to go." The last thing Cord wanted to do was stop, but he knew they would be missed if they didn't return to the social.

"Go where?" she asked, deliberately ignoring reality. "You mean we can't stay right here forever?"

"Don't tempt me."

"I love tempting you," she said in a throaty, seductive voice.

"And I love the way you tempt me, but . . ." He kissed her again, hungrily. When he broke off the kiss, it startled him to realize that he truly didn't want to go back to the social. He wanted to stay there with her.

They could marry—

The thought came unbidden to Cord, and he forced himself to leave her and move away from the bed. The idea of being with Autumn, loving her for the rest of their lives excited him, but he knew he couldn't speak to her of marriage yet. She had professed to love him, but he wondered if she loved him enough to understand that he had to do his job. If the time came when he had to arrest her sister, he would have to do it.

"You look angry. Is something wrong?" she asked, for she'd noticed how his expression had become serious once he'd left her side.

"No—nothing's wrong," he assured her. "I was just thinking about how I would much prefer to stay right here with you."

That much was true. He would have loved to shut out the real world—the world that threatened to tear them apart just as they'd found each other.

"I know." Autumn sighed. She was sorry that their idyllic encounter had to end, but she knew that what they had shared was special and beautiful. For a moment, she thought of being married to him and how wonderful it would be never to have to leave him. But then she realized he could never marry her. She was the sister of an outlaw—the realization saddened her deeply, but she hid her sadness from him, determined to enjoy what they had for as long as it lasted.

Autumn rose with him. They dressed, pausing every now and then to share a quick kiss.

When they were finally ready to leave the house, Cord gathered Autumn to him and simply held her close. She fit perfectly against him, and they were happy.

For now, that was all that mattered.

Chapter Twenty-four

Sam was making his way back to the pavilion when he caught sight of Miles Harris standing in the entrance to an alleyway. He hadn't seen the former deputy around since Cord had fired him. He wondered why the man was back in town.

"How are you doing?" Sam asked.

"I'm fine," Miles answered.

By his slurred speech, Sam could tell he'd been drinking.

"Where have you been? I haven't seen much of you lately," Sam said trying to make conversation.

"I been around," Miles answered. He pulled a flask out of his pocket and took a deep swallow.

"Things going all right for you?" Sam wasn't

prying, but he always prided himself on being able to find out what was happening in town.

"I been looking for Cord. You know where he is?"

"He was here a few minutes ago. He just broke the bronc Tom brought in. If I see him, I'll tell him you're looking for him," Sam offered.

"Don't bother," Miles replied tersely. "I'll find him myself."

With that, Miles walked away.

Sam watched him go. He thought Miles was acting strange, and he hoped that didn't mean trouble for the sheriff.

Miles was angry, and he was drunk. In the time since Cord had fired him, he'd made a trip to Dry Spring, hoping to get hired on there, but Sheriff Bannecker didn't need another deputy. Miles's fury with Cord had grown, and he'd headed back to Sagebrush, wanting to have it out with him. Today was the day, and he'd needed to bolster his courage with whiskey.

Miles never had held his liquor well. Today proved no exception. The more whiskey he'd drunk, the more furious he'd become with Cord. It still made no sense to him that Cord had gotten Mike's job. It should have been his for the asking. He had worked for Mike the longest. What right did Cord have to just step in and take over the way he had? And then Cord had hit him and fired him just for trying to have a little fun with the Thomas woman. He was going to find Cord and confront him about it.

Miles made his way toward the pavilion to take another look around. He still didn't see any sign of Cord, so he decided to head for the sheriff's house in search of him. He went up the walk and was crossing the porch just as Cord came outside.

"Miles—what are you doing here?" Cord demanded cautiously as Autumn followed him out of the house. "I thought I told you to get out of town."

"I'm just paying a little social call." Miles looked at Autumn, then back at Cord.

"You're drunk," Cord said in disgust.

"I may have been drinking, but it looks like you two have been doing more than that." Miles smiled a leering, knowing smile at them.

"Autumn, go back inside."

She quickly obeyed Cord, but she worried about leaving him with Miles. She knew what a mean man the ex-deputy was, and she didn't trust him.

"Did I interrupt something, *Sheriff?* What did you have going on here? Were you and the prisoner having some fun at your house instead of down at the jail?"

"Miss Thomas is not a prisoner."

"That's right," Miles chuckled evilly. "It's her sister who's the slut, not her."

"Watch your mouth, Miles," Cord ordered.

"To hell with you, Randolph! I should be sheriff now, not you! You didn't have no right to fire me! I was only taking what she was offering that day, like you were doing just now!"

Cord would stand for no slur on Autumn's honor. He hit Miles in the jaw. The force of the blow knocked the drunken man to the ground.

"I told you to watch what you were saying."

"You son of a bitch!" Miles snarled as he charged to his feet. "You ain't got no right to be the law here in Sagebrush! I was a deputy longer than you were! I should have the job!"

"It doesn't work that way, Miles," Cord told him coldly. "You've already shown what kind of man you really are. I can't trust you anymore. You're supposed to protect prisoners in your custody, not abuse them!"

"I wasn't abusing her! She wanted me!"

"Get out of here now, Miles, or I'll lock you up for trespassing," Cord ordered. "Get off my property."

Miles was furious, and his drunken state made him that much wilder. He turned as if to go, wanting to catch Cord off guard.

Autumn had been nervous as she'd watched the confrontation between the two men from inside the house. Cord was a strong, honest man, but she knew Miles was capable of anything. She relaxed a bit when he finally started to leave.

As Cord turned to come back inside with Autumn, Miles launched himself at the sheriff, tackling him before he could reach the door. Cord hadn't been expecting his attack, but he recovered quickly. They struggled fiercely, grappling together, each trying to land a solid blow. Miles was beyond caring. He fought blindly, hating his opponent, wanting revenge for the wrongs he believed had been done him.

Autumn knew she had to do something to help Cord. She looked around frantically for some kind of weapon and saw a heavy pitcher in the kitchen. She ran to get it and then charged outside. As she came through the door, Miles had just managed to throw himself on Cord. Autumn did not hesitate to act. She swung the pitcher as hard as she could at Miles and hit him on the back of the head. The force of her blow knocked him unconscious and shattered the pitcher.

Cord pushed Miles's limp body away and got to his feet.

"Thanks," he told Autumn with a half-grin.

"Are you all right?" She went to his side.

"I'm fine, thanks to you," he answered. "You saved *me* this time." His grin broadened. "If you're ever looking for a job, I'll hire you on as a deputy."

"I'm not very good with a gun yet."

"No, but you swing a mean pitcher." He gave her a quick hug, sorry that she'd been subjected to Miles's ugliness again; then he put her from him.

"What are you going to do with him?"

"I'll take him down to the jail and have Thatch lock him up. Why don't you go back to the pavilion, and I'll meet you there."

She looked down at the drunk, who was slowly coming around. "Be careful."

"I will," Cord promised her as he reached down and took Miles's gun out of his holster. "He won't be causing anybody any more trouble today."

Autumn hurried off. As she made her way back to join Muriel and Ralph, she found herself thinking of all that had happened, since she'd seen them, and she smiled. Miles's attack had been frightening, but all that was really important was that Cord loved her and she loved him.

"Here she comes now," Muriel was saying as Autumn drew near.

"You look awfully happy," Muriel told her.

"It's been a wonderful day," she said.

"Where's Cord?"

"We ran into his old deputy, Miles. He was drunk and looking for a fight."

"Is everything all right?" Muriel asked, suddenly concerned about Cord.

"Cord handled it. He's on his way to the jail with Miles right now to lock him up."

"Miles isn't the smartest man around, that's for sure," Ralph remarked.

A short time later, Autumn saw Cord coming their way. She watched him walking down the street toward them and found she couldn't take her eyes off him. The emotions that rocked her left her wondering how she had ever thought herself in love with James. Memories of Cord's passionate lovemaking sent a flush of heat pulsing through her, and she struggled not to blush. She didn't know what the future held for her.

She prayed that Cord would be a part of it—that somehow they would find a way to be together.

"Did he cause you any trouble?" Autumn asked Cord.

"No. Thatch was at the office, so I turned Miles over to him."

"You've had an exciting afternoon, but I guess that's the way it is when you're the law in town," Ralph said. "You never get a minute to call your own."

Cord and Autumn shared a private look at his statement, knowing they had somehow been lucky enough to have those few minutes together today.

"Being sheriff is a big responsibility, but the rewards can be great." He smiled at Autumn. "If I hadn't been the sheriff, I wouldn't have had such an interesting introduction to Autumn."

"It was unforgettable," Muriel agreed, remembering far too clearly the terror of the events on the stage that day.

"I'll say, but that's over now," Autumn put in. "I never intend to see the inside of a jail cell again."

"That's a worthy goal for a lady," Ralph quipped in good humor.

It was getting late in the afternoon, and Autumn and Muriel knew it was almost time for them to start on the return trip to the ranch. They wanted to get back before sundown.

The men escorted them to their carriage to see them safely on their way.

"Would you like to come out for dinner tomorrow night?" Autumn invited Cord, not wanting to be apart from him. She included Ralph in the invitation out of politeness.

Cord was sorely regretting that she had to leave him at all, so he was eager to take her up on her invitation. "I'd like that. What about you, Ralph?"

Ralph looked at Muriel and found her gaze upon him as she eagerly awaited his answer. "That would be wonderful."

"What time should we be there?" Cord asked.

"How's six-thirty?"

"Six-thirty is fine. We'll see you then," he promised.

His gaze darkened as it met and held Autumn's. He helped her into the carriage. He wanted to hold her. He wanted to kiss her. But he couldn't. He settled on just kissing her hand before he stepped away. Autumn was thrilled by his simple, romantic gesture.

Ralph helped Muriel get in on the other side.

"Don't be late tomorrow," Muriel told the two men as Autumn took up the reins.

The women waved as they drove off toward the Lazy T.

"He kissed your hand!" Muriel sighed dreamily.

"Yes, he did." Autumn actually blushed a bit.

"Breaking your engagement with James may have been a very wise decision on your part."

"I think so."

The trip passed quickly for them. They spoke of all the excitement of the day and how they were looking forward to the dinner the following evening.

Autumn could tell that after spending the afternoon with him, Muriel was even more smitten with Ralph than before. She was glad. She hoped her friend found true happiness with the lawyer.

Her thoughts turned to her own happiness. She loved Cord. She knew that now. It should have been so simple, but there was nothing simple about their relationship. Her heart ached as she realized how complicated things were. Though they had not spoken of it, Cord was a man of honor and integrity and bound to do his job as sheriff. If Grace ever did return, Autumn feared what might happen; she did not know how she would ever choose between them.

Tormented, Autumn pushed the worry from her. She told herself to enjoy the beauty of what she had shared with Cord that day. She would be seeing him soon. She smiled at the thought.

Sherry saw the carriage driving up and went out to welcome the women home.

"How was the social?" she asked when they'd reined in.

"We had a wonderful time," Muriel told her.

They climbed down and went inside with Sherry as one of the hands took charge of the horse and carriage. They told her about the activities of the day and of the guests who would be coming to dinner the next evening. Sherry and Muriel began to plan the meal.

"You did have a visitor today," Sherry informed Autumn. "Pete Miller came by."

Autumn was surprised. "Did he say what he wanted?"

"Only that he wanted to talk to you. I told him you were coming home tonight, so he may be back in the morning."

"Thanks."

Sherry left them for the evening, and they settled in, tired but happy from their excursion into town.

"Pete Miller is a nice young man," Muriel remarked, believing he'd come to call to begin courting Autumn. "He's rather handsome, too, don't you think?"

"Yes, he is."

"How exciting for you to have two gentlemen calling on you."

"I wonder if he really will come back tomorrow."

Autumn thought Pete was a nice man, but she had no romantic interest in him. There was only one man in her life, only one man who held her heart. Still, she couldn't help wondering why Pete had sought her out.

Cord checked in with Thatch at the sheriff's office after Autumn had gone. Things were quiet there, and Miles wasn't giving Thatch any trouble, so Cord went home.

As he lay in his bed late that night, he was haunted by the memories of what he and Autumn had shared there that day. She was beautiful and spirited and everything he'd ever wanted in a woman.

He loved her.

Only the shadow of her sister's criminal involvement stood between them and kept them from happiness.

Cord knew that somehow he had to find a way for them to be together.

Chapter Twenty-five

Grace had thought she was nervous the day before when Pete had ridden off to the Lazy T, but what she'd been feeling then was nothing compared to her nervousness this day. It was noon. Pete had left to get Autumn an hour before, and she wasn't sure how soon he'd be back.

Yesterday, Grace had been waiting and watching for his return. Each minute had seemed an hour. When at last Pete had come back, she'd seen him riding in by himself from her bedroom window.

Grace had immediately assumed that Autumn had refused to come with him or have anything to do with her. Her devastation had surprised her. She hadn't realized that she'd allowed herself to care that much. Only Pete's reassurance that he hadn't spoken with Autumn yet eased her heartbreak.

As she waited impatiently now, Grace was reliving all those tormenting emotions. Today, however, she had prepared herself for the worst. Still, she allowed herself to hope that when Pete returned this time, her sister would be with him.

Pete hoped there wouldn't be many people around when he got to the Lazy T. What he had to say to Autumn needed to be said in private. He could not risk alerting anyone else to Grace's presence. As he rode up to the house, he was glad to see that Autumn was at the stable. He was surprised to find that she was wearing pants, just as Grace had done on the ranch. He realized he shouldn't have been surprised by the similarity in their dress—they were twins, after all.

"Autumn—I see you're back from town," Pete greeted her as he dismounted and tied up his horse.

"Hello, Pete," she said, smiling in welcome. "Sherry told me you came over to see me yesterday. I'm sorry I missed you. Muriel and I were in town for the social."

"That's what she said. Did you have a good time?"

"Yes, as a matter of fact, we did. It was fun, but I'm sure you know all about the town socials."

"I have been to a few, that's true."

"So, what brings you to the Lazy T?" she asked.

"Well, I wondered if you'd have time to go for a ride with me today."

Autumn wasn't quite sure what to make of his invitation. "Where did you want to go?"

"Over to my ranch for a while. There's something I want to show you."

She remembered Muriel's remark and thought he was trying to court her. She did like him, but Cord was the man she loved, and she didn't want to give Pete any false encouragement. "Things are a little busy here today, Pete."

He frowned slightly, trying to figure out the best way to convince her to come with him without revealing the whole truth right away. "This is important."

"Can you tell me what it is you want me to see?" Autumn asked innocently enough.

Pete cast a quick look around, then decided to tell her the plain truth. "Your sister."

Autumn stared at him, her eyes widening in amazement. "Grace? You know where she is?"

He kept his voice low. "She came to me for help, and I'm hiding her at my place. I'm the only one who knows she's there. I told her about you."

"You did?"

"Yes, and she wants to meet you. Will you come with me? Grace will understand if you don't want to, but I know it would mean a lot to her to see you."

"Of course I'll come with you—right now!" she answered. "Let me go tell Muriel that I'm going for a ride with you and I'll be right back."

"Your friend won't suspect anything, will she?"

Autumn gave him a warm smile. "No. When she heard you were here yesterday, she thought you were coming to court me."

Pete blushed a little at her words. "We'll just let her go on believing that."

"Come with me. We'll make this look very real for her."

He smiled at her invitation, and they walked together up to the main house.

Autumn took great care to keep her expression calm as she sought out Muriel. She introduced her to Pete and told her that she was riding out with him for a while and would be back that afternoon.

"Have a good time," Muriel bade them.

Autumn started to leave the house with Pete, when she realized there was one thing she needed to take for Grace. She went back and was glad that Muriel was busy in her bedroom, so she didn't have to explain her actions. Autumn got the family picture off the desk, then hurried back to join Pete.

They returned to the stable to get their horses. She stowed the picture in her saddlebag, and they rode away together.

Only when they were away from the Lazy T did Autumn start questioning Pete.

"When did Grace come to you? Has she been at your ranch very long?"

"Only a few days," he told her, explaining how he'd found her in the house. "She's afraid of Martin. He's one deadly bastard—oh, excuse me, Autumn."

"It's all right, Pete. You're right about Martin. Cord's told me a little about him."

"I've got to keep her safe from him. I've got to find a way to help her."

"*We've* got to find a way to help her," she corrected him. "Do you think she'll trust me?"

"I hope so. I've been trying to convince her to turn herself in to Sheriff Randolph. I think it would be the smartest thing for her to do, but so far, she's against the idea."

"I'll talk to her about it, too. There's no future for her, living like she's been living on the wrong side of the law."

"She's talked about running away, but I want her to stay." He looked over at Autumn.

"I want her to stay, too," she told him, and their gazes met in understanding.

It wasn't a long trip to the Miller ranch, but it seemed to take forever to Autumn.

"How have you managed to keep her hidden?"

"We've been lucky so far. She's stayed in the house since she got here, but it's only a matter of time before somebody figures out what's going on. I hope she'll listen to you."

"So do I."

They rode up to the house and tied their horses out front.

Autumn wanted to run straight inside to her sister, but she knew that some of Pete's hands were working nearby and might wonder what was going on. So she tried to act as normal as possible.

"Are you ready?" Pete asked.

"I've been waiting for this my whole life. I just didn't know it," she answered.

They walked up the front steps together. Pete opened the door for her. Autumn stepped inside and he followed.

"Hello, Autumn," Grace said softly from where she stood in the doorway of her bedroom.

Autumn went still as she stared at her twin, the sister she had never known.

"Grace—" she whispered. She was unable to move for a moment, and unable to look away from the woman who was her mirror image.

They stood there in silence for a breathless moment, staring at each other in wonder, each trying to understand what the other was feeling.

Autumn made the first move. She crossed the room to Grace.

She stopped before her.

And then, with pure love, she took her sister in her arms.

"Oh—Grace—" Autumn held her close as she gave vent to her tears. They were tears of loneliness and of happiness.

They had been lost, but now were found.

Grace was stiff in Autumn's embrace, but only

307

for a moment. When she felt the unquestioning love and acceptance in Autumn's arms, she hugged her back.

Relief swept through Grace as she realized it was true. She did have a sister—a twin.

It was an emotional moment for Pete, too. He stood back, looking on and saying nothing. He wasn't sure he could have spoken even if he'd wanted to.

When Autumn and Grace finally moved apart, they went to sit on the sofa. Autumn wanted to stay as close to Grace as she could. She held her hand as she sat down beside her.

"Tell me everything, Grace. I want to know all there is to know about you."

"And I want to know everything about you," Grace returned. She paused to look at Pete, her love for him shining in her eyes. "Thank you, Pete."

He smiled gently at her. "You're welcome."

The resemblance between the two was amazing, he had to admit. From their blond hair to their dark eyes and warm smiles, they were identical. He watched them as they sat side by side, talking, and he knew he was glad they'd been reunited.

"Did you know anything about me?" Grace asked Autumn.

"No, nothing. I didn't even know our father was still alive until I got a letter from the lawyer telling me that I'd inherited his estate. Mother had told me that he'd died when I was an infant, and she never mentioned that I had a sister."

The knowledge that her own mother could

deny her existence still had the power to hurt Grace, but the pain in her heart was eased by Autumn's presence.

"Pa told me she'd died when I was little, and he didn't tell me anything about you, either," Grace said, amazed. "They sure were good liars, weren't they?"

Autumn realized with sadness that Grace was right. "I don't know how 'good' they were, but yes, they were obviously very accomplished at lying."

"Well, there will never be any need for lies between us," Grace said.

"You're right. I love you, and I am thrilled we've found each other. I am so glad you came here to Pete."

It had been so long since Grace had known unconditional love, she wasn't sure quite how to react. "I love you, too, Autumn."

"There's something I have to show you."

Autumn started to get up, but Pete knew what she was talking about. "I'll get it for you."

He went for the picture and came back to hand it to Autumn.

"What is it?" Grace asked, curious.

"It's us."

"Us?" Grace was confused until Autumn handed her the cherished picture.

"Oh—" She stared down at the family she'd never known. When she looked up at Autumn, her eyes were filled with tears. "I always felt that something was missing in my life, but I thought it was because I didn't have a mother. Now I know it's because you weren't with me."

The two women embraced again, rejoicing in the love they had found.

The hours passed quickly as they told each other all that had happened in their lives. Autumn and Grace cried often, but they laughed, too, as they shared stories of their childhoods.

Pete remained quietly with them, watching Grace. He was relieved that everything had turned out so well between the two women, but he knew they were still in danger. He and Autumn had to find a way to keep Grace safe from Rod Martin. Pete was ready to bring the subject up, when Autumn spoke of it first.

"Have you given any thought to what we can do about your situation? Pete and I want to help you in any way we can," she said.

"I know," Grace said gratefully as she looked at Pete. "Rod could still be looking for me, and I'm also wanted by the law."

"You have to turn yourself in—the sooner, the better," Autumn told her.

"No! All I want is to get away from here. Pete told me a long time ago that if I ever needed help, he'd help me. That's why I came here."

"Grace, I can tell you're afraid, but running away isn't the answer. That's what you did before, and it only made things worse and got you into deeper trouble."

Her words touched Grace.

"You're right," she said in a soft voice, tormented by what she faced. "But what can I do?"

"There's only one way to make sure you're going to be safe for the rest of your life," Autumn told her. "You have to go to Sheriff Randolph and give yourself up. He can put you in jail and keep you safe there. Could you help him catch the gang?"

"I could try," she answered hesitantly, still fearful, "but what if I turned myself in and the sheriff didn't believe what I told him?"

"I know him. Cord Randolph is a good man. He'll believe you, and he'll protect you. You can trust him."

"I don't trust any lawman," Grace declared, her fear winning over momentarily. "I should leave—"

"Grace, you don't have to keep running," Autumn insisted, taking her hand. "I'm sure that if you tried to help Sheriff Randolph catch the gang, he'd go easy on you. Stay here. Face up to what you've done."

"That's easy for you to say. You're not the one who might be spending time in jail."

Autumn grew a bit angry at her sister's obstinacy. "You're wrong, Grace. I have spent time in jail."

"You have? When?"

"Sheriff Randolph arrested me on my way into Sagebrush because he thought I was you. It took a while for me to prove my true identity, so I was locked up overnight."

"I'm sorry."

"It's all right. I got to know him then. If you cooperate with him, things could go easier on you."

"I don't know . . ."

"Grace," Pete said softly.

She looked at him.

"If you want a life with me, if you want to be safe here on the ranch with me, then you have to turn yourself in. You have to help Sheriff Randolph get Rod Martin," he explained. "I love you. You know that."

Her gaze met his, and she saw the truth of his love for her in his eyes. "Yes, I know."

"You know, too, that if you want me to do it, I will sell the ranch and go anywhere with you. But we both know that Martin isn't going to quit looking for you. As long as he knows you're alive, he'll be searching for you."

"And if he finds me, he'll kill me."

"Martin isn't going to give up," he warned her. "That's why you have to go to the sheriff. You won't be completely safe until Martin's dead or locked up."

Grace looked even more worried. "I'm not sure what to do."

"We've just found each other. I want us to be together," Autumn said with heartfelt emotion.

"Think about what Autumn and I have said," Pete said gently, wanting to ease the pressure they'd put on her.

"But I'm wanted by the law, too."

"If you help Sheriff Randolph, I'm sure he'll find a way to help you. Once Martin's been arrested, you'll be safe again. We wouldn't have to run. We could stay here and have our life together," he told her.

"Do you know where the gang is right now,

or what they're planning next?" Autumn asked.

"They spoke of a few different things."

"You could let Cord know, so he can be ready for them if they come to town," she urged.

Autumn could see Grace's torment, and she hugged her.

"Sleep on it overnight. I know it's hard. You've been through a lot lately, but you've got me and you've got Pete. You're never going to be alone again, I promise."

Autumn stood up to go, wanting to give Grace more time to think things through.

"I'll come back again tomorrow," she told her. "We can talk more then."

Autumn smiled at Pete as she started to leave.

"Do you want me to ride with you?" he offered.

"No, I'll be fine. Just take care of Grace."

"I will," he said firmly.

Chapter Twenty-six

Muriel was worried. It was late afternoon, and there had been no sign of Autumn returning from Pete's ranch. Cord and Ralph were due to arrive within the next few hours for dinner, and she had no idea where Autumn could be. She should have been home long ago.

"Are you worried about something?" Sherry asked, noticing her troubled expression.

"I was just wondering when Autumn would be back."

"It's about a half-hour ride to the Miller place. She should be showing up soon—especially since you've got your gentleman callers coming tonight. She wouldn't want to miss them."

"I know." Muriel frowned again. She wondered if it was possible for Autumn to get so busy with Pete that she would forget Cord and Ralph were coming to dinner. She hoped not, for it would be awkward to explain her absence to them.

This had been one of the most memorable days of Autumn's life, and as she rode home, she took her time, wanting to treasure every second. Grace was alive and well.

Autumn knew she and Pete were going to have to find a way to convince her sister to do the right thing. It wasn't going to be easy to convince her to turn herself in, but they had to do it—for her sake.

Autumn wished she could talk to Cord about Grace, but that was impossible. He was bound by the law to do his job, and she couldn't betray her sister's trust. She couldn't reveal to anyone that her sister was hiding out at Pete's ranch.

Autumn felt trapped between saving her sister and doing the right thing. As she thought of Cord, she was suddenly stricken by the realization that it must be after six. She had been so caught up in the wonder of her reunion with Grace that she'd completely forgotten Cord and Ralph were due at the Lazy T for dinner that very evening!

Panic struck her, along with mortification that she could have forgotten. Autumn put her heels to her horse's sides and raced for the ranch. It was bad enough that she was going to be late to her own dinner party, but somehow she had to keep herself from revealing the truth about Grace to Cord. Though her parents had obviously been accomplished liars, Autumn had never been one. It was going to be a difficult night for her and a true test of her acting abilities.

Her nerves were stretched taut as she raced toward home.

Home—

Autumn realized suddenly that she'd thought of the ranch as home. The idea astounded her and calmed her. In her heart, she knew she was finally right where she belonged.

"How long has Autumn been gone?" Cord asked, concerned. He and Ralph had arrived early for dinner to find Muriel worrying about Autumn's absence.

"She left just before noon. Pete Miller came over and invited her to his ranch for a visit. I knew she'd be gone awhile, but I never thought she'd stay away this long."

"Pete's a good man, and if there was any kind of trouble, he'd take care of it," Ralph said.

"It'll be dark soon, so I'd better ride out and take a look around," Cord told them and mounted up again.

"Thank you, Cord," Muriel said.

As Cord headed off toward the Miller ranch, he admitted to himself that he had felt jealous when Muriel told him Autumn had gone off with Pete. Logically, he told himself he had no claim on Autumn. She was free to do what she wanted, but it didn't change the way he felt. Concerned about her safety, he quickened his pace. He wanted to cover as many miles as he could while it was still light out.

Autumn saw the lone rider coming toward her and wasn't sure what to do. She was carrying her derringer as Sherry had advised, but until this moment she'd never imagined she'd have to use it.

Then she recognized Cord.

Autumn was both thrilled to see him and worried that she wouldn't be a good enough actress to hide the truth from him. She told herself she had to be. Too much depended on her. Even as she worried about Grace, her gaze remained fixed on Cord. She thought he looked most handsome as he came toward her, and she remembered how wonderful it had been to be in his arms. The conflict in her heart was real, but she managed a smile as she rode to meet him.

"I'm sorry I'm late," Autumn apologized as she reined in beside Cord.

"We were worried about you, so I rode out to look for you," he told her. "Are you all right?"

"Oh, yes. I just stayed at Pete's longer than I had planned."

"I'm glad nothing was wrong."

Now that his fear had been relieved, he found himself wondering what she'd been doing at Miller's all this time. He forced the thought away.

He had no claim on her. All that mattered was that she was safe.

"The only thing wrong is that I'm hungry. What about you?"

"I'm hungry all right," he said, "but not for food."

He urged his horse nearer to hers and leaned over to give her a kiss.

At the touch of his lips, Autumn sighed. His kiss was her heaven—and right now, her hell. She longed to be honest with him about Grace, but she couldn't. She had to draw upon her meager thespian skills and try to act as if nothing had changed, when everything was different. It wasn't going to be easy, but she would do it. She had to—for Grace.

When the horses stirred, Cord reluctantly ended the exchange and drew away. He would have liked to stay there all night, alone with Autumn, but he knew they couldn't. Muriel and Ralph were waiting for them at the Lazy T.

"We'd better get back. Muriel's worried about you."

They started for the ranch at a quickened pace that didn't allow for much conversation. Autumn was glad. She needed more time to collect her thoughts and prepare herself for the evening to come.

"Here they come now, Muriel," Ralph told her as Cord and Autumn rode in.

"Thank heaven!" She hurried outside to meet them.

"Is dinner ready?" Autumn asked, trying to make light of her late arrival.

"Is that the reason you stayed away so long? So you wouldn't have to cook?" Muriel teased, glad that Autumn was back.

"That's right. You're a much better cook than I am."

Everyone laughed and went inside to relax and enjoy the evening.

Autumn took a few minutes to freshen up and change clothes.

Cord looked up as she rejoined them, and he smiled.

"You look lovely," he complimented her.

"Thank you." She felt a little more ladylike after trading her riding clothes for a gown.

"Shall we eat?" Muriel invited.

The meal was delicious, and they ate their fill.

"You were right, Autumn. Muriel is a good cook," Ralph praised.

"Thank you." Muriel was pleased that he appreciated her cooking.

"How were things in Sagebrush today?" Autumn asked, looking at Cord.

"Peaceful," he answered.

"That must mean you're a good sheriff," Muriel said with a smile.

Cord appreciated her compliment, but he wouldn't believe he was doing a good job until he'd taken care of Martin and his gang.

"What did you do about Miles?" Autumn asked curiously. She'd worried about what he might try at the jail.

"Thatch and I decided it would do him good to stay locked up an extra day or two. I want to make an impression on him, so he doesn't end up there again."

"It will," Autumn said. "It made an impression on me. I don't plan on going back to jail anytime soon."

Everyone laughed.

"Pity. I'd much rather have you locked up in back than Miles," Cord told her.

Their gazes met, and they both remembered the kiss they'd shared during her last visit to the jail. She struggled not to blush at the memory.

"That was a terrible time for me," Muriel added. "I was so worried about you—and frightened."

"I was safe. I was with Cord," Autumn said.

"We know that now, but that first day we didn't. Why, James was fit to be tied!"

Autumn hadn't thought of James for a few days, and she hadn't missed him. She could just imagine what he'd be saying if he knew that Grace was so nearby.

"As troubling as it was to have him along, I'm still glad James made the trip with us. If he hadn't, I would never have found out what kind of man he really was until after we'd married— and then it would have been too late."

"Which just goes to show, you can always find

a blessing in every difficult situation. It's just that sometimes it's harder to find the blessings," Muriel remarked.

"I can agree with that," Cord said gruffly, thinking of his frustration over the hunt for Rod Martin.

"Have you heard anything new on the Martin gang?" Autumn asked, understanding the direction of his thoughts. She hoped that while they discussed the subject, he might reveal something that would help her with Grace.

"No. Nothing," he answered curtly.

"They're bound to make a mistake one of these days, Cord, and when they do, you'll get them. I know you will." Ralph was confident in the sheriff's abilities.

"I'm looking forward to that day," Cord said.

Autumn supposed it was good that there had been no news about Martin. That meant he wasn't close by, and Grace would be safe with Pete for a little while longer.

Muriel had been watching Autumn all evening, and she noticed that her young friend seemed a bit unsettled. She doubted that anyone else noticed, but she knew her so well she could often read her moods. She was curious about her day with Pete, and wondered if the rancher had made an impression on Autumn. She, herself, wouldn't have had any difficulty choosing between Cord and Pete. Though Pete seemed nice enough, Cord was more the man for Autumn.

"Well, thank you, ladies, for dinner," Cord

said as he and Ralph prepared to leave.

The evening had been enjoyable, but it was getting late and they had to ride back to town.

"As Autumn said," Ralph added, "you are a wonderful cook, Muriel."

"Compliments like that will get you invited back, Ralph," Muriel told him.

"Good. I'm looking forward to the invitation."

Everyone laughed.

Cord and Autumn went outside to have a moment alone, leaving Muriel and Ralph by themselves in the house.

"It's a beautiful night," Autumn sighed as she went to stand at the edge of the porch and look up at the sky.

The moon was bright, and stars spangled the heavens.

"Yes, it is," Cord said as he followed her.

The sound of his voice so close behind her sent a shiver of sensual awareness through her. She turned and smiled up at him. He gazed down at her and thought her the most beautiful woman he'd ever seen. There was no need for words as they went into each other's arms.

Autumn held tightly to Cord, reveling in the strength and security she found in his embrace. From the first time he'd held her there in the jail cell, she had sensed that this was where she wanted to be—in Cord's arms, close to his heart. She lifted her lips to his.

As she kissed him, she offered up a fervent

prayer that Grace would make the right decision, and soon.

"I'm glad you came tonight, Ralph," Muriel told him as they lingered inside for a moment to give Cord and Autumn a few minutes alone.

"So am I," he answered.

Widower that he was, Ralph hadn't thought about courting anyone else since his wife, Sharon, had died seven years before. But now that he'd met Muriel, all that had changed. She had taught him how to smile and laugh again. He was beginning to enjoy life again. He hadn't thought it possible, for he'd loved Sharon very much. But it had happened.

Feeling like a callow, untried youth, Ralph closed the distance between them. He took the stunned Muriel in his arms and kissed her. Muriel wasn't stunned for long. She returned Ralph's embrace with abandon. She had never thought she would experience these feelings again.

The embrace was rapturous. Caught up in the splendor of their newly discovered love, they didn't speak but merely held on to one another. When at last they finally moved apart, they were both a bit shy and embarrassed.

"Will I see you again?" Ralph asked.

"Any time you want to," Muriel answered straight out, not about to waste time being coy.

He kissed her again, this time sweetly. "Good. I'm looking forward to it."

* * *

Grace couldn't sleep. She'd tried, but that welcome and needed rest had proven elusive. Memories of her visit with Autumn stayed with her. It had been a wonderful reunion, and she would always be grateful to Pete for bringing them together.

Those were the only happy thoughts she had, though. Grace was deeply troubled as she relived in her mind all that had happened in her life, and the mistakes she had made. Those mistakes had been made out of desperation. They had seemed the right choices at the time; they had seemed the way to happiness, but now she knew better.

Grace got out of bed, restless. She needed to talk to someone, and she knew Pete would listen. She took the blanket from the bed and wrapped it around her, then left the room to waken Pete.

Her soft knock on his bedroom door was answered quickly.

"Grace—what is it?" he asked as he came out and stood before her clad in only the pants he'd hurriedly tugged on.

"I need to talk, Pete."

She sounded so sad and troubled that he immediately took her in his arms and held her close. He thought about taking her back into his bedroom to talk, but decided against it. He considered himself a reasonably strong man, but tonight he wasn't feeling strong. He led her to the sofa. He did not light any lamps, for he didn't want anyone else on the ranch to know he was awake. If they saw lights, they might think there was trouble and come up to help. He did not want to be interrupted right now.

"I think I've made my decision, but I wanted to talk to you about it first."

"What have you decided?" he asked, gently urging her to go on.

"I love you, Pete."

At her words, he leaned toward her and kissed her softly. "I love you, too."

She smiled tightly and went on. "I will turn myself in to the sheriff. Tomorrow—if you and Autumn want me to."

"Grace—it's got to be what you want to do. Have you thought this through completely? You know what you're facing?"

"Oh, yes," she answered as she drew a ragged breath. "And I'm ready to do it."

"It won't be easy."

"My life has never been easy."

"Then you've got something to look forward to. Once you marry me, I am going to spend the rest of my life making you happy."

"Marry you?"

"Oh, yes, love, and the sooner the better. We'll work this out—together."

She went into his embrace, feeling completely safe from harm for the first time in so long.

He held her near, stroking the silken length of her hair and fighting down his need to make love to her. As he'd told her before, he was going to wait, and he intended to stick to his word.

"Autumn will be back tomorrow, and when she gets here, we'll head straight into Sage-brush."

"Thank you, Pete."

"For what?" He was puzzled.

"For loving me."

He kissed her sweetly, adoringly, and held her to his heart.

Chapter Twenty-seven

Autumn had lain awake for most of the night, trying to figure out what she was going to do if Grace decided to run away again. The question had tormented her for hours.

As dawn brightened the sky, Autumn got up and dressed. She was ready to ride to Pete's. She had to know Grace's answer.

Glad that Muriel wasn't up yet, Autumn left her a note saying she'd be at Pete's ranch, then rode out. She was anxious to be back with Grace again.

Pete was working in the stable when one of his men came to get him.

"Autumn Thomas is riding in, Pete," the hand told him.

"Thanks."

Pete quit working and went to meet her. He was eager to tell her the news.

"Let's go inside. There's something I've got to tell you," he said as he walked with her up to the house.

"Good news?" she asked hopefully.

"Very good news," he answered.

They went in to find Grace waiting for them.

"Did Pete tell you?" Grace asked Autumn.

"Tell me what?"

"I've made my decision."

Autumn waited, her nerves stretched taut.

"I'll go with you to town and turn myself in to the sheriff."

Autumn gathered Grace in her arms and hugged her. "You won't be sorry. Trust me."

Grace looked at her and nodded. "I do trust you—and Pete." It felt so wonderful to have them to rely on and to love.

"How soon do you want to go?" Pete asked Autumn.

"We can leave this morning. There's no reason to wait any longer. The sooner you're safe with Cord, the better," Autumn told her sister.

"I never thought of being with a lawman as safe," Grace remarked.

"Start," Autumn declared.

Cord was in the office working at his desk. He'd released Miles earlier that morning and had given him a stern warning about what would

happen if he ever caused any trouble in Sagebrush again. He'd told his former deputy to get
out of town and stay out, and this time Miles had
agreed. Cord hoped the extra time in jail had
made a lasting impression on him.

Cord was surprised when he heard a knock at
the back door. It was unusual for anyone to come
in that way. Fearing trouble, he got the keys and
went to check. The knock came again as he
reached the door. He quickly unlocked it and
opened it wide to find Autumn there.

"Autumn? What's wrong? What are you doing
back here?"

"Cord—we didn't want to cause any trouble
in town."

"We?" He hadn't seen anyone else, but just
then Pete came forward with Grace.

"This is my sister, Grace," Autumn told him.

"Grace?" He looked between them. He was
amazed by the resemblance, although he knew
he shouldn't have been.

"She's come to turn herself in to you."

"Get in here now," he directed, taking a quick
look down the alleyway to make sure no one had
seen them. He stepped back to let them in, then
closed and locked the door behind them. "Wait
here for a minute."

Cord went to the front office and pulled down
the shades and locked the door.

"You can come in here now," he directed.

Cord remained standing as they came into the
room. He watched Grace's every move, not fully

trusting her even though Autumn was with her.

"Where's Rod Martin?" Cord demanded.

"Right now, I'm not sure," Grace answered honestly.

She was nervous, and she watched the lawman warily as she went to sit down.

"It's all right," Pete told her as he stood behind her chair and put a hand on her shoulder for comfort.

Cord looked from Pete to Autumn and suddenly understood what had happened yesterday. He looked back at Autumn. "So this was why you were late for dinner last night."

"Yes," Autumn answered. "Pete came over to let me know Grace was at his house and wanted to meet me. Not telling you the truth last night was one of the hardest things I've ever done, but I couldn't betray Grace. She still hadn't made her decision about what to do, but now she has."

"I'm giving myself up to you. I want to help you any way I can," Grace said. She'd been watching Cord with Autumn and was beginning to understand more about her sister and the lawman. "Autumn says I can trust you."

"You can, but do you?" Cord met her gaze as he waited for her response.

Grace looked him straight in the eye and was quiet for a moment, studying him. Then she answered, "Yes."

"Good. You're under arrest, Miss Thomas," Cord declared.

She only nodded.

Autumn spoke up. "Grace has some information about Martin that might help you."

He looked at Grace, trying not to get excited. He'd been disappointed too many times to let that happen again. "What can you tell me?"

"I don't know how much good it will do you."

"Let me decide that."

Grace quickly told him what she knew about Rod's plans for upcoming robberies and how the gang had used Charley's ranch as a hideout.

"So he did talk about the army payroll coming through?"

"Yes, he mentioned the payroll here in Sagebrush and the bank in Dry Spring. Before I ran off, he hadn't made up his mind which one to hit next."

"How did you get away?" Cord was wondering if Martin had sent her there to give him the wrong information.

Grace explained what had happened, gazing up at Pete when she finished. Her love for him was obvious. "I should never have run off with Rod. I should have listened to you that day and come home with you then."

Pete knelt beside her chair and held her hand. "It's going to be all right now. You don't have to run anymore. You're home."

Grace hugged him as she began to cry. She'd been strong for so long, but suddenly she didn't feel strong anymore. She felt like the same lost, abandoned young girl who'd fled into the night after being beaten by her father.

Cord went to Autumn, whose eyes were filled with tears.

"Thank you," he said in a low voice. "This can't have been easy for you."

"It wasn't, but you were right—it was the right thing to do."

"I have to lock her up."

"She understands, and she's willing to cooperate with you."

"Good."

He turned away to get the cell keys.

"Miss Thomas, I'm going to have to take you in back now."

Grace was nervous but stood up to follow him. Autumn quickly went to her.

She managed a small grin as she said, "The cot isn't the most comfortable, but I did manage to get some sleep on it."

Grace smiled, too.

Pete embraced her one last time. He hated the idea of her in jail, but he knew it was the best thing to do. She would be safe here, and soon, he hoped, she would be free. He walked with her as she followed Cord.

Cord locked her in the cell and left Pete there to keep her company. He returned to the office and Autumn.

They were alone. He went straight to her, took her in his arms and kissed her gently.

"I was jealous of Pete last night," he told her when he'd ended the kiss.

"There was no reason to be," Autumn responded.

"I didn't know that at the time."

"Now you do." She lifted one hand to caress the lean line of his jaw, and he pressed a kiss to her palm. "Grace will help you any way she can. I told her I'd stay here in town at the hotel, so I could be close to her in case she needed me. Now that I've finally found her, I don't want us to be separated. She's scared, Cord."

"She should be. Martin's as deadly as they come. You be careful, too, now," he warned her. "The man may show up around here, and if he sees you, he might mistake you for Grace. Carry your derringer."

"I've got it in my saddlebags."

"Start keeping it on you, just in case."

"A sheriff once told me that it was a deadly weapon and I shouldn't be carrying it," she said with a smile.

"That lawman was a very wise man, but a lot has happened since then. I want you to be able to protect yourself."

"I will."

Cord gave her one more kiss, then moved away. He had a lot to do. The payroll would be coming through town at the end of the week, and he had to be ready for trouble. He wasn't going to take any chances. He was also going to wire to the lawman in Dry Spring to alert him that Martin might show up there.

"Cord—will the law go easier on Grace because she turned herself in and tried to help you?" Autumn was afraid her sister would still have to serve a long sentence.

"I'll do everything I can for her. I'll talk to the judge and let him know that she surrendered on her own and provided information to me."

"Thank you. I'll talk to Ralph, too, and see if there's anything else I can do. She's had a rough time, and I want to make things better for her."

"You and Pete did the right thing when you got her to turn herself in. Everything will work out."

"I hope you're right."

"I do, too. I never thought I'd be wanting Martin to come into town to pull off a robbery, but I really hope he shows up and tries to steal the payroll," he said grimly.

"You'll be ready for him," Autumn said with confidence.

"Ready and waiting," he confirmed.

They shared a powerful look of understanding, for Autumn knew how much it would mean to Cord to apprehend Martin.

Rod was in a bad mood, and he had been ever since he'd returned without Grace. He'd stayed drunk most of the time since then, but once the gang started the trip to Sagebrush, he'd sobered up. It was time to get serious.

"You think this is going to be easy without Sheriff Gallagher around?" Joe asked as he rode next to Rod.

"Hell, it's got to be. He was the best lawman in these parts," Rod answered.

"There's been talk about his deputy, though. We'd better not be too confident," Lou put in.

"Don't worry, everything's going to work out just fine," Rod told him.

"Hey, Rod—wasn't Grace from Sagebrush? Maybe you'll run into her while we're there," Joe taunted him.

Rod only smiled at him coldly. "We won't have any time for women in Sagebrush. We got more important things to worry about—like the payroll."

They all laughed in agreement. The payroll was a big one, and they were going to enjoy spending it.

As Rod thought about it, though, he liked the idea that he might run into Grace in town. He wanted to see her again. They had some unfinished business.

"Is there anything more I can do for Grace, Ralph?" Autumn asked as she met with the lawyer at his office.

"No, you and Pete have done a fine job. Grace is going to thank you when this is over."

"I hope so. I felt bad leaving her alone at the jail."

"She'll be okay. We both know what a fine, upstanding man Cord is."

"How soon is the judge due back in town?"

"In a week or two. I'll talk to Cord, and we'll

see about sending him a wire to let him know what's going on. With Cord offering testimony for her, I think she'll have a good chance of winning the judge's favor."

Autumn sighed with relief. "Good. I want her home with me where she belongs."

"I'll do my best to make sure that happens."

Autumn left his office and started back for the ranch to give everyone the news of what had happened. She would pick up the things she needed for Grace and for herself, and return immediately to town.

Chapter Twenty-eight

It was Friday, and the army payroll was due in town late that afternoon.

Cord and his deputies were ready.

"I appreciate your help, Sheriff Randolph," John Backe, the president of the Sagebrush Bank, told Cord as they met in mid-afternoon. "If there's anything else you need us to do, just let me know."

"I will, but I think we've covered everything," Cord assured him. They had just finished discussing the security arrangements, and everything seemed to be in order.

"Has anyone seen Martin around?"

"No. It's been quiet."

"If we're lucky, all our worrying will be for

nothing," the banker said, nervous about the possibility of a robbery attempt.

"I'm not putting any trust in luck." Cord was tense in anticipation of the night to come.

"I understand."

They shook hands, and Cord left the bank and returned to the sheriff's office.

Cord had worked with Thatch and Jared earlier to pick the best vantage points from which to guard the bank. They were prepared for any trouble. Several armed guards traveled with the payroll, so he would have their help, too, if need be. No matter what happened, though, it was going to be a long night.

Cord reached the office, ready to bide his time.

"Everything all set with Mr. Backe?" Thatch asked as Cord came in.

"Yes. All we have to do now is wait. We're due at the bank in a couple of hours. The payroll should be rolling into town about then, and we'll be ready and waiting for it."

"I'm looking forward to tomorrow when the payroll is rolling out of town," the deputy said with a grimace. "I'll be glad when this is all over."

"You're not alone." Cord sat down at his desk. "How's our prisoner?"

"She's fine. Autumn was here with Muriel earlier for a visit, but I haven't seen Pete today. I guess he hasn't returned from his ranch yet."

"He'll be back soon. He told me he'd stay here

and keep an eye on things for us while we were at the bank."

"Autumn said she'd be back for another visit this afternoon."

Cord frowned. "I want to make sure she stays at the hotel all evening."

"That will be the safest place for her tonight," Thatch agreed.

Since Grace's arrest, Autumn had returned to the Lazy T only once to give everyone the news. Muriel had accompanied her back to town, as had Sherry, to see Grace and welcome her home. Sherry had gone back to the ranch, but Muriel had remained in town with Autumn. They'd taken rooms at the hotel and visited Grace every day.

Cord started on his paperwork, expecting the two women and Pete to show up at any time. He had trouble concentrating, but forced himself to keep working.

It wasn't long until Autumn and Muriel came in.

"Hello, Cord," Autumn greeted him with a smile.

"Hello, Autumn," he returned.

"How did your meeting with the banker go?"

"Everything is set. We're meeting him at four o'clock."

It was almost three now. The time was drawing near.

"Is it all right if we pay Grace another visit?" Muriel asked.

"Yes, but I want you to go back to the hotel when I leave with Thatch and Jared."

"All right. Is there anything we can do to help you?" Autumn asked.

"The best way you can help me is to stay in your hotel rooms tonight. I don't want to be worrying about you. I want to know you're safe."

"We will," they promised.

Cord admitted the two women to see Grace, then returned to speak with Thatch.

"I'll go on down to the restaurant and get dinner for the prisoner," Thatch volunteered.

"Thanks. When is Jared due back?"

"He was out making rounds. He should be here in about half an hour."

"Good. As soon as Jared returns, we'll head over to the bank."

Thatch agreed and hurried off. He had an ulterior motive for wanting to get the meal. It gave him an opportunity to court Gail a little more. Ever since he'd kissed her at the social, she'd been paying more attention to him, and he was glad. He'd been secretly in love with her for a long time. When he got up his nerve, he planned to propose to her, but he hadn't felt brave enough yet. The thought bothered Thatch; he wasn't afraid to face down men like Martin, but he was afraid to propose to the woman of his dreams. His shyness didn't stop him from wanting to see her, though. He was smiling when he entered the restaurant.

Cord returned to his desk, but gave up the

effort to work. He put the stack of papers aside and turned his thoughts to the hours to come.

"Cord."

He glanced up at the sound of Autumn's voice.

"Be careful tonight," she told him earnestly. She'd slipped away from Muriel and Grace to speak with him alone.

"I will."

"I couldn't bear it if anything happened to you," she said as she went to him.

Cord stood up. Though someone could have walked in on them, he didn't care. He framed her face with his hands as he gazed down at her.

His expression was so serious that, for a moment, Autumn almost thought something was wrong.

"I love you, Autumn," he told her quietly. "And I have every intention of marrying you just as soon as this is over."

Autumn was thrilled. Tears burned in her eyes. "Was that a proposal, Sheriff Randolph?"

He gave her a sardonic half-grin. "Yes, Autumn, I guess it was."

She gazed up at him. It was the moment she'd been hoping for. "I love you, too, Cord—and yes, I'll marry you."

She pulled him down to her for a kiss.

For that brief moment in time, it was just the two of them, alone in the world. Nothing existed except the beauty of their love.

Autumn wished it could stay that way, but reality intruded as Thatch returned with Grace's meal.

Autumn and Cord both managed to look composed, although Autumn wasn't sure how she did it. Certainly, her heart was pounding, and she wanted nothing more than to go back into Cord's embrace. She controlled the desire with an effort and went to help Thatch with the food.

Pete arrived at the office shortly before Jared returned. Cord was satisfied that everything was going according to plan. He went to get Autumn and Muriel, and Pete went with him.

"Pete's going to take over here for me overnight," he informed the women. "It's time for us to go to the bank, so I want you to return to the hotel now. We'll walk you over."

Autumn and Muriel said their goodbyes; then Cord and his men escorted them to the hotel.

Autumn wanted to throw herself in Cord's arms when it was time for them to part. She wanted to hold on to him and never let him go, but she knew he was a man with a job to do, and he would not be deterred.

"Take care," Autumn told him.

Cord nodded. He waited until the women had disappeared inside; then he and the deputies headed for the bank.

Autumn and Muriel watched them walk away from the hotel's front window.

"I wish there was something more I could do," Autumn agonized.

342

"There is," Muriel said gently. "You can pray."

They shared a look of tortured understanding as they went upstairs to their rooms, prepared for a long and troubled night.

As Cord led the way to the bank, tension ate at him. When they reached the building, he checked his gun again, then began to issue orders.

"I want you on the roof of the mercantile," he told Thatch, directing him to the store across the street from the front of the bank. "And Jared, I want you on the roof of the building in back, so you can watch the alley."

Both men hurried off to take up their positions. The night was going to be a long one, but they would be ready. They had their sidearms and rifles and extra ammunition, just in case there was big trouble.

Cord knew Martin never operated the same way twice, so there was no way of knowing exactly what he might try this time. The only thing they could be certain of was that if Martin did show up, his plan would be deadly. The outlaw believed in shooting first. He didn't bother to ask any questions. He went after what he wanted and took it, and he didn't care who got in his way.

Cord went inside the bank to find Mr. Backe.

Rod and his men were ready. It was normal for two guards to be posted with any payroll, so they would have to take care of them first and then go after the prize they sought. They had considered robbing the payroll farther out of town, but there were few places along the way that offered the cover they needed for a surprise attack.

"They'll be unloading the strongbox around back," Rod told them, reviewing one last time their plan of action. "We'll go in shooting. We need to kill the guards right away to give ourselves the time we need to grab the strongbox and make a run for it."

"What about the sheriff?"

"Be watching for him. From what I remember, there were two deputies, too, so there may be three more gunmen waiting for us. Keep an eye out."

"Here they come now," Cord told the banker as he saw Thatch signaling from the rooftop.

They'd been waiting in front of the bank for the guarded stagecoach to arrive. They saw it turn down the side street that would take it to the alley and the bank's back entrance. They hurried to unlock the back door so the guards could bring the strongbox inside once they'd reined in out back.

The Martin gang's attack was swift and deadly.

Rod and his men had seen the payroll arriving, and when the stagecoach turned down the narrow alley, they made their move. With guns blazing, they swooped down from both ends of the alley. The guard who was holding the strongbox was felled by their gunfire. He collapsed and dropped the box beside him.

Cord charged out of the bank's back door and took cover by the stagecoach, shooting determinedly at the attacking outlaws as Jared fired down on them from the rooftop.

Rod and his men had expected some trouble from the guards, but they hadn't realized anyone would be on the roof.

"Damn! It's a trap! It's almost like they knew we were coming!" Rod swore to Joe.

"Let's get out of here!" Frank shouted to them, knowing it was hopeless.

The outlaws tried to turn their horses and flee from the alley as Cord and the others continued to fire at them. Frank was downed first. With a scream of pain, he fell from his horse and lay still. Lou turned around, trying to escape the deadly fire. The other guard chased after him on foot, but Thatch was ready. As Lou emerged from the alley, Thatch shot him down.

Cord and Jared concentrated on Rod and Joe. Even in the growing darkness, Cord recognized Rod Martin. He took careful aim and got off his shot. Rod was hit and fell from his horse. Cord hoped the man was dead, and he was furious when he saw him get to his feet and stagger down the alley. Cord kept firing at him, but Rod somehow managed to dodge his bullets and disappear from view.

Cord wanted to go after him immediately, but Jared and the other outlaw were still engaged in a fierce gun battle. Turning his sights on the gunman, Cord fired off several rounds. He was relieved when the man gave a scream of pain and fell from his horse.

"Did you see which way Martin ran?" Cord called up to Jared.

"No! I'll come down and help you look for him."

Cord turned the strongbox over to the bank president, then ran around to the front of the building to get the guard and Thatch and enlist their help in finding the wounded outlaw leader.

Cord was not going to let Rod Martin get away.

Autumn had been in her room trying to rest when she first heard the gunshots. She ran to the window to try to see where the shots were coming from, but could see nothing.

Autumn knew Cord had told her to stay in her room, but fear for him and for Grace filled her. She desperately wanted to go to the bank to check on Cord, but she knew he'd be furious with her. Instead, she decided to go to the jail. She could stay with Grace and wait there for word from Cord.

Autumn turned away from the window and grabbed up her purse. She got out the derringer and put it in her skirt pocket. She hoped she wouldn't need it, but she wanted to be prepared—just in case. Running from the room, she stopped only long enough to tell Muriel where she was going.

"No! I heard the shooting, too. You should wait here until Cord comes for you."

"I can't, Muriel. What if Cord was hurt or Grace is in trouble? I have to go the jail and find out what happened."

"But—"

Autumn gave her no time to argue further. She left the hotel. The street was almost deserted as she stepped outside.

"Somebody's trying to rob the bank!" a man shouted to her as he rushed past.

"Was anybody hurt?" she called after him.

"Yes—several men were killed."

Fear struck at the very heart of her. Autumn prayed fervently that Cord had not been one of those who'd been shot. She ran for the sheriff's office.

Rod was in agony. He'd suffered enough gunshots in his time to know that this wound was serious. The pain was excruciating, and he was bleeding heavily. He wasn't about to let any lawman take him alive, though. He was going to find a place to hole up, and then hold them off for as long as he could. He planned to take a few of them with him when he died.

Stumbling through the alleyways, he stayed in the shadows. He circled back to the main street and looked out, waiting for the chance to run across it.

It was then that he saw her come out of the hotel.

Grace—

Rod stood completely still. Shocked, he was suddenly filled with such rage that he no longer felt any pain.

That was how the sheriff had known they were coming into Sagebrush! The bitch had betrayed him to the law!

Unbridled anger drove him. He followed Grace, gun in hand, ready to exact his revenge.

Chapter Twenty-nine

Autumn rushed into the sheriff's office to find Pete in back talking with Grace.

"I heard the shooting. Do you know what happened? A man I saw on the street told me people were killed," Autumn called to him.

"I haven't heard anything yet." Pete was grim as he came out of the cell area.

He got no chance to say any more as the door to the office crashed open.

Rod ran into the office, gun in hand. Pete recognized the outlaw leader and went for his own sidearm, but Rod was too fast. The outlaw shot him down and smiled as he watched him fall.

"No!" Autumn cried out, going for her derringer.

"Pete!" Grace screamed in horror. She

couldn't see everything that was transpiring, but she feared the worst.

At their screams, Rod turned toward the women. He saw Autumn standing near the door to the cell area and thought she was Grace.

"Grace—you no-good bitch!" he raged, taking a menacing step toward her.

It was Grace's worst nightmare coming true. She was trapped in the jail cell unable to defend herself against Rod, and Autumn was caught in the middle of it all. She wanted to save her sister if she could.

"No—Rod!"

At her cry, Rod looked past the woman he'd thought was Grace to see the real Grace standing in the cell. He was stunned as he stared at the two.

"What the—? Well, now, which one of you do I kill first?" he asked with savage intent, looking between them. He smiled a feral grin as he started to lift his gun.

Autumn was frozen in terror, but then she heard Grace's whispered warning.

"Shoot him. Shoot him. It's our only chance!"

Autumn realized they were facing certain death. When Rod aimed his gun at them, she turned, ready to fire.

At that instant, Cord charged violently into the office. He had been following the outlaw's bloody trail and had grown even more worried when he discovered Rod had made his way to the jail. Gun in hand, he was ready for his final showdown with Mike's killer.

Cord saw Rod taking aim at the women and reacted instantly. He fired at Rod at the same time as Autumn pulled her trigger.

Both the shots were deadly. Rod was spun around by their violent power. He crashed to the floor, the last of his life's blood draining from his body.

"Oh, Cord!" Autumn threw her derringer aside and ran straight into his arms. "Thank God, you're all right!"

Cord holstered his gun and embraced her, turning her away so she couldn't see Rod. He didn't know whether to be furious with her for being at the jail or ecstatic that she was safe. His arms closed powerfully around her for a moment, then he put her from him.

"You're not hurt?"

"No. Grace and I are fine, but Pete—"

Cord went to Pete, fearing the worst. Rod's shot had hit the rancher in the chest. He was unconscious, but still breathing.

"Autumn—get the keys and let Grace out of the cell. She can help me while you go get Dr. Murray!" he ordered as he tore open Pete's shirt to try to stanch the flow of blood from his wound.

When Autumn unlocked the door, Grace was trembling fiercely. She had to get to Pete. She ran to Pete's side while Autumn hurried to get the doctor.

"How is he?" Grace asked as she knelt beside Cord.

"He's still alive," he reassured her.

"Thank heaven." Silently she begged God not to take Pete from her now that they had finally found each other again.

Only a few minutes later Autumn returned with the doctor. They all stood back to give him room to work.

"We need to get him over to my office," the physician told them almost immediately.

"Is he going to live?" Grace asked, frightened and desperate to know.

"I won't know until I get the bullet out."

Cord went outside and flagged down a man driving by in a buckboard. With the driver's help, Cord and Dr. Murray were able to carry Pete out to the vehicle and lay him in back.

"Cord—can Grace go with him?" Autumn asked, knowing how her sister was suffering.

He looked at Grace and nodded. "Go on and ride in the buckboard with the doc. Autumn and I will be along in a minute."

"Thank you," Grace said with heartfelt sincerity.

Thatch, Jared and the other guard from the payroll came running up just then. They had been spread out around town trying to find Rod and had heard the gunfire at the jail. Cord told them all that had occurred. He put Jared in charge of getting Rod Martin's body out of the sheriff's office and sent Thatch back to the bank to finish taking care of things there.

"I'll be over at the doc's until we find out how Pete's doing."

Cord and Autumn left Jared there.

An hour later, Autumn, Grace and Cord were still waiting in the doctor's outer office for word of Pete's condition.

"That was a brave thing you did, Autumn," Cord said.

"I've never shot anyone before." She shuddered visibly as she relived the horror of the shooting in her mind.

"Martin gave you no choice. You did what you had to do to save yourself and your sister."

"If it hadn't been for Grace, I don't know if I could have done it." Autumn looked at her sister.

"You were wonderful," Grace said. "You had no way of knowing Sheriff Randolph would show up when he did. You saved our lives."

Autumn's gaze met Cord's. "I should have known Cord would come. He always shows up when I need him the most."

Dr. Murray finally came out to speak to them, and Grace rose nervously to her feet.

"Is he going to make it?" she asked.

"Yes," he answered. "It was a clean wound, and I got the bullet out. He's a very fortunate man. It missed his vital organs. He should make a full recovery."

Grace began to cry with relief and thanksgiving.

"He's conscious now, and he asked to see you, Miss Thomas."

She turned to Cord. "Is it all right? Can I go in?"

"Go ahead."

She went into the room, elated over the good news that Pete was going to recover.

Pete lay on the examining table, his chest swathed in bandages, his eyes closed. Grace approached quietly and stood beside him, gazing down at him.

"Pete—" she said softly.

His eyes opened at the sound of her voice and he managed to smile up at her in spite of his pain. "Are you and Autumn all right?"

She was astounded that his first thoughts were of them, and her love for him grew even more. "We're fine, but how can you even be worrying about us? You're the one who was shot."

"What about Martin?"

"He's dead."

Pete nodded and closed his eyes for a moment to gather his strength. "I love you, Grace."

"I love you, too, Pete."

She leaned down to kiss him. It was a soft, gentle kiss that told him of her devotion.

"You rest. I'll stay here with you as long as they'll let me," Grace promised.

"If I had my way, you'd never be away from me again."

Dr. Murray came back for her a short time

later. Pete had fallen asleep, so they went into the outer office to talk.

"Pete needs to rest now. He told me you were his fiancée, so if there are any changes, I'll notify you at once. Where will I be able to reach you?"

Grace looked shamefaced, but answered straightforwardly, "I'll be in the jail."

The doctor nodded in understanding. He had heard all the talk in town. "I'll let you know how he's doing."

"Thank you." She turned to Cord. "Sheriff Randolph—"

"I think you can call me Cord, Grace," he said gently.

"I'm ready to go back."

They returned to the jail. Cord was glad to see that Jared had taken care of everything at the office.

"I hate to do this, Grace, but I have to lock you up again," Cord said.

"I understand." She went into the cell of her own free will.

"How long will it be until Grace can be released?" Autumn asked.

"The judge won't be here for another week or two. We'll have the hearing with a prosecutor when he gets here."

"Do you think there's any hope for me?" Grace asked.

"It's because of you that we were able to get Martin and his men tonight. That will carry a lot of weight with the judge. I'll tell him how much you cooperated with me."

Cord was about to say more when they heard someone come into the office.

"Is it true?" Beth Gallagher demanded of Jared. "Did you get Martin tonight?"

Cord recognized her voice and told Autumn to stay in back with Grace while he went to speak with her.

"Hello, Beth," he said as he entered the office.

"Oh, Cord. Jared was just telling me what happened. So it's true! You got them—you got all of them!"

"Yes, Beth, it's true. The Martin gang will never hurt anyone again."

She began to cry. She went to him and kissed his cheek. "Thank you, Cord. Mike said you were a good lawman, and he was right."

Cord appreciated her praise.

"What are you going to do about the Thomas woman?" she asked, her voice turning cold.

He had known this moment was coming, and he faced her squarely. "Grace Thomas is the reason we were able to trap the gang tonight."

"She is?" Beth sounded shocked.

"She gave me the information I needed so I could be ready for Martin when he showed up."

"Oh—But she's not going to get off, is she?"

"Honestly, Beth, I hope she does. I'll testify on her behalf if I need to."

"But she was one of them."

He went on in Grace's defense, "Without

Grace Thomas's help, Rod Martin might still be running loose. I hope I'm able to convince the judge and prosecutor of that."

"I see." Troubled by her mixed feelings, Beth turned and left without another word.

Cord watched her go, and he worried about her. He wanted Grace's hearing to go smoothly, but if Beth came to argue against her being released, things might prove more difficult.

"Is everything all right?" Autumn asked, coming to the doorway.

"I hope so," he told her. "We won't know until we go before the judge."

She went to him. She needed his strength to get through these hard times. "That day can't come soon enough for me."

"I know," Cord said as he put his arms around her. He knew Jared was there, but he didn't care. He wanted to comfort her as best he could. There was nothing else they could do now but wait.

Cord finished his positive testimony about Grace before Judge Stevenson and stepped down as the judge directed. Cord smiled reassuringly at Grace as he walked past the table where she sat with Ralph Baxter by her side. Cord went to sit with Autumn, Muriel and Pete. In the two weeks since the shootout, Pete had surprised everyone with the progress he'd made in his recovery. He had been determined to attend the hearing in support of Grace.

The time leading up to this court date had seemed endless for all of them. Judge Stevenson brought in Prosecutor Dan Lesseg from Dry Spring to help with the case, and they were now about to conclude the hearing.

Judge Stevenson looked at the prosecutor. "I understand we have one last witness."

"Yes. Mrs. Beth Gallagher."

The moment Cord had been dreading had arrived. He cared about Beth, and he understood her need to voice her opinion, but he didn't want Grace to suffer any more.

"Mrs. Gallagher, please tell us of your involvement with this case," the prosecutor requested after she'd been sworn in and had taken her seat.

"I'm the widow of Sheriff Gallagher, who was killed by the Martin gang," she said.

Beth's expression was unreadable as she looked straight at Grace.

Grace was afraid, but she met Beth Gallagher's regard without flinching. She knew the woman might sway the judge's opinion, and she waited tensely for what was to come.

"Mrs. Gallagher, what would you like to add to what we've heard today?"

"I would like to commend Sheriff Randolph for his handling of this whole matter. It's been very painful for me." She paused to gather her strength to go on. "I just want you to know that I will be forever grateful to Grace Thomas for her part in helping Sheriff Randolph."

Grace had been sitting frozen in her seat, and

at the woman's words, she began to cry quietly.

"I cannot say that I have forgiven her yet for being a part of Rod Martin's gang for a time, but I do not feel justice would be served by keeping her imprisoned any longer."

"Thank you, Mrs. Gallagher."

The judge looked at the prosecutor. "Mr. Lesseg—"

"Because Miss Thomas provided Sheriff Randolph with information that helped stop the Martin gang, it is my opinion that we should accept the recommendation that she be released from jail."

"No further jail time needed?"

"No, Your Honor."

"Miss Thomas—"

Grace and Ralph stood up to face the judge.

He ruled, "It is the opinion of this court that Grace Thomas is to be freed from jail today. Miss Thomas—"

Grace was trembling with the force of her emotions. "Yes, Your Honor?"

"You are a very fortunate young woman. You are surrounded by people who care about you and you are getting a second chance. Not everyone is so lucky. Make the most of this opportunity."

"Yes, Your Honor."

"You may go."

Grace hugged Ralph. "Thank you."

She turned to Autumn, tears falling unheeded

as she embraced her sister. "I could never have done this without you and Pete."

"We love you, Grace," Autumn told her, crying, too.

"I love you, too."

When they moved apart, Grace looked up to see Pete standing, waiting for her. She left Autumn and went to him.

They didn't speak. There was no need for words between them.

Pete held his hand out to her, and Grace took it. They knew they would never be apart again as they walked together from the courtroom.

"Your sister's been through a lot, but she's a strong woman. She deserves to have some happiness in her life," Cord told Autumn.

"I think Pete is going to see to that," she said with a smile as she watched the other couple leave.

They followed them outside into the sunshine, knowing their futures were as bright as the day before them.

Epilogue

Six weeks later

The church was crowded with well-wishers all eagerly anticipating the weddings to come. There had never been a double wedding in Sagebrush before. The brides were beautiful as they stood with their grooms before the pastor at the altar. All were attentive as he began the ceremony that would bind them together forever in the eyes of God.

"Dearly beloved, we are gathered here today to join these couples in matrimony," the pastor intoned.

Autumn gazed up at Cord. She had never dreamed that her life could change so completely, so quickly, but it had. She was going to be Mrs. Cord Randolph. He was everything she'd ever wanted in a man, and she had been blessed to have him come into her life.

As if sensing her gaze upon him, Cord looked down at Autumn and flashed her a smile. Autumn's heartbeat quickened, and she knew she was going to spend the rest of her life showing him just how much she loved him.

Pete stood with Grace at his side, his expression serious. There had been times when he'd thought this day would never come, but now it was here at last. Soon they would be man and wife, joined as one forever. He loved Grace. He had made the mistake once of not telling her of his love, and it had cost them both dearly. From this day forward, he would never let a day go by without telling her how much she meant to him.

"Do you, Grace Thomas, take this man, Peter Miller, to be your lawfully wedded husband, to have and to hold, for richer or poorer, for better or worse, in sickness and in health, 'til death do you part?"

Grace turned to gaze up to Pete. She had come so close to losing him that she knew she was going to treasure every minute they had together.

"I do," she said without hesitation.

The pastor repeated the vow for Pete.

"I do," Pete responded in an unfaltering voice.

The pastor turned to Autumn and Cord. "Do you, Autumn Thomas, take this man, Cord Randolph, to be your lawfully wedded husband, to have and to hold, for richer or poorer, for better or worse, in sickness and in health, 'til death do you part?"

"I do," she answered breathlessly.

He turned to Cord and repeated the wedding vow.

"I do," Cord told him.

"The rings, please."

Cord and Pete took the wedding bands out of their pockets and slipped them onto Autumn's and Grace's fingers.

"By the power vested in me, I now pronounce you man and wife," he told Pete and Grace. Then he faced Autumn and Cord. "I now pronounce you man and wife. What God has joined together, let no man put asunder."

A cheer resounded through the church.

"Gentlemen, you may kiss your brides."

Cord and Pete needed no further encouragement.

Cord turned to Autumn and bent down to kiss her almost reverently.

Pete drew Grace to him and kissed her most lovingly.

In the front pew, Ralph looked at Muriel and gave her a knowing grin.

"Very soon, that will be us," he told her.

"I can't wait." Muriel blushed like a young girl.

She smiled happily as she looked down at the engagement ring she wore. Ralph had given it to her several weeks before. He had told her he had waited that long to propose only because he wasn't sure she wanted to remain in Texas. Once she and Autumn had made arrangements for a solicitor in Philadelphia to close out their interests and transfer their holdings to Sagebrush, he'd known she was the woman for him.

The organist began to play, and the two couples began their procession up the aisle. In the last pew, Gail sat watching as Cord walked by. Instead of being miserable over his marriage, though, she was smiling, for Thatch was sitting right beside her, and she had grown quite fond of the deputy.

A small reception was held afterward at the church. Everyone congratulated the newlyweds and wished them great happiness. It was several hours later before the happy couples could slip away.

Cord and Autumn escaped to the privacy of Cord's house, while Pete and Grace went to the room they had taken at the hotel.

Cord swept Autumn up into his arms and carried her across the threshold.

"You can put me down now," Autumn told him as he kicked the door shut and carried her farther into the house.

"I'm going to put you down, all right," he chuckled.

Cord kept on walking and took her straight into the bedroom, where he laid her upon the bed. He kept his arms around her and kissed her passionately.

"I love you, Mrs. Randolph," he growled seductively.

He started to draw away, but Autumn wouldn't let him go.

"I love you, too." She kissed him again, hungry to know the full glory of his lovemaking once again.

Cord needed no further encouragement. He had been waiting for this moment.

With eager hands, they stripped away their clothing. They were desperate to be together. They wanted to know the perfection of being one. Each kiss and caress heated their passion. As they came together in a firestorm of desire, their love for one another took them to unscaled heights of ecstasy. They reached rapture's peak and crested there, clinging to each other in the splendor of love's gift.

Grace and Pete lay on the bed together, wrapped in each other's arms. Pete's touch was cherishing as he explored her soft, silken curves. Grace held him close. She loved him with all her heart and thrilled to his arousing caresses. Her passion grew as they met in kiss after devouring kiss. The glory of their loving transported them to passion's pleasure and beyond. Throughout the night, they cherished the exquisite beauty of the love they had almost lost. Only when dawn brightened the eastern sky did they fall into an exhausted slumber, secure in the promise of happiness the future held for them.

* * *

Cord awoke first and stared down at Autumn as she slept on, curled against him. He thought of the night just past and realized he had never known that love could be so powerful. Unable to resist, he bent to her and kissed her awake. A low, sensual sound escaped her as she rolled over on top of him.

"Good morning, my husband."

"I like the sound of that."

"So do I." She leaned down to kiss him.

Having her pressed so intimately to him stirred Cord's need for her. He rolled her beneath him again and took her in a breathtakingly passionate possession that left them both panting. Autumn was the first to speak as she lay in his arms in the aftermath of the tempest of their loving.

"Have you thought of our having children?" she asked softly.

"I would love to have children someday," Cord answered, thinking how wonderful it would be to have a family.

Autumn raised herself on one elbow to gaze down at him. Her smile was a bit mischievous. "We could have twins. They run in my family, you know."

He grinned back. "If you love me, you'll only give me one baby at a time. I don't know if I can handle another set of twins, after dealing with you and your sister."

Autumn only smiled as she kissed him.

Author's Note

Dear Readers,

Hi! Leisure Books is the world's best publisher! They're allowing me to publish another of my early works here in *Forever Autumn*.

Those of you who read *Brides of Durango: Jenny* are familiar with my very first book—*Flood!* I wrote it when I was ten years old, and Leisure printed it for me in *Jenny*, so I could let parents and teachers know what to look for in aspiring authors. Now, I am thrilled to have "Good-Bye" in print. I wrote it during my freshman year at Harris Teachers' College here in St. Louis, and it was published in the *Harris Quarterly*—its literary magazine—in the spring of 1968. I hope you enjoy it.

GOOD-BYE
ROBERTA SMITH

As the call came for the boarding of the plane the thought that I had burned out of my mind for a few relieving seconds came back and haunted me again: This might be the last time, the last good-bye—forever and ever. I watched silently as he said, "So long," to his mom and family. He then turned to me. I vaguely remembered to keep my face clear of emotion, and I was fairly successful.

I searched his face, especially his eyes, and found what I had expected—all the grief and worry that came from leaving his home and his loved ones. His mouth was smiling that kind of smile that was completely disconnected from his thoughts, but covered his anguish quite well. I had convinced myself that I was perfecting a beautiful act, until his eyes challenged mine, and we locked in mental combat. He could penetrate my Pollyanna performance, just as I could see through his. His entire facial expression saddened, until I had to glance away to save my own composure.

My eyes were filled with tears and my heart was pounding in my throat, creating that one lump that is so hard to dissolve. Over and over I repeated to myself—Don't break down! Don't break down!

By help from God, I didn't. I gave him that

reassuring smile that he had been waiting for and with this he held me close and gave me the kiss that would be our last for such a long time. Before I knew it he had disappeared up the ramp into the jet.

I hurried out to the observation platform to catch a last glimpse of the plane as it rose into the cloudy gray sky to the west. I wanted to jump down and run to the plane with its engines roaring. I wanted to escape from what was to be my "existence" for the next thirteen months. But then the plane was gone, and I felt totally drained of strength and emotion. I turned the hollow shell of my former self back to what was left of my life.

It was then I knew how long those months were really going to be for me, here, and for him, in Viet Nam.

BROKEN
BLOSSOMS
PAM CROOKS

Trig Mathison knows the danger of opium's spell—his brother died from it. And though he vows vengeance, the undercover agent wonders if a forbidden yearning will destroy him as well. The beauty he pursues—one whose very blood marks her his enemy—arouses in Trig not a desire for justice, but a hunger for love.

The flower of her innocence crushed by her father's lies, Carleigh Chandler is on the run. Chased by a handsome bounty hunter, she succumbs to temptation in his arms. But will their passion be strong enough to untangle the web of deceit that ensnares them?

CHASE THE WIND
CINDY HOLBY

From the moment he sets eyes on Faith, Ian Duncan knows she is the only girl for him.   But her unbreakable betrothal to his employer's vicious son forces him to steal his love away on the very eve of her marriage. Faith and Ian are married clandestinely, their only possessions a magnificent horse, a family Bible, a wedding-ring quilt and their unshakable belief in each other. While their homestead waits to be carved out of the Iowa wilderness, Faith presents Ian with the most precious gift of all: a son and a daughter, born of the winter snows into the spring of their lives.   The golden years are still ahead, their dream is coming true, but this is just the beginning. . . .
